THE

Anna could see the slick trail of moisture the finger left in its wake. She could feel her own nipples hardening, as though they had experienced the delights of Hera's touch. A slow, steady pulse began to beat between her legs and she tried to ignore the sensation. As she had told herself earlier, there would be plenty of time to enjoy the memory of these incidents from the comfort of her own bed. The thought did not help. Instead, she found the anticipation of the moment only added to her excitement.

By the same author:

THE BLACK ROOM
AMAZON SLAVE
FAIRGROUND ATTRACTIONS
THE BLACK WIDOW
THE BLACK MASQUE
DANCE OF SUBMISSION
THE SLAVE AUCTION
SLAVE SENTENCE
THE TORTURE CHAMBER
THE BLACK FLAME
PROPERTY
ORIGINAL SINS
HOT PURSUIT

A NEXUS CLASSIC

THE BLACK GARTER

Lisette Ashton

This book is a work of fiction.
In real life, make sure you practise safe, sane and consensual sex.

First published in 1998 by
Nexus
Thames Wharf Studios
Rainville Road
London W6 9HA

This Nexus Classic edition 2004

www.nexus-books.co.uk

Typeset by TW Typesetting, Plymouth, Devon

ISBN 0 352 33919 5

Printed and bound in Great Britain by Clays Ltd, St Ives PLC

One

Anna was breathless. She ran into the gym, her eyes quickly adjusting to the macabre flicker of candlelight that barely illuminated the room. She glanced at the circle of cowled figures and found Hera easily. Even in the shrouds of darkness that accompanied the ceremony it would have been difficult to miss her. She was taller than the others, broader, and she stood with more natural confidence in her poise. The radiance of her commanding personality shone like a beacon in the dark.

Anna's heartbeat quickened in the faltering shadows of the supernatural light. A smile broke her lips. She walked towards the woman, stood silently beside her and waited to be acknowledged. She would not have behaved in such a way if it had been daylight. Under any other circumstances, Anna would have confidently marched up to Hera, tapped her briskly on the shoulder and said what she had to say. But this was different.

This was a meeting of the Black Garter. And not just an ordinary meeting. This was a punishment ceremony.

'Is everything quiet?' Hera asked.

Anna nodded. 'So far.'

She was careful not to use the woman's name. The Black Garter had to maintain an air of secrecy: that was something Hera insisted upon. Not that Anna minded. She did not like having to say Hera's name aloud. It was difficult even to mutter it without her voice filling with reverence. For the same reason, Anna was happy to tolerate the semi-darkness of the candlelit gym. In this light, Hera was unlikely to see her infatuated smile.

It was not that she wanted to keep her feelings a secret from Hera. She simply did not want to embarrass her mentor with declarations of a love that was most likely unrequited.

'Join the circle and grab a paddle,' Hera said curtly. 'Felicity is ready for her second bout of correction.'

Kneeling on the floor, within the shadow of the six cowled figures, a young woman moaned unhappily. Her cry seemed to embody feelings of fear and anguish yet held a whispered undercurrent of awakening desire.

Anna glanced at her, unable to suppress a shiver of excitement. Felicity had been stripped naked and was being held on her hands and knees in the centre of the gym. There were no bindings on her wrists or ankles. She stayed in the centre of the circle because she was terrified not to. The only things on her body were the two red garters she had received as a sign of punishment. One covered her eyes, effectively blindfolding her in the room's dim light, while the second covered her mouth, holding her own knickers as a gag.

Anna smiled excitedly at the scene, grabbed a paddle and joined the rest of the circle. Like the other women, she too was wearing a hooded cloak and in this light she knew she looked like some medieval recluse. They all did. It was an unflattering garment that showed off none of her curves or shapeliness;

however, it was obligatory for a meeting of the Black Garter and, like the others, Anna wore it with pride. The fact that this evening she was naked beneath the outfit should have excited her. Hera had insisted she wear nothing beneath the cloak tonight and Anna would have visited hell before refusing the woman.

She wondered idly if the other women were dressed similarly, then stopped herself. The atmosphere was already charged with enough electric anticipation. She did not need to add to it with her own erotic thoughts.

'Ladies, we will begin,' Hera said.

Felicity moaned although the sound was muffled against the gag. Her body trembled nervously, each quiver subtly augmented by the flickering candlelight.

Hera raised the table-tennis paddle and brought it down against the exposed cheek of Felicity's arse. Standing close to her, Anna could hear the woman's grunt of satisfaction as she inflicted the first blow. The bulky charm bracelet she wore tinkled musically as her hand fell through the air. Felicity released a soft moan.

Each member of the circle moved around one pace. Anna smiled grimly as she realised it was her turn to deliver a punishing blow. She gazed at the moon-like orbs of Felicity's arse and her smile broadened. She brought the table-tennis paddle down smartly against the young woman's cheeks. The resounding slap echoed through the gym.

Felicity tried to cry out but the gag was doing its job properly. The muted sound that escaped her lips was barely more than a whisper. The circle moved around.

The girl at Anna's side struck hard at Felicity's arse with her paddle. The slap of rubber against flesh echoed hollowly in the darkened gym. From the corner of her eye, Anna could see Felicity quake with the force of the blow. The anguished rasp of her breath was a constant growl in the darkness. Her arms and legs trembled fearfully as she braced herself for the next strike of the paddle.

Each of the six cowled figures took their turn slapping at Felicity's backside. When it came around to Hera again, the whole cycle began for a second time. Without breaking pace Hera led the group around Felicity again and again. Each time, Anna could see that Hera was striking harder and harder. Dimly, she realised that she too was inflicting more and more punishing blows. Before they had finished, each girl had been allowed to strike Felicity six times.

Anna could not take her eyes from the scene. She was transfixed by the sight of the woman on the floor as she endured her punishment. Each time she inflicted a blow to Felicity's backside, she it did with all the force she could muster. The woman's arse cheeks glowed a dull red in the pale light of the gym. The swell of her sex was clearly visible and Anna realised Felicity was becoming more excited. The lips of her pussy had started to spread open and a trickle of wetness glistened on the pink silk of her sex. Anna was convinced that Felicity was enjoying her punishment.

She could empathise with that emotion as her own loins were burning furiously. It was a dull sexual ache that yearned for satisfaction and she looked forward to the release her own fingers would give later in the evening.

By the time they had finished with their paddles, Felicity was panting steadily. Her arms and legs trembled with a combination of exhaustion and emotion and the flickering candlelight exaggerated the tremors of her body profusely. She had a fairly attractive figure, Anna thought. She had small pert breasts, which quivered with each vibration of her body, and a narrow waist which gave way to wide hips and a large, pear-shaped arse that looked incredibly inviting, especially with the reddened marks that covered her cheeks. Her skin was pale with golden tints from the yellow flames in the gym. Anna thought Hera had chosen this evening's victim well. She knew the leader had something special planned for tonight and she wondered idly if it had anything to do with Felicity's alluring figure or the rumours of her sexual ambiguity.

After the last blow had been struck, Hera held up her hand and carelessly threw the paddle away. The other cowled figures followed her lead and tossed their bats to the side of the gym.

Anna could not stop herself from grinning at Hera in the darkness. The woman had such a natural flair for leadership she was truly inspiring. She had to be the most innovative leader the Black Garter had ever had. Before, the group had been little more than a social circle for the school's older girls who wanted to drink, smoke and talk about boys. Admittedly, they had kept the other girls in line, like a secret society of prefects, but never with such outrageous audacity. Under Hera's leadership, the group had moved a long way.

Hera led the circle until she was standing in front of Felicity's face. 'Release her gag,' she commanded. As an afterthought she added, 'The blindfold stays.'

Anna watched one of the figures move towards Felicity and carefully ease the red garter from her mouth. The girl on the floor spat out the pants and sucked in ragged gasps of air.

'You have been charged with consistently failing to meet an expected standard, Felicity,' Hera said. 'You pleaded guilty and you have just accepted the punishment handed out by your peers. Is that correct?'

On the floor, Felicity nodded. 'Yes,' she whispered. 'That's correct.'

Anna watched eagerly. Because of her earlier look-out duties, she had missed Felicity's admission of guilt and her first bout of punishment. She held her breath, wondering exactly what else Hera had in store. Normally the Black Garter finished their meeting after this point. The guilty party was left to make her own way back to her dorm and the incident was never spoken of again.

Glancing slyly at Hera, Anna realised tonight was going to be different. Judging by the heady tension that tightened the air in the room, she guessed it was going to be very different.

'The Kilgrimol School for Young Ladies has always been proud of its high standard,' Hera said. 'That standard has been maintained, to a great degree, by the vigilance of the Black Garter. It is the job of the Garter to show errant students the error of their ways. Do you think we have shown you the error of your ways?'

Anna frowned, puzzled by Hera's words. This was not something she had heard being mentioned before. Hera's entire speech was completely unprecedented. She watched the scene progress, her excitement holding her enthralled. She could tell that Felicity would agree to anything in her present position but she had no idea what Hera might be planning.

'I've seen the error,' Felicity mumbled softly. 'I won't let my grades slip again,' she promised. 'You have my word.'

In the candlelit gloom Hera was shaking her head. Anna caught a glimpse of the brilliant white smile on the leader's lips. It was a voracious expression, simultaneously unnerving and exciting.

'I don't think your word is good enough,' Hera

told her. 'This is the second time you've offended. This is the second time you've had to be punished. You ought to realise how serious we are. You ought to realise that you have an obligation to the school and to the rest of us. Before you leave this room tonight, I want a token of your respect.'

Anna's frown deepened. She had no idea what Hera was talking about and she puzzled over her own lack of comprehension. Nervously, she chewed her lower lip, wondering what Hera intended to do now.

Her thoughts turned to the spate of scandals they had endured recently. Defamatory articles had been appearing in the local paper, each one chipping away at the carefully nurtured reputation of the school. Hera had said that the source of the stories had to be one of the school's students and she wanted the culprit found. Quite what she would do to such a sneak, Anna did not know, but she doubted it would be pleasant. The good name of the school was of paramount importance to every girl in the Black Garter, particularly the leader.

If Felicity was the source they were all looking for, Anna knew that Hera was bound to have an exceptionally cruel punishment lined up. She knew how much it had been bothering the Black Garter's leader. Hera had confided to Anna that the problem would soon be solved and, whilst she had seemed sincere, Anna still remained sceptical.

'Crawl towards me and kiss my feet,' Hera whispered.

A murmur of shocked surprise rippled across the silent room.

Anna could not tell if the sound came from Felicity or one of the cowled figures. She could only empathise with the murmurers as she experienced her own shock at the command. Paddling Felicity's arse was one thing. That was standard procedure for the ceremony of a Black Garter punishment. This was completely different.

Anna tried not to give in to ungracious thoughts concerning Hera's order. She was painfully aware of the stimulation it afforded her.

As they all watched, Felicity made her way blindfold towards Hera's voice. She stopped when her head brushed against the woman's legs and she slowly lowered her lips until they touched the tips of her toes. Each one of the cowled figures was watching intently. The silence seemed heavier than ever and Anna realised that all of the girls were holding their breath in excited anticipation.

'Are you prepared to give me your token of obedience?' Hera asked. Her calm voice carried effortlessly to every corner of the deserted gym.

In contrast, Felicity's voice was a strangled whisper. 'Yes,' she hissed, shaping the word around a nervous lump in her throat.

Hera smiled. 'Then kiss higher,' she instructed. 'Kiss higher.'

The meaning of her words was all too obvious. Even before she threw back the cowl and stepped out of her robe, Anna had realised exactly what she meant. When she saw Hera standing naked, save for a single black garter at the top of her right leg, her fears were confirmed.

If the sight had not been so darkly exciting, she would have fled from the gym and resigned her position in the Black Garter there and then. If Hera's body had not been such a joy to behold, she would have run away, never to return.

There were a lot of things she would have done if she had been blessed with the willpower. Instead, she stayed where she was and enjoyed the dark, thrilling eroticism of the moment.

She tried to snatch her gaze away from Hera's naked body. At the tender age of twenty she had the full feminine figure of a mature woman. Her stomach was flat and lean; the faint swell of capable, athletic muscles rippled beneath the surface of her pallid skin; long muscular legs led up to an enviably narrow waist. Her slenderness was accentuated by a pair of voluptuous breasts that rose and fell gently with each breath.

Anna found her gaze being drawn to Hera's breasts and her arousal heightened as she studied them. She was disturbed by the hard thrust of the woman's nipples, signalling her obvious sexual enjoyment.

Moving her lips slowly up from Hera's feet, Felicity began to kiss the woman's ankles and shins. Her mouth worked its way above her knees and up to her thighs.

Anna's breath deepened when she saw Felicity's lips brush blindly against Hera's black garter. Her nose was less than an inch from the top of the leader's legs. Anna drew air deeply and imagined the musky scent of Hera's sex filling Felicity's nostrils. It was an intoxicating thought and she felt dizzy by the wave of desire it provoked.

'That's right,' Hera encouraged, thrusting her pelvis slightly forward. 'You know what to do, Felicity. Stop being a tease.'

Anna shivered. Her gaze went down to Hera's neatly trimmed triangle of dark curly hairs. Felicity's hesitant mouth was barely a whisper away from the heart of Hera's arousal. Anna watched as she moistened her lips then pushed her tongue forward. Hair fell across Felicity's face, snatching the sight from Anna's view.

It was only when she heard Hera's sigh of appreciation that she realised Felicity had obeyed the command. The deed had been done. In an act of absolute servility she had pressed her mouth against Hera's sex. Anna shivered, her thoughts lost between feelings of outright disbelief and unspeakable envy.

Hera's tone deepened, and a growl of pleasure oozed from her throat. She raised her hands to her head. Brushing splayed fingers lazily through her luxuriant jet hair, she held the pose for an instant. Each of the cowled figures had fixed their gaze on her and she seemed to revel in their admiration.

Anna glanced at the woman's nipples, aware that they were erect and thrusting eagerly forward. She had always admired Hera's body. When she had glimpsed her in the showers, Anna had felt a curious excitement touch her. Before, the sensation had been puzzling but now she realised exactly what the source of that excitement was. It would have been impossible not to be aroused by the sight of the woman. Looking at Hera, Anna knew that anyone, male or female, regardless of their sexual predilection, would have succumbed to the same excitement and arousal.

She still chewed her lower lip as she tested a smile in the darkness. It was suddenly clear to her exactly what Hera had in mind, and Anna wanted to show that she was wholly in tune with the woman's thoughts.

Reaching for the cord that fastened her cowl, Anna quickly tore the garment open and shrugged it from her shoulders. She stood naked next to Hera; displaying her nudity with arrogant pride.

As though they saw Anna's gesture as an indication of what to do next, the rest of the Black Garter disrobed. Aside from the black garter that each of the young women wore, close to the top of their right legs, they were all entirely naked.

Anna took a moment to glance at each of the girls,

surprised that they all appeared exciting and desirable in their own individual way. She did not know if it was the sight of so much naked flesh, or the special quality that was born into a Black Garter girl: whatever the cause, she could feel her excitement mounting. A delightful yearning began to tickle deep within the cleft of her loins.

Hera reached out an arm and touched the cool sensitive skin at the base of Anna's back. Her fingers were warm, yet her touch inspired a shiver. She leant her head towards Anna and whispered the words, 'Thank you.' She took hold of Anna's hand and squeezed tightly, conveying her heartfelt gratitude in one simple gesture.

Anna had found most of the evening to be darkly exciting but this had to be the best thing yet. Felicity's servility was truly exhilarating to watch. Hera's nudity was breathtaking and the rest of the Black Garter, displaying their nubile young bodies, looked almost as desirable. Yet none of these things could compare to the stimulation she received from Hera's whispered words of thanks and the tender touch of her fingers.

She returned the squeeze and then reached out for the girl to her right. In the darkness she could not tell if it was Melanie or Grace. Shadows covered the woman's face and Anna's cursory glance only took in a pair of small, pert breasts with erect nipples. Their fingers met before she could work out who it was. Then they were holding hands. Movement around the circle caught Anna's attention and she realised that at her signal, the rest of the Black Garter had followed suit, and now, all six of the women were holding hands.

Grinning broadly, Hera bucked her hips forward, allowing Felicity to tongue the lips of her sex more easily. She released a mewl of pleasure and Anna heard an excited parody of the sound being echoed by the rest of the circle. The guttural moan of the other girls seemed to combine revulsion, envy and excitement in one soft whisper.

Anna stared at the cleft between Hera's legs. The thick swatch of dark pubic curls stopped abruptly before it met the lips of her vagina. She could see the glistening pink lips of the woman's sex, exposed and flushed with excitement. As she watched, Felicity trailed her tongue slowly along the flesh.

'Good,' Hera whispered. 'Very good.' She took a step to her left and Anna felt her arm being tugged.

An explosion of nervous panic erupted in her chest as she realised what was expected of her. She froze, terrified by the prospect of what Hera had planned. Her heart beat rapidly, sending a torrent of adrenaline-charged blood pounding through her temples. In the candlelit shadows, she felt sure that the rest of the Black Garter would be able to hear her nervousness.

Hera tugged harder on Anna's hand. A frown of concern twisted her lips and her eyes shone with a glimmer of mild annoyance as she glared forcefully at Anna.

Swallowing thickly, Anna took a step to her left, standing in the spot Hera had vacated. She could feel Felicity's nose brushing against the thick curls of her blonde pubic hair. She was so close, she could feel the gentle warmth of the woman's breath as she exhaled softly. The sensation was disturbingly arousing.

Thankful for the darkness, aware that her blushes could not be seen in this dim light, Anna tried to glance around the circle. Five shadowed faces stared back at her expectantly. She knew what she had to do and even though this was something she had never contemplated before, she was prepared to do it. Hera had managed it, therefore Anna knew she would be capable. After all, she was a member of the Black Garter.

'Kiss me, Felicity,' she instructed. Her voice sounded calm and confident, surprising her with its even timbre.

A shocked, excited whisper erupted from four of the women. Hera squeezed Anna's hand again. The shape of her smile was clearly visible in the poor light.

Felicity pushed her head forward until her nose was buried in the thatch of hairs covering Anna's pubic mound. This closeness was something Anna had never experienced. She held her breath, knowing what to expect and not daring to contemplate it. She had never had a tongue touch her down there before and, whilst the idea had occurred to her in the more exotic moments of lurid, masturbatory fantasies, she had never imagined she could have a woman doing it to her.

Felicity's tongue touched softly against the lips of Anna's sex. The wet tip began to draw against the sensitive flesh of her perineum. She drew it slowly along the tight folds of Anna's labia, coating her pussy lips with a slippery layer of wetness. Then, with the same languid movement, Felicity brought her tongue up slightly and pressed hard against the pulsing nub of Anna's clitoris.

Anna held herself rigid, aware that the rest of the circle were watching intently. Perhaps Hera was the leader of the group, and perhaps it was her command that everyone followed, but Anna realised the importance of her own position. She knew that the rest of the Black Garter looked to her for confirmation of Hera's orders.

When Hera had proposed they have a weekly

punishment patrol, Anna was the one who had seconded the motion. Consequently, it had been carried unanimously. When Hera had suggested they strip and paddle offenders, Anna had enthused about the idea. After that, everyone had agreed. Earlier this evening, Grace had called on Anna to ask if she thought Hera was serious about being naked beneath their cloaks. Daringly, Anna had opened her cowl and given Grace a glimpse of her body, nude save for the black garter at the top of her right leg. Grace had grinned and left her alone. In the corridor, outside her room, Anna had heard Grace mumbling something to two or three women. Aware of the way things worked in the Black Garter she knew those women were staring at her now.

Hera was the leader but, as second in command, Anna knew she had her own control over the group. She was the voice of reason to whom the Black Garter looked for guidance. It was an awesome responsibility but she had always managed to cope with it in the past. Despite the magnitude of what they were doing this evening, she saw no reason why she shouldn't continue to guide the women in the way she thought most suitable.

Felicity licked her tongue slowly against Anna's pussy for a second time. The sensation was electric.

She released the breath she had been holding. A whispered sigh of pleasure fell from her lips. The subtle sensation of the woman's mouth against the heated pulse of her sex was more thrilling than Anna would have believed. A wealth of excitement began to tingle between her legs. She could feel an acute awareness steal over her flesh, making every square inch of skin more sensitive than ever. The pulse of her sex beat harder. The nervous drumbeat of her heart continued to throb hard and loud but Anna realised it was no longer beating with apprehension. Now there was an obvious physical cause for her excitement.

A broad grin split her face when she felt Felicity's tongue continue on its exquisite journey. The mounting explosion of pleasure continued to well deep inside her and, in an unconscious imitation of Hera, Anna thrust her pelvis forward. She felt Felicity's tongue probe gently against the inner lips of her sex and a growl of absolute satisfaction trembled from her throat. The tingle of pleasure had given way to tremors of joy that seemed to be building to seismic proportions.

Dimly aware of her surroundings, Anna felt her hand being squeezed and she half-turned to see Hera smiling indulgently at her.

Anna returned the grin although she could happily have stood in front of Felicity for the rest of the evening. The woman had a gift for pleasuring that Anna would never have believed. Her tongue felt heavenly on Anna's body.

Hera squeezed Anna's hand again and tugged it gently. Anna glanced at her, a misty smile twisting her lips. Hera tugged once more to remind her that the circle needed to continue and reluctantly Anna nodded. She allowed Felicity to trail her beautiful tongue against the sensitive flesh of her sex for one last time. 'Good,' she said, remembering the words of praise Hera had used before relinquishing her position. 'Very good,' she assured her. She took a firm, definite step to her left, and tugged the woman on her right in front of Felicity. It was Grace, she realised, and the tall mousy-blonde took the position with a nervous stumble.

Hera pressed her mouth close to Anna's ear. 'Thanks again,' she whispered. Her warmth breath tickled the sensitive flesh of Anna's neck, exciting a poignant memory of the pleasure she had just experienced.

'I think I should be thanking you,' Anna replied, keeping her voice low.

She saw Hera nod in the darkness. 'Felicity is quite gifted, isn't she?'

Anna grinned wickedly. 'I just hope her grades continue to slip,' she whispered. 'I could have enjoyed a lot more of that.'

Hera nodded. In the darkness she pressed her lips against Anna's neck and kissed her softly. 'Visit my dorm tonight,' she whispered. 'Perhaps we can both enjoy some more.' She delivered another small, soft kiss, then took a step away as the circle moved around.

Anna's heart began to trip at a helter-skelter pace. The flurry of excitement she had enjoyed from Felicity's tongue was nothing compared to the exhilaration that came from Hera's suggestion. The idea of going to her dorm this evening filled Anna with a nervous delight that left her breathless. She did not even entertain the thought of refusal. Her acceptance was a foregone conclusion.

With another step she was standing directly behind Felicity. Melanie was having her pussy licked by the submissive blonde and Anna had a splendid view of the pair of them. She could see a broad smile illuminating Melanie's face and Anna grinned back at her, empathising with her pleasure.

She glanced down at Felicity's backside and studied the cleft of her sex. The pale coating of downy hairs that edged her labia were sodden with pussy juice. Her lower lips had parted fully now and the dark pink inner flesh pulsed softly with desire.

Feeling another tug on her arm, Anna moved reluctantly round the circle again.

When Hera was finally returned to her position in front of Felicity, she released her hands from the two women on either side of her and moved her fingers towards her legs. Teasing the lips of her labia apart she spread her sex so that Felicity could use her tongue directly against the pulsing nub of her clitoris.

Hera groaned softly, a warm smile breaking her lips. 'You have given us the token of your obedience,' she said stiffly. 'And because of that, we are going to trust you when you say you won't reoffend. Do you understand?'

Felicity nodded and whispered, 'Yes.'

'Good,' Hera murmured. 'Then it only . . .'

'FAIRCHILD!!!'

The name cut through Hera's speech like a knife. All six of the circle glanced towards the gym door where the shouted warning had come from. Edwina Fairchild was the school's senior principal and her wrath was legendary. The fact that she was on her way to the gym was an intimidating prospect.

'Bitch!' Hera exclaimed angrily.

Anna was already tugging her cowl back on and glancing around to make sure the others were doing the same thing. The fire-exit doors were open and she watched four of the Black Garter flee quickly through them. Hera stood next to her, calmly fastening her cowl.

'Interfering old cow,' she muttered.

'What do we do about her?' Anna asked, nodding at Felicity. The blonde still knelt on the floor with the blindfold covering her eyes.

Hera shrugged. 'Leave her. We're in a rush.'

Anna nodded and started quickly towards the fire exit. Hera's hand on her arm stopped her from fleeing into the night.

'Will you be visiting me later?' Hera asked.

Anna paused. She was nervous at the prospect of being caught, but Hera's repeated offer made her heart beat even faster. 'I don't know,' she began. 'I mean . . .'

Hera stopped her hesitancy with a kiss. 'Twelve o'clock tonight,' she said firmly. 'I'll have something for us to drink when you arrive.' Without waiting for a response, she grabbed Anna's arm, dragged her through the fire exit and out into the night.

As the cool air caught her flesh, Anna shivered. She had never been so excited in her entire life.

Two

Jo Valentine flicked the double-headed sovereign high in the air. As it spun upward, she watched it catch the occasional dull red glint from the flashing sign outside her office. She caught it halfway through its descent. As always, her reactions were lightning fast and she smacked the coin swiftly on to the careworn surface of her desk.

Five hard, relentless raps fell heavily on the door of her office.

Jo glanced up. 'Fuck off,' she snapped miserably. 'There's no one here.' She flicked the coin again and caught it easily in the dark. The lights were off and the room's only illumination came from a sign outside the twenty-four-hour petrol station opposite her office. Cloaked in the scarlet-edged shadows, Jo's pale skin glistened a dark crimson. Her long dark hair looked jet-black. They were colours that matched her mood.

The knock was repeated. Five hard, relentless raps, an exact repetition of the first five.

A month ago, she would have been intrigued. It was ten o'clock at night and if someone wanted her at this late hour, they had to have a bloody good reason. But it wasn't a month ago; it was today and that made a difference. In the last thirty days her life had changed completely and she was still trying to come to terms with it. She stared sullenly at the door. In the filtered cerise light her eyes were black glowering coals.

The five raps were repeated. 'Open up, Valentine. I know you're in there.'

Jo grunted sourly when she heard the voice. She recognised the owner instantly and stayed in her chair. She might have opened the door for Brad Pitt or k. d. lang, but not for this visitor. Again, she tossed the coin and caught it. A wry smile crossed her lips when she saw it was heads again.

She blamed herself for not seeing the signs. She was a private investigator and it was her job to notice the small details that others overlooked. Philip Marlowe would not have missed it, she told herself miserably. The fact that Philip Marlowe would not have been living in a *ménage à trois* with a lesbian lover and an old boyfriend was a detail she tried to ignore. Jo was unhappy and she felt justified to wallow in self-pity.

The handle of the door began to rattle and Jo heard a key being pressed into the lock. The door swung slowly open and the shadow of a man filled the frame. When he flicked the light switch on, Jo was not surprised to see Mr Smith standing there. Tall, dark and forbidding, he looked as austere and unapproachable as ever.

'Stephanie gave me the key,' he explained in reply to her unasked question. 'She was worried about you.'

'Tell her I'm fine. Leave the key on my desk and close the door on your way out,' Jo replied shortly.

He smiled tightly and ignored her. He closed the door and walked over to her desk then sat down in the facing chair. 'It hit you pretty hard when they got married, didn't it?'

Jo stared at him impassively, determined she would

not reveal her emotions to the man. She had never liked Mr Smith and in her current mood she was unwilling to offer him even the simplest courtesy. 'When who got married?' she asked coolly.

He shook his head. 'Don't try and play clever word games with me, Valentine,' he snapped crisply. 'Nick and Stephanie's marriage hurt you, didn't it? Tell me I'm right. It hit you hard, didn't it?'

Jo shrugged. 'You've hit me harder.'

He laughed dryly. 'You're a tough bitch.'

'You have to be in this life,' she replied. She tossed her coin again. 'Are you going to tell me why you're here?'

'I have a case for you,' he began.

'I'm not taking cases at the moment,' Jo said flatly. 'I'm on sabbatical.'

He continued talking as though she hadn't spoken. 'It's not the sort of thing you're used to, but I think you might appreciate the break it offers.'

'Do you want me to go undercover in a distillery?' Jo asked. 'I could appreciate that at the moment.' She flicked the coin again, caught it, and then climbed restlessly from her chair. 'Talking of distilleries, do you want a drink?'

He nodded and sat in silence as she went to the drinks cabinet. He watched her thoughtfully as she poured two neat scotches.

Jo was aware of him studying the sleek contours of her legs and the ample swell of her breasts above her thin waist. Because she was in the office, she was dressed for work, even though she had no intention of doing any. She wore a dark blue suit, long-line jacket and short skirt, completing the ensemble with a low-cut blouse revealing a deep, inviting cleavage. She knew how good she was looking, in spite of her current problems, and she was pleased to note Mr

Smith's appreciative response. As much as she despised the man, she was grateful for his lustful admiration. She caught his eye as he glanced at the tops of her legs and he looked away quickly.

Clearing his throat gruffly he told her, 'My daughter's finishing school has been suffering a series of scandals.' He was glancing distractedly around the room, trying to fix his eye on anything now except for Jo. 'Students have been found drunk in the local public house, men have been found in the boarding rooms. Alcohol has also been found on the premises.'

Jo's grin was a cruel line as she passed him his drink. 'It sounds like you've sent her to a very prestigious place. What do you want me to do? Should I ask for a refund on your school fees?'

'None of these matters are very serious,' he went on, ignoring her unconcealed mirth. 'I'm sure this sort of thing happens at most finishing schools. After all, these are young women, not girls. The scandals themselves don't concern me.'

'So what's the problem?' Jo asked, hating herself for being intrigued.

He snorted derisively. 'The real problem is the local newspaper. They keep printing these stories, discovering them almost as soon as they happen. The scandals are ruining the Kilgrimol's good name.'

'Kilgrimol?' Jo repeated.

'The Kilgrimol School for Young Ladies,' Mr Smith said tiredly. 'Surely you've heard of it?'

Jo shook her head. 'I'm a private investigator,' she reminded him softly. 'I need to know about a lot of things in my job. I need to keep tracks on the hierarchy of the local underworld. I need to keep abreast of the best things available for headaches, bruises and nettle-rash.' She stared poignantly at him and Mr Smith had the good grace to turn away.

'What I don't need to know about, is the quality of the nation's finishing schools,' Jo told him. She settled herself back in her chair and kicked her long, stocking-clad legs on to the desk. The heels of her stilettos rested on the battered leather top. 'Go on,' she told him, after taking a careful sip at her drink. 'You've managed to catch my interest. Tell me the rest.'

He grinned warmly at her. It was an unfamiliar expression for him to wear, Jo thought, and she could not stop herself from returning the unexpected smile.

'The Kilgrimol is one of the best schools in the country,' he explained. 'They have had an outstanding reputation for the last hundred years or so but these incessant scandals are going to kill that.'

'Why don't you pay off the newspaper?' Jo suggested. 'You and your friends at the Pentagon Agency have enough money to do that, don't you?'

He shook his head. 'It's not the business of the Pentagon Agency,' he told her. 'This is personal. It's my daughter's school. It's my problem. And besides,' he added bitterly, 'I've already tried to buy off the editor and he refused my offer. He even suggested there might be a story in my trying to bribe him.'

'So how do I fit into this little problem of yours?'

He drained his glass and slammed the empty vessel heavily down on her desk. 'There's only one way the newspaper can be getting the stories they've printed. Someone at the Kilgrimol has to be giving them information. I want you to go to the school and find out who it is.'

Jo considered him silently for a moment. 'And what will you do with this information once I've got it for you?'

He shook his head and a tight smile twisted his lips. 'If you accept this case, my involvement ends here, tonight. You'll be going to the school undercover, posing as an assistant to the gym instructor. Once you've had a chance to work out who the source is, you will give your findings to the school's principal, Edwina Fairchild.'

'Is she a friend of yours?' Jo asked carefully.

He nodded, missing the subtle inflection of her question. 'Once she knows who is talking to the newspaper, she will deal with the problem. If it's a pupil, she will have the girl expelled. If it's a member of staff, she will dismiss them instantly.'

Jo considered this, then nodded her agreement. 'Why am I going as an assistant to a gym instructor?' she asked suddenly.

He coughed apologetically and glanced uncertainly at the top of her desk. 'I was taking into account your lack of an academic background.'

Jo bit back a rueful grin. 'Thank you,' she said tersely. 'I'd almost forgotten that I dislike you.' A thought occurred to her and she leant forward in her chair. 'If this isn't Pentagon Agency business, who's picking up the tab?'

'I'll pay all your expenses and meet your usual fee,' he said quickly. His hand went to the pocket of his trench coat and he produced a cheque book in a leather-bound wallet.

As she watched him write the amount in a neat, precise script, Jo asked quietly, 'Was Stephanie really concerned about me?'

Mr Smith glanced up from the cheque book. A hard, uncompromising smile sat on his lips. 'You ought to be paying me for this assignment,' he said quietly. 'A month in the heart of Scotland, away from this town, away from the memories. It's just what you need. You'll have a chance to relax in quiet surroundings and forget about all your problems.'

Jo sat back in her chair and grunted rudely at him. 'I won't have much of a chance to relax,' she reminded him. 'I am meant to be on a case, remember.'

He shook her argument away with a wave of the cheque. 'I'm sure you'll have it all solved within a couple of days,' he said generously. 'I have a lot of faith in you.'

Jo studied him doubtfully, wondering if there was something he had neglected to tell her. 'I'll still be undercover,' she reminded him. 'That's always dangerous.'

He laughed; a harsh powerful sound that echoed hollowly in the tight confines of Jo's office. 'Dangerous?' he repeated, chuckling as though he found mirth in the word. 'What danger could you possibly encounter in a girls' school?'

Jo quietly took the cheque from him, and wondered.

The three of them sat in silence watching the video tape. The TV screen came alive with the vibrant pinks of naked flesh.

Two broad-shouldered, well-hung men were stroking and caressing a willing blonde. Between plastic moans of delight and satisfaction, she returned their caresses, touching herself, then touching them.

'Suck me, baby,' one man told her.

The blonde smiled crazily at him, fell to her knees and moved her mouth around his huge glistening cock. After the camera had focused on the intimacy of her tongue against his penis, the blonde began to suck furiously on him, taking all of his length in her mouth.

'That looks good,' the other man grinned. 'I'm going to stick this up your cunt,' he said, brandishing his huge tool like a truncheon.

She sucked greedily on one cock as the other plunged roughly between her legs. The camera shifted from one end of the blonde to the other. All the time, the screen was either filled with the image of the shaft sliding between her legs or the other pushing into her mouth. The groans and sighs of the trio's mutual pleasure overlaid the background music.

On the couch, sitting between the pair of them, Bunny giggled. Her tiny snub nose twitched slightly but neither of the men noticed. Both were staring intently at the TV screen, their attention fixed. Bunny cast a discreet glance at Steven and saw the bulge thrusting at the front of his pants. She released a second giggle and tried to stifle it with her hand.

Glancing slyly towards Peter she saw the smooth front of his jeans was pushing forward urgently. Suddenly aware of her attention, Peter squirmed in his seat and crossed his legs, trying to hide his excitement.

'Peter's got a stiffy!' Bunny exclaimed loudly.

Steven rolled his eyes impatiently. 'Of course Peter's got a stiffy,' he told her wearily. 'We're watching a porn film. That's what happens when you watch them.' He stood up and went to the kitchenette. When he returned he was carrying three cans of cola. 'All guys get stiffies when they watch porn films,' he explained carefully. 'Peter's got one, and so have I.'

Bunny glanced up at him from the couch and looked at the bulge distorting the front of his pants. She wondered if part of his excitement was for her. She had made a special effort to look sexy for him this evening. Her long blonde curls were swept up in a sophisticated style that drew attention to the elegant length of her neck and she wore a tight-fitting white blouse that accentuated the swell of her large bosom.

The short black skirt she wore displayed her long, coltish legs to their best advantage. She knew both men had been steadily appraising her throughout the evening.

She accepted her drink from Steven with one hand and trailed her fingers over the bulge with the other. 'You feel really excited,' she observed. 'Is that what those films do for you?' Her sparkling blue eyes shone wickedly.

He shrugged and passed a can to Peter. 'I guess they must. I imagine you're wet after watching it.'

Bunny continued to grin at him but the shine of the smile had left her eyes. 'Don't be so fucking coarse,' she growled threateningly. 'What do you think I am? Some sort of pervert or a slut? Those are the only people who get turned on by filth like this.'

A broad grin split his face as he watched her anger mounting. 'Bullshit, Bunny,' he laughed. 'You don't expect me to believe that you're not wet between the legs.'

'I am not!' Bunny declared indignantly.

He snorted derisively and placed his can of coke on the coffee table. With a sudden sly movement, he lunged forward and pushed her back on to the couch.

Bunny had not expected this and was surprised to feel his hand pressing between her breasts. She glared furiously at him as he placed his hand on her knee and slowly began to work his fingers up her leg. 'No!' she exclaimed angrily. 'Stop it!'

'Let's see if you're wet or not,' he said grinning cheerfully.

'NO!' Bunny repeated. She began to swing her arms, scoring ill-marked blows against his shoulder and neck.

Steven kept on grinning and his fingers worked their way swiftly beneath the hem of the short skirt she wore.

Bunny could feel Peter shifting uncomfortably on the seat beside her. He was trying to keep his gaze fixed on the TV screen but she could see him sneaking surreptitious glances at her. The focus of his attention seemed to be Steven's hand as it worked its way deliberately upwards.

'Fucking stop it, Steven,' Bunny exclaimed.

Steven smiled coolly into the depths of her angry glare. 'Let's just see if you've got a damp-on,' he said. 'If I'm wrong, I'll apologise.'

She grunted angrily at him and threw another couple of mock punches but none of them had any effect. When she felt his hand reach the gusset of her panties, she stopped hitting at him and tried to twist her legs so they were protecting her modesty. He parted them effortlessly.

There was a momentary struggle of wills. Bunny tried pressing her thighs hard together but Steven was strong and capable. He pushed hard against her vice-like grip and because the pressure was so strong, Bunny relented. He grinned at her and drew the tip of his finger slowly between her legs.

Bunny glared at him defiantly, trying not to think of how excited she was. She was aware that Peter had now given up all pretence of watching the film. He glanced over Steven's shoulder, mesmerised by the movement of the other man's finger as it rubbed slowly backwards and forwards over the fabric that covered her heated pubis. A broad, lecherous smile split his lips.

'You feel pretty wet,' Steven said thickly.

She stared angrily at him. 'The knickers were damp when I put them on,' she said coldly. 'They were only washed today.'

He nodded seriously, as though he had expected her to say this. 'You lie like an MP during a general election,' he said quietly. 'But just so that I can prove you're telling the truth . . .'

He did not bother to finish the sentence. Instead, she felt his fingers teasing against the top of her leg, pushing beneath the flimsy material of her panties.

Peter made a small sound of excitement and Bunny glanced at him. He was staring directly between her legs and she knew that he was staring at the exposed lips of her sex. Her cheeks coloured bright red, although she did not know if the cause was anger, embarrassment or some other emotion. Her confusion heightened when she felt Steven's finger draw gently against the sensitive flesh of her labia. His touch was strong and cool and she vainly resisted the urge to shiver.

His broad smile widened and he moved his fingers away. 'So what's your excuse for your quim being wet?' he asked, releasing his hold on her chest. 'Was that damp when you put it on tonight?' Peter chuckled thickly and Bunny cast daggers of hatred at them both.

Steven ignored her. He moved the finger to his nose and inhaled the scented wetness.

'All right,' Bunny declared defiantly. 'So I'm wet. So what?'

'You're horny,' Steven told her. 'Why don't you do something about it?'

She scowled up at him and straightened the hem of her dress. 'I didn't come here to get horny,' she said flatly. 'I came here to show you that video. I thought you could use it.'

He shook his head and took a swig from his can. 'I think you're lying again, Bunny,' he said calmly. 'Just like before. Just like yesterday. Just like since the first time I met you.'

Her mood shifted again. This time her bottom lip

quivered and she stared unhappily at him. 'I don't lie,' she whispered meekly.

'Bullshit,' Steven replied. 'You were lying about the last video you brought here and you're lying about this one.'

'I am not!' Bunny declared. 'I'm telling the truth. It belongs to one of the girls at the Kilgrimol School for Young Ladies.'

He was still shaking his head. 'I did a bit of research after I'd run that last story,' he explained. 'There's only one video recorder at the school and that's kept under lock and key for the use of documentaries and educational films.'

Bunny's expression was so cold it was positively threatening. She had been seeing Steven for a month now and she had thought he believed all the stories she had told him. They had met in a pub in Kilgrimol, the small town closest to the school. Recalling the evening, Bunny remembered she had been deeply unhappy that night. She had endured the shame and embarrassment of an initiation ceremony the night before. To her chagrin, she had failed the test miserably. Throughout the following day she had been trying not to think of the perversity she had been forced to suffer. The fact that she had enjoyed it only made her feelings of revulsion that much stronger. Memories of the anguish and the delightful torment were still too poignant for her to even dare to face them. The heady sense of shame was enough to cause tears of self-disgust to brim on her lower lids.

One of the school's first-year students had delivered a short message to her that fateful night. Even though Bunny knew who they all were, the Black Garter had chosen an unrelated intermediary so they could maintain their secrecy.

'The Black Garter say they don't want you,' the girl had explained meekly.

Bunny was furious. To become a member of the Black Garter had been a driving ambition for her throughout the summer. She envied the air of dark secrecy that the girls maintained and she wanted to be a part of it. When Bunny wanted something, she invariably got it and this sharp, anonymous rebuke was her first taste of rejection.

She did not bother venting her spleen on the first-year student. Because the girl had no involvement with the Black Garter, Bunny knew it would be pointless to exact retribution on the timid creature and instead she had stormed out of the school and walked the arduous two-mile journey into Kilgrimol. Once there, she had gone into the Royal Oak and started to get deliberately drunk.

Sitting alone at a table, she had not been surprised when someone like Steven approached her. He was tall, good-looking, with an intelligent smile and sharp, steel-grey eyes. When Bunny had discovered he was a reporter she had acted as though journalism fascinated her. She had pretended to be intrigued by his stories and anecdotes about life on a provincial newspaper. According to the expression on her face, she had never been more interested in a topic as fascinating as the *Kilgrimol Weekly Clarion*; all the time, a plan had been formulating at the back of her mind. As Steven spoke quickly and easily about his work she began to see a way of getting her own back on the bitches of the Black Garter.

'Have you ever done a story on the Kilgrimol School for Young Ladies?' She asked him.

He shook his head. 'There's never anything to write about. Besides, the locals aren't that interested in the school. Most of the students are from England or out of the country and our readership have a rather parochial outlook.'

Bunny nodded as though she understood him perfectly. 'So you wouldn't be interested in any of the scandals that go on there,' she said tiredly. 'All right. Never mind.'

Watching him, she had seen his eyes light up with excitement. 'I said they were parochial,' he told her carefully. 'But they're still readers, and scandals sell papers. What's happening?' The steel-grey eyes had sharpened and his entire attitude towards her changed. He hung attentively on her every word.

'No,' she said softly. 'Before I tell you anything, I want to see my name in print. I want you to do a story about finding me drunk in this bar. Is it a deal?'

He frowned. 'I'm not sure I understand,' he said. 'I can make a story out of it. "Elite schoolgirl, found drunk", will make an OK piece, but why would you want me to write it?'

Bunny shook her head. 'I want to cover myself,' she explained. 'Promise me you'll do that story for me, then I'll tell you whatever you want to know about the Kilgrimol School.' Everything you want to know, and whatever else I can make up, she thought with dark excitement.

'I promise,' he replied quickly.

Bunny realised she had him in the palm of her hand. After extracting the assurance of his promise, she fed him the wildest story she could concoct. The following evening she delivered a video cassette to him, claiming it belonged to one of the senior girls. The headline of that week's *Clarion* read: 'KILGRIMOL SCHOOL LESBIAN VIDEO SHOCK!'

Bunny had been delighted. It was the first story of many.

Staring into his eyes as he frowned down at her, she realised now that Steven was no longer going to accept every tale she told him. She purposefully ignored Peter. He was only a photographer and of no use to her. 'You don't believe me then?'

Steven smiled easily. 'I want to believe the stories you're telling me,' he began carefully. 'But if you keep lying to me, then I'm going to have to treat everything you say with a certain degree of scepticism.'

'But I haven't been lying,' Bunny insisted. 'I've been honest with you, all of the time. Really.'

He raised his finger to his nostrils and sniffed the scent of her juice. 'You said you weren't horny,' he reminded her. 'Yet you smell horny.'

She blushed and turned away. 'Don't be coarse, Steven,' she hissed. 'You know I don't approve of coarseness.'

Steven ignored her. 'Does that smell like she's horny to you?'

Bunny glanced up and saw that he was offering his finger to Peter. She watched the photographer sniff Steven's finger and smile salaciously. He grinned broadly at Bunny, not disguising the lust that brimmed in his eyes.

'All right, all right,' Bunny declared angrily. She glared at Steven. 'So I'm horny and I didn't want to admit it. Is that a crime?'

His smile was so smug it was infuriating. He sipped at his cola and said, 'And what are you going to do about it?'

She stared uncertainly at him. 'I'm not going to do anything about it. I've already told you. I'm saving myself for when I get married.'

He shook his head from side to side and settled himself back down on the couch next to her. After placing his arm around her shoulders, he shifted position so that she had to move. Uneasily, she realised she was trapped on the couch between the pair of them. She fixed her gaze on the TV screen and watched the video progress.

She had not been lying when she said she was saving herself. Before she had left for college, her father had taken her on one side and delivered a sharp, cold ultimatum. He wanted her to be a success, that was important to him. He had pointed out that he would give her every opportunity to become a success, but if she did not make a good beginning to her life, there would only be one other option. He would have to marry her off.

'You'll either have a career or a husband,' he'd said coldly. 'Whichever it is, you'll stop draining my finances.'

Bunny had felt chilled by his cool, uncompromising tone.

'Whichever it is,' he had continued, 'you'll go into it a virgin.'

'Daddy!' Bunny had exclaimed, shocked by his talk of such personal things.

He had not allowed her to interrupt him. 'If I have to marry you off, I'll marry you off as a virgin,' he said sharply. 'If I learn you've been indulging yourself, I'll cut you off, penniless.'

The menacing glint of his cold dark eyes had left Bunny in no doubt that he was serious. In that instant she had seen why her mother had divorced him. She had also seen that she had no choice other than to go along with his wishes.

She had three options; a career, marriage or penury. Of the three, she had supposed that the career would be best. At least with that choice, she would have enough independence to get away from her father. She tried not to think of her father and his cold, stern threats and focused her attention on the movie. Things had moved on since she had last looked at it. The camera zoomed in on a double-penetration close-up. Two hard cocks hammered forcefully into the blonde's eager orifices and her squeals of passion poured from the stereo speakers.

Bunny swallowed nervously. Steven's fingers brushed against the sensitive skin of her neck and his touch was so subtle and unexpected that Bunny shivered with pleasure. She turned to face him and found his mouth was already moving to hers. As they kissed she wondered if he had forgiven her. He seemed in an unusual mood this evening and she wondered if he was angry with her for having lied to him. It was not as though any of her lies were traceable, she thought and, as he had pointed out after a week of knowing her, he was gaining a reputation for getting stories that sold papers.

His hand fell to her breast and she felt herself leaning towards him. The touch of his fingers, cupping and caressing the eager swell of her flesh, was dangerously exciting. Her nipples stood hard within her bra and she felt his fingers pressing roughly against them. The sensation inspired so many pleasurable feelings she could not stop herself from sighing contentedly.

She moved her hand towards him and stroked the swollen bulge at the front of his pants. 'Are we friends again?' she asked quietly. Her fingers rubbed backwards and forwards as she asked the question.

He nodded, still kissing her. 'We're friends,' he assured her. His hand squeezed hard against her breast and she moaned softly. 'Perhaps we could be more than friends?' he suggested.

'I've told you,' she whispered. 'I'm saving myself.'

He shook his head and smiled at her again. 'I wasn't suggesting that I spoil you,' he said carefully. His fingers continued to manipulate her breast as he spoke, stoking the fuel of her arousal. 'I just thought I could help with your education a little.'

She smiled into his kiss and pushed her tongue in his mouth. The eager throb of her excitement was a heady beat that seemed louder than a rock concert. She continued to stroke the thrusting steel of his erection, aware that he was enjoying her touch just as much as she was. 'You'd call it educational, would you?' she said, and grinned.

'I wouldn't want to deflower you,' he replied gallantly. 'I just want to please you.'

She shivered excitedly. Staring carefully into his face she asked, 'You won't break my virginity?'

He shook his head. His smile was warm, friendly and understanding. 'Like I said,' he repeated. 'It will be educational. I'll get pleasure from pleasing you. You'll get the experience of learning about the male body. Trust me,' he said softly. 'I wouldn't ask you to do anything that I didn't think you wanted to do.'

Bunny considered him warily. She knew that Steven was not going to print any more of her stories if she did not do as he asked. The thought of that ending was something she could not bear. She had already managed to cause a fantastic stir at the Kilgrimol. The succession of scandals was infuriating everyone, from the members of the Black Garter to the principal herself. It was all going too well for Bunny to want it to stop and she realised how limited her options were. If she wanted to keep hurting the Black Garter, she knew that she had to go along with whatever Steven had in mind.

'Do you trust me?' she asked. 'Will you believe me in future, when I tell you about the things going on at the school?'

He kissed her and nodded. 'Of course,' he said. 'And we'll talk some more about it later but for now –' He paused for an instant, his mouth finding hers and his tongue exploring. 'But for now,' he continued, 'we're both excited and I think we should do something about that. Don't you?' He studied her wary frown.

Bunny nodded. 'What do you want me to do?'

He pressed his mouth against her ear, then kissed her gently on the neck and whispered, 'Why don't you undress?'

Bunny felt a shiver thrill through her body. 'I can't,' she hissed, not injecting much refusal into the words. 'Peter's sitting next to me.'

Steven grinned, showing his understanding. 'Peter won't mind,' he assured her. 'And he won't touch you, unless you ask him to.'

Bunny swallowed. Her emotions were a conflicting whirlpool of excitement and fear. She glanced hesitantly at Peter but he seemed oblivious to them, his attention fixed on the pornographic video. She could see the bulge at the front of his trousers and wondered what that swelling would look like uncovered. The thought made her heart race faster.

'All right,' she decided suddenly. She stood up and stepped past the coffee table, placing herself in front of the TV screen. Her heart was beating so fast she could taste the excitement in the back of her mouth. She took a drink of cola and placed the can back down. Slowly, she began swaying her hips from side to side as though she was listening to an unheard dance rhythm. As the two men watched, she kicked off one shoe, then the other.

Steven grinned broadly at her. 'A strip?' He sounded surprised.

Bunny nodded. She cast a nervous glance at Peter and saw that he was also grinning eagerly at her. With her cheeks burning crimson, she turned away and began to dance from side to side in the tight space of the lounge. She kicked her legs high as she danced, aware that she was displaying more and more of her long legs.

Steven and Peter made small sounds of approval, encouraging her with good-natured cries of, 'More, more.'

Enjoying the role of the stripper, Bunny released her hair, allowing the flaxen curls to spill over her shoulders. She shook her head sharply then continued with her dance. Slowly, she began to ease the buttons free at the front of her blouse. She performed the task without breaking the rhythm of her movements. When she had released the last one, she turned her back to the pair and made a great show of concealing herself, still swaying rhythmically. At one point, she daringly bent over, displaying her skirt-covered backside. Knowing that they were staring at her with rapt attention, Bunny reached behind herself and pulled the hem of her skirt high. For an instant, she granted the two men a tantalising glimpse of her buttocks.

Their combined roars of approval warmed her.

She slung the blouse to an empty corner of the room, and continued to dance in front of the pair wearing only her bra and skirt. Their grins were so broad and eager she could feel her excitement mounting. Peter was rubbing impatiently at the swelling between his legs whilst Steven sat calmly back on the couch, allowing her to glance at the swollen bulge he was sporting whenever she deigned to.

Bunny reached down and discreetly eased off her panties. The wetness of her arousal had soaked the crotch and she enjoyed a cool chill between her thighs when she tugged the garment off. She removed the pants without revealing herself to the two men and grinned at their disappointed frowns. Continuing with the dance, she unfastened her bra and eased her breasts free as she swayed from side to side. Her breasts were large, their size seeming greater because of her narrow waist and flat stomach and, as she tossed the bra away, they bounced gently with the rhythm of her dance.

Peter groaned. Steven released a sigh of approval.

Bunny could feel their heated gaze burning her flesh and she rubbed the scorched skin of her breasts with splayed fingers. Her hands accidentally touched the excited brown areolae and she felt a surge of pleasure rush through her body. Her nipples stood hard and proud and she allowed her fingers to tease them. The sensation was so exquisite she felt a scream of joy building in her chest. The blushes of embarrassment were long forgotten and now she felt her skin colouring darkly but for a different reason. This was the flush of an impending orgasm and she savoured the heady moment.

Aware that the two men were expecting more from her, Bunny continued to dance before them. Reaching for the zip at the side of her skirt she held it between forefinger and thumb and graced the pair with a questioning expression. 'Should I?' she asked teasingly. Steven returned her grin quietly.

Peter was moving his head up and down like a nodding dog. 'Go on,' he begged her. 'Go on.'

As Bunny giggled, her nose wrinkled lightly. She tugged the zip downwards and spun quickly round. Turning a full circle, she spread out her arms as the skirt pooled at her ankles. She stood in front of them stark naked, listening to the sound of their applause. The pale curly hairs of her pubic mound were being displayed to the two men and instead of experiencing shame or embarrassment, all she could feel was the dull throb of her own aching desire.

'Gorgeous,' Steven said simply.

Peter nodded eager approval. 'Real beautiful,' he agreed.

'What are you going to do now, Bunny?' Steven asked calmly. He held his can in one hand and sipped casually from it.

She grinned at him. 'I want to see you naked,' she said quickly. She glanced shyly at Peter and said, 'And you. I want to see both of you naked, so I can see what a man looks like without any clothes.'

'Didn't you see enough on that video?' Steven teased lightly.

Bunny frowned. 'That's just a video,' she replied. 'I want to see the real thing.' She leant towards him, her breasts swaying provocatively as she moved. Her hand fell on the huge lump pushing against his pants. 'You said you'd educate me,' she reminded him. 'Aren't you going to honour your promise?'

Steven stood up and gestured for Peter to follow suit. The two men quickly stripped themselves of their shirts and jeans and stood naked beside her.

Bunny took a second to admire them both. Peter was a couple of inches shorter than she was. His hair was a dark crew cut and his body was lean and muscular. She stared excitedly at the modest length of his eager cock. The circumcised end had a swollen purple head that seemed to pulse with the barely contained heat of his excitement. He rubbed himself as she watched, unable to stop himself from grinning at her.

She returned his smile easily, then turned her attention to Steven. He had a broader body. The muscular pectorals and flat stomach were so smooth and hairless she felt an almost irresistible urge to touch his naked form. Between his legs, he held a long, thick cock that seemed to tremble beneath the weight of her gaze. Unable to stop herself, she reached forward and placed a cool finger against the angry heat of his arousal. Steven shivered and tried to stop his cock from twitching beneath her touch.

Her nose twitched slightly and she suppressed a smile. She glanced at Peter and pushed her fingers along his length. He groaned loudly and reached a hand towards her breast.

Bunny held her breath for a second, not knowing what to expect. Her own touch had been divine and Steven's rough manipulation of her orbs had been exciting but she could feel a degree of hesitancy about having Peter touch her.

As his fingers brushed against the dark brown rim of her areola, Bunny released a squeal of delight. The tips of his fingers touched the stiff flesh of her nipple and she felt her body begin to swoon with mounting feelings of joy. When Steven's hand touched her other breast, Bunny felt her excitement move on to a higher plateau. The sensation of having two men stroke her nipples and tease the sensitive flesh of her tingling orbs was something she had never imagined. A misty euphoria began to sweep over her and she realised she was already in the throes of orgasm. She had experienced the pleasure before; being a curious woman, it had only been natural for her fingers to explore the crease between her legs, but she had never experienced pleasure like this. She smiled delightedly at the pair of them and found each of her hands was holding a cock.

As he fondled her bosom, Steven placed a tender kiss on her ear. 'How would you like to continue your education tonight?' he asked.

Bunny did not even need to contemplate the question. 'I want to see one of you come,' she whispered. 'I want to see that.'

He nodded, as though he had been expecting this much. 'That shouldn't be too hard to manage,' he replied. He kissed her again and then guided her to the floor. She lay with her back on the thick shag pile and stared up at the two men. From this angle, they looked huge and, as they towered above her, she thought their cocks looked bigger than ever. The sight was so thrilling she could feel herself on the brink of another explosion of pleasure.

'Would you like to see Peter come first?' Steven asked calmly.

Bunny nodded. She did not care which of them came if she was being honest with herself. Her needs and desires were too great for her to be picky about such a detail. She simply wanted to watch one of them ejaculate. Nothing went above that thought in her mind.

'Then we'll do it this way,' Steven said. 'Like this, you'll be able to feel how much Peter's enjoying himself.'

Bunny groaned and her body trembled with desire. She watched as Steven guided Peter into position so he was standing over her with a foot at either side of her narrow waist. He knelt down slowly, careful not to put his weight on her and then she felt the tickle of his pubic hairs against her chest. His cock was frighteningly close to her and she stared at it longingly. A small pearl of pre-come had grown at the end and Bunny marvelled at the sight. She glanced nervously up at him and saw he was grinning down at her.

'Are you ready?' he whispered.

She nodded, not knowing if she was ready or not. She watched as he reached for her breasts and began to fondle the orbs tenderly with his fingers. The sensations he inspired thrilled her and she moaned happily. The floor should have been an uncomfortable place for her to writhe around but the deep carpet caressed the back of her body, just as Peter was stroking the front.

Peter pressed his tight sac against her chest and she could feel the distant throb of his pleasure. Her gaze was drawn between his eager grin and his huge cock. As she watched he squeezed both her breasts together and forced his length between the deep cleavage he had created. The swollen purple end then appeared between the huge mounds of her soft white flesh. The single eye of his cock was only inches from her face and she shivered, excited by his nearness.

Peter slid himself backward and forward between the crevice he was making, not bothering to disguise his pleasure. His groans and cries of excitement began to build as he pushed himself back and forth along her chest.

Bunny watched his cock appear then disappear between the mountainous cleft of her breasts. The end of his penis seeming to grow whenever it appeared. The single dark eye seemed wider each time and she knew it would not be long before he came. She would have known that much without his half-pained shouts of elation.

'I want to taste you,' she declared suddenly. The idea had come to her as she watched a trickle of pre-come slide languidly from the tip of his cock and slide wetly against her fair skin. As always with Bunny's ideas, when it occurred to her, she wanted to put it into practice instantly. 'I want to taste your cock and I want to feel you come in my mouth.' She grinned wantonly up at him. 'Can I?'

The suggestion itself was too much for Peter.

Bunny felt the pulsing explosion begin at his balls and travel along the tightly squeezed cleavage he was fucking. Peter cried out and then she felt a thick, warm spray burst from the end of his length. His seed coated her chest and neck with the first pulse, then the second showered her mouth and cheeks with creamy globules of his climax. The salty scent of his orgasm filled her nostrils and Bunny growled delightedly.

She licked her lips greedily, aware that some of his seed was on her chin and just below her nose. Desperate to taste his cream, she dragged her tongue as far around her own face as she could manage.

Peter climbed from her and Steven took his place, towering impressively over her. 'You want to taste cock, do you?' he asked, lowering himself on top of her.

Bunny nodded eagerly, smiling into his steel-grey eyes. She glanced lovingly at his magnificent length and watched as he stroked his finger against her cheek. It drew wetly against the flesh and she realised he was coating it with the fruit of Peter's explosion. He held the outstretched finger up to her and she saw it was dripping with the dewy white fluid that Peter had sprayed on to her face.

A shiver of delight coursed through her body. Even with such little stimulation she could feel her excitement welling to climactic proportions. She caught a breath in her throat, acutely aware of her impending orgasm.

As Steven put the finger to her lips, she licked it greedily. Then the orgasm struck her. Her cheeks darkened to a glorious red, her eyes squeezed tightly shut and she released a growl of euphoric proportions. Pinpricks of pleasure stabbed into every pore of her body. Her breasts tingled with the joyous pain of climax and the cleft between her legs throbbed with elation. She took Steven's finger into her mouth and sucked the wetness from him. The creamy taste of Peter's salty come filled her mouth, fulfilling every expectation she had with its glorious flavour.

Breathing in broken gasps of delight, Bunny glanced shyly at up Steven. He was still grinning and she realised his cock was closer to her face than it had been before. 'Are you ready to taste me?' he asked.

She nodded and lifted her head from the floor.

Steven pushed forward and Bunny felt the tip of his shaft press against her lower lip. The scent of his cock's sweat touched her nostrils. She inhaled the aroma deeply, eagerly anticipating the taste of his arousal. She traced the tip of her tongue wetly against his swollen length.

He shivered and grinned down at her. 'You're developing quite a taste for that,' he observed.

She smiled up at him, then moved her lips around his length taking him into her mouth. She could feel the dull throb of his cock beating against her tongue. The shaft seemed to fill her mouth, the bulbous end pressing heavily against the back of her throat. It was an exquisite sensation and she dared not concentrate on it too hard as she could not endure the pleasure of another orgasm yet. She pressed her lips tight around his length and moved her head back slowly. At the same time, she sucked gently, relishing the quickening pulse she could feel from his shaft.

She moved her head up and down him, sucking harder all the time. Using her tongue, she teased the rounded tip of his cock, aware that he was close to coming.

When Steven finally climaxed, Bunny shivered with the force of his orgasm. His white-hot seed filled her mouth, shooting forcefully to the back of her throat. Bunny could feel the liquid building up inside her. The taste and scent were so strong and exciting she felt overwhelmed. A rush of pleasure began to course through her body and she opened her mouth wide to groan with elation.

As the cry escaped her, his cock fell from between her lips. Bunny felt one last spurt shoot from the tip of his length then a spray of his thick white come spattered against her chin. The delight of experiencing his climax was intoxicating and Bunny shivered happily. She swallowed the thick warm fluid that filled her mouth, savouring the flavour of his sex with an elated grin. Smiling up at him she saw that his failing cock was still close to her face. Without even thinking about it, she moved her mouth forward and ran her tongue over the end.

'No more, please.' Steven smiled down at her.

'Perhaps later?' she asked.

He laughed. 'I don't think that's an offer I could refuse,' he replied honestly. 'But first, you and I need to talk.'

She stared at him quizzically. 'Talk? About what?'

She watched Peter disappear from the room and wondered if he was deliberately making himself scarce. Steven offered her his shirt and she took it, draping it modestly over her shoulders.

'Let's lay our cards on the table, Bunny,' he said quietly, sitting next to her. 'You and I both know why you're feeding me these stories. You've got a grudge against someone at the Kilgrimol and you're trying to hurt them. Am I right?'

Bunny looked away. 'Perhaps,' she conceded. 'Why?'

He grinned warmly at her. 'If that's the case, I think we can really help one another.'

Three

Anna stood in the corridor trembling nervously. The lack of illumination and the precariousness of her position added to her disquiet. After lights out, it was against the rules for any girl to be found out of her dorm. Glancing at the luminous display on her digital watch she saw the figures change from 11:59 to 12:00. That was more than enough past the curfew to make her stomach churn. She stood outside Hera's door and swallowed, wondering if she was doing the right thing.

Hera's earlier intimations had excited Anna but, at the same time, they unnerved her. She had been in awe of the leader of the Black Garter since their first meeting. Hera had such a powerful command over the rest of the group that Anna could not stop herself from admiring the woman and, although her thoughts had never properly progressed to any notions of intimacy, she knew the idea must have been at the back of her mind. Her ready acceptance of Hera's offer had been easier than she would ever have believed.

Not that anything would happen tonight, Anna assured herself. Hera had no sexual interest in her, she felt certain of that. With such a gorgeous figure and domineering personality, Anna believed that Hera had to be one hundred percent heterosexual.

She chastised herself for fretting about the meeting: Hera would simply want to discuss Black Garter business, Anna realised; it would be nothing more exciting than that.

Light fell on her face and she realised the door to Hera's room had opened. The woman stood there, a welcoming smile on her lips.

'Anna, you're here. Prompt as ever.' She stepped to one side, allowing Anna to move briskly into the room.

Anna felt a surge of relief as she entered Hera's private room. She had half-expected the woman to be standing naked in the doorway, ready to pounce. Instead, she was wearing a short floral dress that revealed her tanned arms and long sun-bronzed legs. The cotton-print fabric clung to each swell and curve of her body, emphasising her shapeliness. Anna took comfort from the fact that the woman was clothed and began to rationalise her earlier fears. The whole idea of Hera trying to seduce her seemed ridiculous in retrospect and she grinned at her own foolishness.

'Take a seat,' Hera said easily. She reached for a glass of wine and passed it to Anna.

Anna accepted the drink and took a sip before settling herself in a chair. She risked an admiring glance at Hera's legs, wishing she had worn something similar for this discreet meeting. Because of the late hour, and the rules that forbade her from being out, Anna had tried to blend with the darkness. She had dressed in a pair of black jeans and a black, shapeless jumper. The garments made her feel positively masculine in Hera's company. In an attempt to regain some degree of femininity, she released her tied-back hair and allowed the golden tresses to cascade over her shoulders. Pushing her fingers carelessly through the locks she said quietly, 'The meeting went well this evening.'

Hera nodded. She filled her own glass and settled herself in a facing chair. 'It went very well,' she agreed.

In the moment's silence, Anna glanced around Hera's single dorm. It was one of the more spacious rooms that the Kilgrimol offered its boarders. These rooms usually went to the daughters of the wealthiest parents or the really high achievers. Hera fitted into both categories. Her grades were always As and her parents were big, successful names in the media industry. Anna was not sure exactly who they were or what they did. It was not part of the Kilgrimol etiquette to discuss one's parents, no matter how exceptional they were.

Anna glanced around the tasteful decor of Hera's room, trying to suppress a tingle of jealousy. This was a three-roomed apartment, self-contained with so much luxury Anna could even see a bowl of fruit at the centre of the coffee table. It was difficult to contain her envy. Anna had to share with a girl named Debbie Chalmers, whom she did not particularly care for. Thinking of Debbie's untidiness, and her constant supply of sweets and chocolates, Anna shuddered. Her jealousy of Hera's good fortune increased when she thought how much she would have relished such privacy.

'I don't think Felicity will be reoffending,' Hera grinned, raising her glass. She brushed a hand between her legs and winked knowingly at Anna. 'I'd say that was a shame really, wouldn't you?'

Anna gulped nervously. She took another sip at her drink and willed her cheeks to stop colouring. 'I couldn't believe some of the things you had her doing,' Anna began carefully. 'I was ...' She struggled to find the right word.

'Excited?' Hera suggested.

'Shocked,' Anna finished, grinning at the frown on Hera's face. 'Shocked and excited a little,' she amended.

Hera nodded. 'I asked you here for two reasons,' she said. 'I think you might be aware of my main one.' She glanced knowingly at the closed bedroom door, then turned back to Anna.

Anna flushed. Her stomach muscles clenched uneasily. The moment's respite she had snatched earlier now seemed ridiculously optimistic. She had known Hera had plans for her. Now, it was a simply a matter of finding out exactly what they were.

'The other reason has a lot more to do with the Black Garter,' Hera continued, fixing Anna with a stern frown. 'This is my last term at the Kilgrimol and, in a week's time, I will have to hand over the reigns of the Black Garter to someone else. I want it to be you.'

A heavy silence fell between them. Anna studied Hera to see if she was joking. She seemed sincere enough but her offer was frightening.

'You want me to lead the Black Garter? You can't be serious?'

Hera smiled but remained silent.

'But I couldn't.' Anna was shaking her head. 'You're the leader. You're the one with the ideas and the command. I couldn't possibly do it. I'm not . . .' She stopped herself abruptly. She had been about say, I'm not you, but she knew the words would have sounded wrong.

'The girls already look to you for leadership,' Hera reminded her patiently.

Anna stayed silent. She could not deny Hera was right about that.

'You have all the qualifications,' Hera pointed out.

'You're attractive, intelligent and well-respected. You'll be a natural.'

Anna shook her head. 'I can't do it,' she insisted. 'I don't have your flair or imagination.'

Hera raised a surprised eyebrow. Her smile was enchantingly enigmatic. 'I never realised I had flair and imagination.' She rose from her seat and reached for the wine bottle. After filling her own glass she replenished Anna's then settled herself in an adjacent chair.

Anna breathed heavily, poignantly aware that Hera was sitting very close to her. She felt uncomfortable with the sensations that the woman's nearness aroused. 'I couldn't have thought up tonight's punishment,' Anna explained quickly. 'The thought of paddling Felicity would have been OK but I could never have told her to . . .' Her voice trailed off as she tried unsuccessfully to think of coy words that explained what Felicity had done.

Hera grinned knowingly. 'You could have told her to do that,' she said, and placed a comforting hand on Anna's knee. 'And you did get her to do that,' she added pointedly. 'When you're in charge, you'll use a lot more imagination in your punishments than I've ever employed.'

Anna closed her eyes and sat back in her chair. 'It's a big decision to make in one night,' she said quietly.

Hera's voice was filled with understanding. 'I'm not expecting a decision tonight. The leadership issue was a secondary matter for this evening.'

With her eyes closed, Anna took another sip of her wine, enjoying the faint sense of light-headedness it was causing. She smiled tiredly and asked, 'What was the main issue?'

Instead of replying, Hera placed her lips against Anna's.

Anna opened her eyes wide, staring timidly into Hera's face. She felt the woman push her tongue into her mouth and accepted it willingly. The intimacy of their exchange was exhilarating. A furious surge of adrenaline made her heart pound faster. The air suddenly felt heavy with the highly charged excitement that had built up between the pair of them. Anna could feel her lips being bruised by the kiss but she enjoyed it all the more for its passion.

When their mouths parted, she saw Hera was smiling eagerly. Her eyes shone with the promise of an excitement that Anna knew she could not properly imagine.

'Did you like what Felicity did?' Hera asked suddenly.

Anna frowned. Her thoughts had been so focused on the intimate exchange that for a second she could not recall who Felicity was. When recollection came to her, she blushed, smiled uncertainly, and then looked away. 'Yes,' she said. 'I guess I did like it.'

Hera placed her hands on either side of Anna's cheeks and held her face so they were staring at one another. The cold metal of her heavy charm bracelet tickled the warm flesh of Anna's face. 'You liked what she did to you,' Hera repeated. 'That's good. Then I'm sure you'll like what I have in mind for tonight.'

Anna stared at Hera. She watched the tall woman stand up and hold out a hand for her. Wordlessly, she took it and allowed Hera to lead her towards the bedroom.

'I'm not sure,' she began. Then stopped herself.

Hera smiled as she turned the bedroom light on. Anna suppressed a nervous gasp. Like the lounge, the bedroom was spacious and tastefully decorated. The magnolia walls were haphazardly speckled with framed abstract paintings, each signed in Hera's own name. They radiated bright reds and yellows in an abundance of garish images. However, the room's most dominant feature was a large, brass bed. In the centre of the bed, a naked woman lay, face upwards. Her arms and legs were spread out, tied at the wrist and ankles to the four corners.

Anna stared at her, her thoughts bouncing between concern and arousal. 'What's Cassandra doing here?' Anna asked, recognising the woman.

'Cassie wants to join the Black Garter,' Hera explained. 'I thought you'd like to help with her initiation.' She gave this last word such a potent meaning Anna shivered. All the time, her gaze remained fixed on the strawberry-blonde girl tied to the bed.

Cassandra certainly had what it took to be a Black Garter girl, she thought critically. She had a full, feminine figure with large beasts, a narrow waist and long, muscular legs. Studying her, Anna saw that her nipples were standing erect. She realised the woman was smiling uncertainly at her and Anna deliberately ignored her.

'I never had to undergo an initiation like this when I joined,' she whispered in Hera's ear.

'Are you jealous?' Hera asked with a grin.

Anna fixed her with a sour look but it was difficult to maintain the expression.

'This is only the second time I've done one of these initiations,' Hera explained. A dark frown crossed her brow. 'The last one didn't go very well,' she admitted quietly. 'It didn't go well at all.'

Anna studied the leader calmly, unsure of what would be the right thing to do or say. 'What do you want me to do?' she asked.

Hera shrugged, her solemn mood passing quickly. 'I want you to watch. You can see how I induct new initiates and, if I need your help, I'm sure you'll give it to me.' Anna nodded, not even considering her loyalty.

'Are you ready to begin, Cassandra?' Hera asked sweetly.

Cassandra nodded, her wide, fearful eyes fixed intently on the tall brunette.

Anna watched Hera slip out of the summer dress she wore. Aside from the stark black garter at the top of her right leg, she was naked beneath the clothing. She was strikingly tall and this accentuated the absolute perfection of her figure. Her breasts were well-rounded orbs, tipped with dark red areolae and large, thrusting nipples. Her narrow waist gave way to a smooth, flat stomach, which in turn led to the neatly trimmed triangle of her pubic mound.

Anna stared at her admiringly. Hera was blessed with an innate sense of self-possession. Coupled with her gorgeous face and beautiful body Anna thought the woman was irresistible. She tried to snatch her gaze away from Hera's naked form, realising her avid attention was bound to be noticed. It was an impossible struggle.

Aware that she was being watched, Hera smiled nonchalantly at Anna and winked. The gesture was enough to make Anna feel a thrill of pleasure touch her soul.

Unembarrassed by her nudity, Hera strolled boldly to the side of the bed and smiled down at Cassandra. 'Cassie's wanted to be in the Black Garter since the beginning of this term,' she explained. 'Haven't you, Cassie?'

Cassandra nodded, staring meekly up at the tall, dark-haired woman who towered over her. Anna could sense the girl's nervousness. In the heady atmosphere of electric anticipation, she felt uneasy herself.

'She's already learnt the three rules that we all adhere to: silence, obedience and loyalty. Tonight, she's going to prove how good she is at following those rules.' A wicked grin cut across her face.

Cassandra seemed to cower into the bed, as though she were terrified of the woman above her. Even though she adored and respected Hera, Anna sympathised with Cassandra's fear. If she had been in such a vulnerable position, she too would have been cowering.

Hera glanced at Anna and for the first time she seemed to notice the shapeless black clothes she was wearing. 'Are you going to undress?' she asked simply.

Anna acted as though it was a command and not simply a question. She began to tug the jumper over her head and step out of the dark jeans she was wearing. She removed her bra and pants, straightened the garter at the top of her right leg, and stood defiantly naked. She noticed that Cassandra was studying her body with an appreciative eye and, with a tremendous effort of will, she stopped herself from blushing. If she had noticed Hera's lascivious expression the task would not have been so easy.

'What the hell do you think you're looking at?' Hera demanded suddenly.

Anna watched as she snatched a fistful of Cassandra's hair and shook the girl on the bed. 'You look at me,' Hera reminded her sharply. 'Not her. Me.'

Cassandra began to apologise, then stopped herself. Anna heard the sound catch in the girl's throat and was puzzled.

Hera grinned. 'You're probably wondering why Cassie's being so quiet,' she observed. 'There is a reason. She's been laying here quietly all night, just to prove that she can fulfil the Black Garter's oath of silence.'

'But . . .' Anna began.

Hera waved her argument away. 'I know it's not a literal vow of silence. This is just a way of showing that she embraces our discipline.' She turned her attention back to Cassandra. 'You've been doing very well so far,' she told her condescendingly. 'Although, there's been no real challenge yet, has there?'

Cassandra looked more terrified than ever.

Anna wanted to go to the aid of the girl; unfasten her wrists and ankles and let her walk free from the room. Instead, curiosity held her where she was.

Cassandra's nipples stood hard and proud, making it obvious that she was extracting some enjoyment from her bondage. It was also obvious that beneath the glimmer of fear sparkling in her eyes, she harboured her own reverential awe for Hera. Seeing the expression, Anna knew that even if she had untied Cassandra, the girl would have remained on the bed until Hera told her to move.

'No,' Hera sounded almost thoughtful as she said the word. 'You've stayed silent all evening but there's not really been any need for you to speak, has there?'

Uncertainly, Cassandra shook her head. Her eyes were wide and a nervous tremble made her body undulate softly on the bed. Anna watched excitedly, wondering what was going to happen next.

Hera reached a hand toward Cassandra's hard nipple. Her finger stroked a soft circle against the pale areola. Cassandra sighed softly. The sound was little more than a whisper of breath but the angry light that glinted in Hera's eyes was enough to tell her such a noise would not be overlooked if it happened a second time. From her corner of the room, Anna could see the dark foreboding in the brunette's fierce expression.

'Silence, remember,' Hera reminded her. 'I won't tolerate another outburst like that. If I hear another sound, I'll untie you and throw you out of here and you kiss your black garter goodbye.'

Cassandra was nodding furiously on the bed. If she had been able to speak, Anna knew the girl would have been screaming apologies at Hera.

Appearing unaware of the terror she was inspiring, Hera continued to stroke her finger against Cassandra's bare breast. The nipple had looked hard before. Now it seemed to pulse with the ardent urgency of arousal. Hera put a finger to her lips and touched the tip of her tongue against it. With the end of her finger moistened, she rubbed it around Cassandra's breast a second time.

Anna could see the slick trail of moisture the finger left in its wake. She could feel her own nipples hardening, as though they had experienced the delights of Hera's touch. A slow, steady pulse began to beat between her legs and she tried to ignore the sensation. As she had told herself earlier, there would be plenty of time to enjoy the memory of these incidents from the comfort of her own bed. The thought did not help. Instead, she found the anticipation of that moment only added to her excitement.

Hera continued to rub the finger around Cassandra's areola until the tip was dry. She raised the digit to her lips and then stopped. 'What am I doing?' she exclaimed, her voice rich with pantomime surprise. 'I shouldn't be wetting my own finger, when you could wet it for me.' A knowing smile crossed her lips and she stared ominously down at the blonde.

Not realising the implication of the words, Cassandra held her mouth slightly open, expecting Hera to place the finger there.

Hera moved her finger towards Cassandra's face and held it a millimetre from the sultry pout of her lower lip. Then, her grin broadening, Hera slowly pushed her hand down toward the cleft of Cassandra's sex. Anna drew a shocked breath.

Hera grinned confidently and winked again. She placed her finger in the thatch of blonde curly hairs that covered Cassandra's pubic mound and pushed closer to the heat of the girl's sex. Aware that she was writhing uncomfortably on the bed, Hera continued regardless.

'What if she wants you to stop?' Anna asked quietly.

Hera shook her head as though this was unlikely to be a consideration. 'If Cassandra wants me to stop, she'll say so.'

'And would you stop?' Anna asked carefully.

Hera's salacious grin was enough of a reply.

'If she did stop you,' Anna went on, 'would you still let her in the Black Garter?'

Hera shook her head. 'Cassie knows the rules,' she explained. 'If she makes another sound, she won't be allowed in.' As she talked, her hand continued to work its way slowly through the wispy bush of Cassandra's pubic mound. The tips of her fingers had reached the heat of the girl's pussy.

Smiling fondly down at the rosebud of her sex, a tender expression appeared in Hera's eyes. With a soft, gentle stroke, she drew her finger against Cassandra's nether lips. They unfurled beneath the stimulation of her finger. Anna could see they were glistening wetly in the bright light of the bedroom and she heard her own breathing deepen. The thought of relieving herself later seemed too distant to even contemplate. The pulse between her legs was a hammering beat that demanded satisfaction and she had to stop herself from placing a hand against her own sex. Anna knew that if she placed even a finger there, her body would explode with the swell of an orgasm that had built inside her.

Hera moved her finger slowly up and down along the inner lips. A slick coating of dewy moisture covered it. When she withdrew the digit she smiled greedily at the wetness. She grinned at Cassandra then moved the finger back to the bound girl's breast and rubbed the tip against the sensitive flesh of her areola.

Cassandra bit back a groan of delight. Her breathing had grown shallow and Anna could see the combined shine of excitement and fear that filled her face. She kept her gaze fixed on the two women, not wanting to miss an instant of their pleasure.

'Light a couple of candles,' Hera commanded absently.

Without thinking, Anna rushed to obey. She had seen two long slender candles in the twin holder on Hera's bedside cabinet. She retrieved a box of matches from her jeans and hurried back. Anna stood close to the woman as she lit both wicks, then Hera stepped back slightly and Anna felt their naked bodies touch. She did not know if it was done deliberately or accidentally; all that she knew was a longing for the divine naked creature who stood next to her. A frisson of overwhelming excitement seemed to emanate from Hera's bare flesh. The intimate caress of her naked skin evoked feelings far more powerful than Anna could cope with and she fixed her attention on lighting the candles, trying to ignore Cassandra's deepening breath and the unnerving arousal of Hera's presence. Her fingers struggled nervously with the matches. As she held the flame to the slender, phallic tip of each candle, she saw her body's nervousness mimicked by the flickering flame.

Once the candles were lit, she stepped back, wondering what to do with herself. She was scared to remain too close to Hera, fearful of her own eager response to the powerful woman and yet she was unwilling to offend her by moving back to the corner of the room she had been cowering in. She almost sighed with relief when Hera asked her to go to the other side of the bed.

'You'll see more from there,' she explained. With a lewd smile, she added, 'And I'll see more of you.'

Anna shivered and started to move. She was aware that Hera was standing too close to her and as Hera's cool flesh brushed her warm skin, Anna's nipples ached dully and the throb between her legs became as heavy and resounding as the beat of a kettle drum. It was fun and exciting to desire someone as powerful and attractive as Hera but overwhelming to think her feelings might be reciprocated.

She moved to the opposite side of the bed and watched as Hera addressed Cassandra.

'You've done yourself proud so far this evening,' Hera encouraged quietly. 'You've stayed silent throughout the night whilst I was out. You've not said a word while I've been touching you.'

Cassandra blushed as Hera reminded her of this but she did not look away. Her gaze was fixed resolutely on the brunette. An expression of burning gratitude lit her eyes as she listened to the praise that was being given.

'The only thing is,' Hera explained, turning to the

candlestick on the bedside cabinet. 'You need to prove you can stay silent when every muscle in your body wants to scream in agony.'

Cassandra's eyes had begun to widen doubtfully, then filled with sheer terror when she saw Hera holding a single candle in her hand.

Anna could see her struggling against the ropes that bound her hands and feet. Every muscle in her body seemed taut with her fear and the desperate need to get away, yet, in spite of her struggles, she realised Cassandra was remaining silent. However threatening or depraved Hera became, Anna knew that Cassandra would go along with whatever she did. Despite the woman's discomfort and suffering, Anna knew she was enjoying herself although she doubted Cassandra was getting as much pleasure from being dominated as she was from watching, but she supposed it was possible.

Standing by the side of the bed, Anna felt a soft pressure brush at the lips of her sex and glanced down warily. She should not have been surprised to see her own fingers slyly touching the heated wetness of her sex. The situation was more than arousing, it was intoxicating. Unable to stop herself, she used one hand to spread the lips of her pussy wide apart. With the other she began to tease lazy circles against the pulsing flesh of her desire.

She was aware that Hera was watching her avidly but, with the urgency of the moment, that did not matter. All that mattered to Anna was that she experience the vital relief of her mounting orgasm. She worked on herself slowly, resisting the urge to rub furiously. She was determined to indulge herself in the heady joys of a powerful, unhurried climax. The wealth of pleasure inspired by her lazy finger-tip was already building to gargantuan proportions and, if she was allowed the chance to continue, Anna knew she would enjoy a climax of stupendous proportions.

With her finger teasing deftly at the tender folds of flesh, Anna was lost in her own thoughts of imminent orgasm. The coolness of Hera's voice startled her out of her reverie.

'Are you ready to prove your loyalty to the Black Garter?' Hera asked sharply.

Anna was surprised by the ominous tone of Hera's voice. She could see a cold, dark smile breaking the woman's lips. Hera was holding the candle over Cassandra's breast; the tip had already melted and Anna saw that the swell of melted wax had raised a delicate meniscus. The surface trembled in Hera's calm hand.

Cassandra was glaring at it with feverish panic. Beads of sweat speckled her brow and she glanced nervously from Hera to the tip of the candle.

'Are you going to stay silent?' Hera asked. Before Cassandra had time to reply, Hera tilted the candle.

Anna saw a stream of molten wax trickle from the tip of the candle. In the brightly lit room, the wax sparkled like silver. Hera grinned broadly.

Either by good luck or spectacular accuracy, and Anna suspected the latter, the wax splashed wetly against the tip of Cassandra's eager nipple. Anna held her breath. The room remained thick with silence.

Cassandra pulled against the ropes that bound her, twisting and writhing from one side to the other. An expression of tortured pain contorted her face and Anna realised numbly that the girl was not in the throes of agony as she had first suspected; her writhing had been brought on by an orgasm. Tossing her head from side to side, Anna saw a grim smile of satisfaction twist Cassandra's lips. The tendons on her neck stood out like cords as she threw her head back into the pillow.

All the time, she maintained enough self-control to stop even a groan of pleasure slipping from her lips.

Anna was under no such constraints. The urgency of her arousal was too great for her to even contemplate stopping now. Entranced by the vision of Cassandra's joy she felt so close to reaching orgasm the moment was almost tangible. Her fingers squeezed and pressed against the pulsing bud of her clitoris. She rubbed slightly, still holding the lips wide apart with her other hand.

When the orgasm struck, Anna screamed with ecstatic jubilation. Waves of pleasure flowed through her body, engulfing her in a warm, wet explosion of pure delight. Her breasts tingled with a dull wave of joy whilst the muscles, deep inside her, clamped furiously. Her fulfilment was so complete it was unnerving. She snatched her fingers away from the pulsing source of her climax, unable to contemplate the thought of enduring any more delight.

'Impressive,' Hera said quietly.

Anna did not know if she was referring to her or Cassandra but she smiled at the brunette through a hazy red mist of her own satisfaction. She was gratified that Hera graced her with a knowing smile before turning her attention back to Cassandra.

'You've done very well, Cassie,' Hera assured the blonde. 'And you'll be allowed to speak as soon as you've completed the last task.' Her warm smile was unnervingly comforting. 'You've shown you can remain silent; you've proved your obedience. Now, will you prove your loyalty?'

Cassandra nodded eagerly.

Anna wondered what the woman was letting herself in for but dared not speculate too much. She could already feel the tingling pulse of her arousal stirring again. Her limbs still ached from the strength of the last orgasm and she doubted she could tolerate a second one just yet.

Hera tipped the candle again. This time the wax splashed against Cassandra's bare stomach. Anna sucked in air, muting the sound as soon as she had made it. Hera cast a warning glance in her direction as she lowered the burning wick of the candle toward Cassandra's stomach. With a lightning quick flick of her wrist, she drew the flame over Cassandra's body. From her position at the side of the bed, Anna could see the candle was being held a couple of inches above the girl. She knew that from Cassandra's angle, it would look as though the flame was being dragged across her bare flesh and she suspected that was what Hera intended the girl to think.

She watched Cassandra struggle helplessly as she tried to move away from the burning flame. Hera moved the candle quickly, dripping spots of wax on the pale pink flesh as she drew it this way and that. She edged the candle lower as she neared Cassandra's pubic bush and, for a second, Anna felt sure she could detect the acrid scent of singed hair.

With the candle held over the heat of Cassandra's sex, Hera turned to the girl and smiled. Her warm expression was greeted by a look of speechless terror. Cassandra glanced first at the candle, then at Hera, then back to the candle. The burning wick was dangerously close to the hypersensitive flesh of her pussy lips. Her breathing had collapsed into a ragged pant and her face looked like that of a frightened rabbit.

With her grin widening, Hera bent down and blew out the candle. At the same time, she twisted her wrist and pressed the base against the sodden wetness of

Cassandra's pussy. The length of wax entered her quickly and smoothly.

Anna watched Cassandra's face contort into a silent groan of elation. Her hips bucked up and down as she fucked the rigid length of candle between her legs. She released a whispered breath of muted delight as she succumbed to the pleasures of absolute joy.

Hera slipped the candle from Cassandra's pussy and placed it carefully back in the candlestick holder. She extinguished the second burning wick with her fingers, smiling as the flame touched her skin, then opened the drawer of her cabinet.

Aware that the initiation was over, Anna began to unfasten Cassandra's wrists and ankles. The blonde smiled gratefully up at her, then turned her face away from Anna when Hera began to unfasten her limbs at the other side. Anna noticed that the girl seemed to widen her smile when she looked at Hera.

'Here,' Hera said, after unfastening Cassandra's ankle. She put her hands around the girl's foot and Anna realised she was placing something around her leg. A smile touched her lips when she saw what it was.

'Congratulations,' Hera told Cassandra. She placed a tender kiss on her lips. 'You've just become a member of the Black Garter.' Aware that Cassandra was staring at her in silence, she added, 'You can talk now, if you want.'

Cassandra stared gratefully at her, not bothering to mask her adulation. 'Thank you,' the girl whispered passionately. She glanced at Anna, smiling softly as she did this. Then she turned back to Hera. 'I really mean it,' she whispered urgently. 'Thank you.'

Hera laughed and kissed her again before standing up. 'The pleasure wasn't all yours,' she said. 'Anna and I owe you a few words of thanks.' Moving to the side of the bed she placed her hand around Anna's waist and squeezed her gently. It was a gesture that went beyond the platonic and Anna could feel her arousal sparking instantly as Hera touched her. 'I should thank you for your help,' she whispered, delivering a small peck on Anna's lips.

Cassandra was smiling wistfully at the black garter that encircled her thigh. Her features were contorted into an expression that was almost reverential.

Hera and Anna ignored her.

'I didn't know what to expect when you asked me here this evening,' Anna said honestly. 'But I never imagined this.'

Hera laughed. 'Could you come back here after you've seen Cassandra safely back to her dorm?'

Anna was nodding before she even had a chance to consider the offer properly. 'Of course,' she said. 'There's still a lot for us to sort out. We need to develop a plan of action about these newspaper stories . . .'

Hera stopped her words with a kiss.

Anna was surprised by the subtle intimacy of the gesture. The brunette did not use any force. She simply allowed their lips to touch. The soft stimulation was infuriatingly arousing. 'I've got Samantha Flowers looking into the newspaper stories,' Hera said quietly. 'I want you to come back here for a reason that has nothing to do with the Black Garter.' Her eyes shone wickedly with the dark meaning of her words.

Anna could not even contemplate refusing. She whispered her eager response as she kissed Hera's lips passionately. 'I'll come back,' she promised. 'As soon as I've got Cassandra safely back to her dorm.'

Hera nodded. Her fingers brushed softly against Anna's breast and she ended the kiss by taking a step away, leaving Anna breathless and impatient with desire.

Hera walked back to the bedside cabinet, aware of the glorious display her naked body presented. She grinned at Anna and reached for the candlestick. 'I'll light one of these for your return.'

Four

'You're not an assistant gym instructor, are you?'

Jo glanced slowly up from the sheaf of newspapers she was leafing through, surprised to hear someone addressing her so loudly in the library. Admittedly it was ten-thirty at night and she suspected they were the only two in the place but the raised voice still seemed out of place in the solemn silence of the book-lined walls.

A tall red-haired woman stood beside her. She had a serious face and sparkling green eyes hidden behind delicate wire-rimmed spectacles. It was only because she wore the cowl-like cloak of the school overcoat that Jo realised the woman was a student and not some junior librarian.

'Hello,' Jo said flatly.

'You're not an assistant gym instructor, are you?' The redhead repeated.

Jo could not stop herself from smiling. Sitting lazily back in the chair she stretched her aching muscles and flexed her fingers. She had dressed in a loose-fitting exercise suit, trying to reinforce the sporty aspect to her assumed persona. Normally she would not have worn such an outfit unless she was going to a fancy-dress party. It was a comfortable garment, she conceded, labelled with a handful of designer names whom she had vaguely heard of, but it did little to make her feel feminine. Staring at the solemn bespectacled face of the cowled young woman next to her, Jo wondered cruelly if a lack of femininity was the norm for the Kilgrimol School for Young Ladies.

'Do they teach students how to begin a conversation at this school?' Jo asked curiously. 'If they do, perhaps you should take those lessons again.'

'Who are you, and what are you doing here?'

Jo blinked a couple of times, surprised by the girl's bluntness. She considered being sarcastic and rude for a second time then stopped herself, aware it was having no effect. From past experience, she knew that the only alternative was plain rudeness.

'Fuck off and stop bothering me,' she growled. 'I'm too busy to come and play with your dolls if that's what you're wanting.' She turned her attention back to the sheaf of newspapers and continued to read the article.

She had arrived at the Kilgrimol School earlier that evening after a long, arduous drive through some of Scotland's most beautiful terrain. The drive had left her feeling melancholy and weary. Her car radio had broken the moment she set off and with only her own thoughts, and the empty scenery for company, she had spent nine unbroken hours wallowing in the most miserable depths of introspection. It had not been an experience she wanted to repeat.

As soon as she had arrived at the school, Jo had sought out the principal and started working on the case. It was not that she felt particularly enthusiastic about the prospect of solving Mr Smith's problem. She simply needed to immerse her thoughts in something other than her own world of broken hearts and lost loves.

'Who are you, and what are you doing here?'

Jo glanced up from the article again. This time she was frowning. 'What are you?' she demanded. 'The school's fucking ghost or something? Why don't you go and haunt someone else?'

'I asked you a question,' the redhead repeated. 'Who are you, and what are you doing here?'

'And I asked you to fuck off and stop bothering me,' Jo retorted. 'But it's made no difference, has it?'

They stared angrily at one another. Jo could see the defiant expression of her own determined face mirrored in the bespectacled young woman's.

A sudden smile broke the redhead's look of consternation. 'The blunt, forceful approach isn't going to work on you, is it?' she said cheerfully. She extended a hand. 'My name's Samantha Flowers. I'm a third-year senior prefect.'

Jo stared uncertainly at the hand. She shook it carefully, unhappy with the woman's sudden mood change. 'And what can I do for you, Samantha?'

'Sam,' the redhead corrected. 'And you can start by telling me who you are and why you're here. I know you're not an assistant to the gym instructor.'

'You seem very confident about that fact,' Jo observed. 'Would you care to take a seat and tell me why?'

Sam shrugged easily and slipped into the seat next to Jo. 'This is my last term at the Kilgrimol,' she explained. 'When I go out into the world, I intend to do some work with the police.'

Jo raised her eyebrows as though she was interested. 'Helping them with their enquiries?' she guessed.

Sam smiled. The expression changed her face, expelling the serious, bookish look and making her seem far prettier than Jo would have believed. 'I hardly think so,' Sam replied. 'I'd like to be a detective and solve crimes.'

'Fascinating,' Jo replied dourly.

Sam nodded. 'I'm sure it will be. Do you enjoy doing that?'

Jo had been trying to maintain a mask of cool, indifferent calm but the girl's question was enough to unsettle her. She knew that a guilty expression had crossed her features before she had a chance to stop it surfacing. 'I thought we were going to talk about you.'

'What's it like being a private investigator?' Sam pushed. 'Is it exciting? Is it as glamorous as it looks in the movies?'

'The best part,' Jo replied, 'is when you get to wring the neck of nosy schoolgirls. Moments like that make the job worth every other sacrifice.'

Sam cheerfully paid no heed to the threat. 'As I see it, you must be here for one of two reasons. You're either trying to find out about our scandals, or you're trying to break up the Black Garter.'

Jo pushed the papers to one side and picked up the notepad she had been scribbling in. 'Goodnight, Inspector Clouseau,' she said, pushing her chair noisily under the library table. 'Perhaps I'll see you again if I ever visit the lunatic asylum you've escaped from.'

'Wait!' Sam had jumped up from her chair and was following Jo. 'You haven't answered any of my questions. I want to talk to you.' Her hand fell on Jo's arm as she pushed through the door. 'I need to talk to you.'

Jo stared at her, wondering if she had mistaken the urgency in the girl's last sentence. She studied the green eyes that stared desperately from behind the wire-rimmed spectacles. Not trusting her own good nature, Jo relented. She glanced around the deserted library, then looked sternly at Sam. 'Is this place secure?'

'Secure?'

'Are we safe to talk in here?' she explained.

Sam nodded quickly. 'It's a school library. No one ever comes in here. Besides, it's after curfew and this is the last place anyone would come after lights out.'

Jo nodded, accepting the redhead's rationalisation. She returned slowly to the desk she had been using and settled herself back in the chair. 'I don't suppose you're carrying a drink beneath that Batman cape, are you?' she asked.

Sam reached into her pocket and produced a silver hip flask. 'I'll say sorry now,' she said as she passed it to Jo. 'It's only Jack Daniels.'

Jo grinned as she unscrewed the top and savoured the familiar, bitter scent of her favourite whisky. 'I think I can find it in my heart to forgive you,' she whispered, sipping greedily at the drink. She smiled, refreshed by the potent taste and wiped her lips dry with the back of her hand. Fixing Sam with a solemn stare she asked, 'What's your problem?'

'I've got several,' Sam replied, sitting next to Jo. 'I'm expected to get the name of the bitch who's been leaking stuff to the papers. I'm meant to work out who you are, and why you're here. I should also be trying to discover who sent you and why. And I need to know if you're involved in the scandals in any way.'

Jo nodded. 'And are you just nosy, or is there a reason for all of this?'

Sam grinned tightly and took the hip flask back from Jo. She sipped delicately at the Jack Daniels and Jo watched her features contort as the liquid filled her mouth. She guessed that Sam was not used to the flavour of the whisky undiluted. A superior smile filled her lips as she realised the redhead was trying to impress her.

'I have to get this information for some friends of mine,' Sam replied carefully.

'The Black Garter?' Jo asked.

Sam frowned sharply. 'How do you know about the Black Garter?'

'They know you have a penchant for playing Sherlock Holmes and they want you to do their dirty work and find the school snitch,' Jo said, not bothering to explain that she was simply guessing at fairly obvious facts. 'So far, you've been working your way through a list of possibilities but you've not found anything that can help you. Is there a threat of retribution if you fail?'

Sam looked positively panic-stricken. 'How do you know so much about the Black Garter?' she demanded. 'Are you a former member, or has someone been telling our secrets? Is the leak coming from one of the group?'

'Slow down,' Jo said, snatching the hip flask from her. She swigged a mouthful and handed the flask back. 'Are you a member?'

Sam turned her face away from Jo's. By way of reply, she pulled the cape of her school overcoat open, revealing the Black Garter at the top of her thigh.

Jo stared at the band of fabric breaking the cool pale beauty of her long muscular leg. Her gaze was drawn above the garter, to the crease of Sam's lap. The top of her leg was held in shadows from the coat and Jo found herself wishing she could see just a little bit more. 'Is that like a membership badge?'

Sam nodded. 'The Black Garter are a secret society. Members are forbidden to divulge their association.'

Jo noticed how carefully Sam phrased her words, neither confirming nor denying her part in the organisation. She nodded her understanding, unable to stop herself from admiring the redhead's integrity. She took a last glance at the black garter, enjoying the sight of the bare leg it encircled, then looked at Sam's face. 'Who's on the top of your whodunnit list?'

'Check the school register,' Sam replied. 'It could be anyone.'

'I doubt that,' Jo said arrogantly. 'But that's the wrong way to start. Have you got a list of the victims?'

Sam frowned. 'Victims?'

'Have you got a list of the girls who've been involved in the scandals?' She watched Sam shake her head, then said quickly, 'Get one. When we have that, we can make a start.'

A heart-warming smile split Sam's lips. 'Can I help you to solve this case?' she asked eagerly. 'Are we working together?'

Jo snatched the hip flask from her and took a long, satisfying drink before answering. 'We're not working together,' she explained calmly. 'But I would appreciate your help.'

Sam nodded, not bothering to conceal the broad grin that filled her face. 'How do we start? What do you want me to do?'

Jo passed her the notepad and a pen. 'You can start with that list I wanted,' she replied.

Sam took the paper and pen and pushed her seat closer to Jo's. As she leafed through the pile of newspapers, she made quick, neat notes on the pad.

Jo watched her, uncomfortable with the redhead's nearness. Her coat had fallen fully open now and Jo saw she was wearing a short skirt and a tight T-shirt. The black garter she wore was only just covered by the hem of the skirt and Jo realised she was staring at it with more interest than was healthy. She stopped herself abruptly, unhappy with the train of thought that Sam was inspiring.

'How did you know I wasn't a gym instructor's assistant?'

Sam glanced shyly up from her notes. 'I went through your things,' she explained. 'I hope you don't mind.'

Jo shrugged. 'Would it matter if I did?'

Smiling, Sam returned to the note she was making. 'I saw you arrive earlier. You asked a prefect where Miss Fairchild was, and you told her you were the new assistant gym instructor. When I discovered which room you had, I went to your room, intending to sound you out.'

She used these last three words with such a lack of familiarity that Jo grinned. She wondered which novel the girl had found the phrase in, then stopped herself from asking the question.

Oblivious to Jo's thoughts, Sam continued. 'After I'd knocked half a dozen times, I realised you'd gone out, so I broke in and went through your things.' She glanced up from the notepad. 'Are you sure you don't mind?'

Jo shook her head, sipping at the hip flask. 'Just so long as my whisky is there when I get back and your findings remain a secret between you and I.'

Sam stopped writing. 'I'm not sure I can agree to that,' she said, staring solemnly at Jo. 'I'm bound by an honour code.'

'Tell your friends and I'll press charges for breaking and entering,' Jo told her, injecting a subtle firmness into the threat. 'I don't want anyone to know why I'm here. Not even your precious Black Garter.'

'But I have an obligation,' Sam insisted. She put

her hand against Jo's leg as she spoke. It was a natural, unaffected gesture but Jo felt a thrill of excitement from the touch. She swallowed nervously, surprised by the effect of such innocent familiarity.

'I have to tell them everything I've discovered,' Sam explained earnestly.

She seemed unaware of Jo's arousal, and the private investigator took a small measure of relief from that fact. 'You don't have to tell them everything,' Jo said firmly. 'A good investigator knows when to indulge in a little selective reporting.'

'I don't know what you mean,' Sam told her. Her hand remained on Jo's leg, moving up slightly as she spoke. The gesture remained unconscious and lacked deliberate intimacy but Jo still felt thrilled by the stimulation. She shivered, disturbed by the excitement of Sam's touch. 'Read that,' Jo said, pointing at an article in the paper. 'Read that to me.'

Dutifully, Sam read the words. 'Roadworks will be causing delays on the East Glen High Street, in Kilgrimol, for the next two weeks. Drivers are advised to avoid the area if at all possible and use alternative routes.' She looked up from the newspaper and stared at Jo. 'I don't understand.'

'Will you be telling the Black Garter all about the roadworks on East Glen High Street?' Jo asked patiently.

'Of course not,' Sam replied.

'Then you'll be doing some selective reporting,' Jo replied.

'But that's different.'

Jo rolled her eyes with exasperation. 'Will you do it for me? As a personal favour? I know it's a lot to ask but . . .' Her voice trailed off and she realised Sam was staring at her. There was something familiar about the sparkle in her green eyes and the pout of her wide, soft lips. Uncomfortable with the woman's admiring gaze, Jo turned away. She tried desperately not to think of her own arousal but it was difficult.

'OK,' Sam said quickly. She gave Jo's leg one last reassuring squeeze, then turned back to the notepad again.

Once she had moved her hand away, Jo could still feel an electric tingling where Sam had been touching her. The dull, aching arousal began to spread through her body and she vainly tried to quell the emotion; sex was definitely not on the agenda, she told herself. Trying to focus her thoughts, Jo wondered if she could trust Sam. Her sudden agreement to side with Jo had been too quick and completely unprecedented. She supposed it was just a lie, to stop her from pursuing the issue. There would be time to get her point across later in the evening and Jo decided to let the matter drop, for the moment. Before they were finished, she would make sure she had reinforced her need for absolute secrecy.

'Who is Stephanie?' Sam asked suddenly.

Jo flinched as though she had been struck. 'Stephanie?' she repeated, trying to give herself time to think. 'Stephanie who?'

Sam continued working on her notes, speaking as she wrote. 'Her name was mentioned in your diary quite a few times. Who is she?'

'You read my diary?' Jo tried to sound aghast. She could not find it in herself to feel properly annoyed. If she had been in Sam's situation, she supposed she would have done the same thing. 'What the hell were you doing reading my diary?'

Sam glanced up from her writing. 'I was trying to find out who you are. A good investigator will use every source available.'

'Does that include a lack of morals?' Jo replied

unhappily. 'I write personal things in there. You had no right to go through it.'

'Sorry,' Sam replied with an indifferent shrug. She turned back to the notepad and began writing quickly.

Jo breathed a soft sigh of relief, thankful that the subject was finished with. Considering her body's eager response to the young redhead beside her, the last thing she needed was to have her arousal heightened by thoughts of Stephanie. It was difficult enough to concentrate on the nuances of this case.

'She was your lover, wasn't she?' Sam said quietly.

Jo stayed silent, glaring at her.

'That doesn't bother me, or offend me,' Sam said quickly.

'Thank you,' Jo sneered. 'I'm glad about that.'

Sam grinned and turned away from her notes. She placed a hand on Jo's leg and smiled warmly at her. 'I've been to bed with a woman once; it was quite exciting.'

Jo tried to remain indifferent beneath the redhead's fingers. The exercise suit was flimsy and she could feel the subtle pressure of Sam's hand as though it was touching bare flesh. Her palm rested halfway above Jo's knee and the tips of her fingers nestled dangerously close to the top of her leg.

Drawing on every last reserve of willpower, Jo said stiffly, 'I'm so pleased you weren't psychologically scarred for life by the experience.'

Sam laughed. It was a small musical sound that echoed merrily around the dry, dusty walls of the library. 'You're a miserable cow, aren't you?'

'If, by that, you mean I don't like schoolgirls reading through my diary, then perhaps you have a point,' Jo said icily.

'Do you still see her?' Sam asked curiously.

'I can't,' Jo replied. 'I murdered her, cut her body into small bits and then buried the remains in a mushroom field near to where I live. She started to annoy me with her questions,' Jo added poignantly.

Sam grinned. 'She must have been very special to you.'

'Should I call an emergency teacher?' Jo asked suddenly. 'You seem to have forgotten how to write. And you seem to be confusing the tasks of making a list, and asking intrusive personal questions.'

'Women make better lovers than men,' Sam said, ignoring Jo's sarcasm. Her fingers inched slowly up Jo's leg. 'Don't you think that's true?'

This time there was nothing accidental or imagined about her touch. Jo shivered in spite of herself. 'They don't once you've buried their bodies,' Jo said sharply. 'Are you going to write this damned list, or spend the rest of the night feeling up my leg?'

Sam's smile widened. 'Well, if I have the choice,' she began eagerly. Her fingers moved further upward. 'I know which I'd rather be doing.'

'It was a rhetorical question,' Jo said coldly.

Sam allowed her fingers to linger a moment longer than was necessary then, smiling into Jo's dark frown of disapproval, she reluctantly moved her hand away and turned back to her notes.

Jo's sigh of relief was clearly audible in the quiet confines of the library. She watched Sam writing quickly in the pad and tried to stop herself from mentally undressing the girl. Her first impression had been wrong, she conceded. Sam was not lacking in femininity. The girl simply managed to hide it well behind unattractive spectacles and a shapeless school cape. Her long hair was the luxuriant colour of fiery autumn leaves.

'Do you want to hear about the first time I did it with a woman?' Sam asked suddenly.

'Not particularly,' Jo retorted.

'I suppose I only did it because I was a little tipsy,' Sam continued. 'This friend of mine, I won't mention her name, that would be indiscreet; she and I had spent the evening in her dorm drinking a bottle of wine.'

'Should I start searching for someone who's interested in what you're saying?' Jo asked rudely.

'After we'd finished drinking the bottle, she kissed me on the mouth. It was amazing really. I wasn't expecting it. I wasn't expecting it when I kissed her back either. I'd have to rate it as one of the most thrilling experiences of my life.'

Jo grunted a noncommittal sound, wishing Sam would shut up. The girl's talk of sex and arousal was unsettling and she was already harbouring lustful thoughts for her. Sordid tales of 'my first time', and 'guess who I kissed', were not helping.

'Then she put a hand inside my blouse,' Sam continued. She pushed the cape down past her shoulders and thrust her small breasts forward, as if to demonstrate. 'I don't have big boobs,' she said coyly, 'but they're really sensitive.'

Jo tried to tug her gaze away from the ardent thrust of Sam's breasts. She was not wearing a bra and her nipples pushed noticeably against the flimsy fabric of her T-shirt. The tender orbs looked excruciatingly desirable beneath the thin cotton and Jo struggled to keep her breathing at a normal rate. As she watched, Sam rubbed a thumb over one of the thrusting nubs, then shivered as though she had been chilled by the touch. She smiled broadly and her eyes shone merrily.

'I suppose women are better at touching boobs

than men,' Sam said thoughtfully. 'We know where to touch them and how to do it properly.'

Jo shrugged and stayed silent, not trusting herself to give a response.

'Anyway, she and I ended up in bed together and we did everything that night. She didn't just kiss my mouth, she kissed me everywhere. I did the same to her; licked her boobs and even put my tongue in her cunny.'

'Why are you telling me all this?' Jo asked quietly.

Sam smiled, as though she did not mind being interrupted too much. 'The next morning, we were both a bit shy with one another. I don't suppose it's the done thing to be a bit lezzie but we'd done it and there was no getting away from it. She asked me why I'd let her do all those things. Do you know what I said? I said that I'd wanted her to do them.'

The silence in the library was thick with anticipation. Jo could feel a band of excitement tightening across her chest. Determined that Sam would not see how she was affecting her, Jo said calmly, 'And your point is?'

Sam shook her head and smiled into Jo's stern face. 'My point is, I do whatever I want,' Sam explained. 'If I want to sleep with a woman, I just go ahead and do it.' She placed her hand on Jo's leg and leant toward her. Her face moved close to Jo's. 'I want to sleep with you,' she whispered softly.

'I'm sorry I can't help you,' Jo said sharply. 'I'm practising to become a Benedictine monk at the moment. I hear they get discounts on the sherry.'

Sam moved her lips close to Jo's face. Their mouths were mere inches apart. 'Kiss me, Jo,' Sam urged her. 'I want you.'

Jo moved her face away. 'I can't kiss you,' she snapped angrily. 'Christ! You're only a fucking schoolgirl. How old are you? You make me feel like a child molester just looking at you!'

'I'm twenty,' Sam said. 'How old are you?'

'None of your fucking business,' Jo retorted.

'I've read your diary,' Sam reminded Jo. 'I've read the things you've written about Stephanie. You know how exciting it is to have a woman touch your boobs, don't you?' Her hand snaked forward and brushed against Jo's breast.

In the tight lycra top of her exercise suit, the hard swell of her nipple was an easy target. Jo felt a rush of delight course through her body and slapped Sam's hand away angrily.

'Why are you fighting it?'

Jo glared at her. 'I'm just not interested, OK?'

Sam shook her head. 'If you weren't interested, you wouldn't have enjoyed my touching you so much. You want me, don't you?'

Jo could not find the strength to lie to the girl. It was easier to avoid the question. 'I don't want anyone. I'm here to solve a case. I'm not here to fuck my way through the whole school.'

Grinning, Sam moved her face closer to Jo's. 'I wasn't going to bring anyone else in, unless you were really good,' she whispered. 'Why don't you just fuck me instead?'

Jo opened her mouth intending to raise a protest but Sam silenced her words with a kiss. Their mouths joined and Jo felt herself responding willingly to the redhead. At Sam's intrusion into her mouth she experienced a heady rush of desire. Their tongues twisted and curled together. One hand was fondling her breast, while the other was caressing her shoulder. All the time they were kissing, Jo could feel the surge of longing well within her like waters pressing at a dam.

It had been two months since Stephanie and Nick had married. It had been a lot longer since Jo had felt someone touch her in this way. All the tension and misery she had endured since Nick and Stephanie announced their engagement seemed to dissipate with Sam's careful caresses.

Unable to stop herself, Jo moved her hand towards Sam's breasts. She rubbed her fingers carefully against the orb, tracing its outline through the thin cotton T-shirt.

Sam groaned excitedly, pushing her breast eagerly into Jo's hand. Her own fingers were squeezing and caressing Jo's pliant flesh, whilst her other hand had started to move downward. Her delight was obvious.

The warning voice of Jo's conscience whispered words of caution. It told her Sam was too young; the timing was inappropriate and the place was unsuitable. Jo ignored the voice. She had always known the difference between right and wrong but she had rarely let such knowledge influence her decisions.

She pulled Sam close to her, embracing the woman tightly. The light scent of perfume filled her nostrils and beneath that scent, subtler but devastatingly more arousing, was the thrilling aroma of her excitement.

Not only could Jo feel the ardent touch and caress of the redhead's eagerly exploring fingers but now she was enjoying the hedonistic pleasure of having the woman's body pressed against her. She ached with desire, relishing the intimacy.

Sam's fingers found their way beneath Jo's lycra top. She released Jo's breasts from their confines, moving back slightly to admire them fully. An appreciative smile lit her lips and she drew a tentative finger against the exposed flesh.

Jo smiled hesitantly at Sam, then closed her eyes and immersed herself in the joy of the redhead's erotic caresses. A warm, wet mouth fell over her breast. The heated moisture would have been exciting enough on its own but, with the added stimulation of the tongue flicking over her nipple, she realised the half-forgotten joy of an orgasm would soon be tearing through her. She sighed excitedly, eagerly anticipating the explosion of pleasure.

The eruption started when Sam moved her mouth to the other breast. Her fingers continued to play with the nipple she had been sucking and she rolled and teased the hardened nub of flesh between her thumb and forefinger. The pressure she applied varied from whisper-soft strokes to merciless clamping. Her wet lips fell around Jo's other nipple and she sucked gently on it.

Jo heard herself release a distant groan. Her breasts had been aching for a touch like this. Their eager response had created a spiralling whirlpool of joy inside her and she could feel herself spinning dizzily downward to dark depths of delight.

The intensity of her response was totally unexpected. Jo had realised she was aroused but it seemed inconceivable she could have been so ready for orgasm. As the waves of pleasure coursed through her, she moaned with elation. Climactic spasms racked her body and her breathing fell into a ragged pant. When she opened her eyes, she stared at Sam with newly earned respect.

'Was that as much fun as it looked?' Sam asked innocently.

Jo laughed softly and kissed her. With experienced hands, she stripped Sam naked and pushed her on top of the desk. Newspapers, notepads and pencils spilt to the floor but neither of the women noticed. Both seemed lost in a heady world filled with longing, desire and impending satisfaction.

Revealed, Sam's breasts were a joy to behold. Small and pert, they were tipped with dark areolae and short, broad nipples. Jo rubbed a casual thumb over each breast and every muscle of the redhead's body shook as waves of delight rippled through her. Jo smiled down at her, her grin a twisted grimace of joy.

'You're ready for this, aren't you?' Jo murmured.

Sam nodded. 'I'm more than ready.'

The words were encouragement enough for Jo. She stroked her hands over the silky smooth flesh of Sam's thighs, relishing the shiver of excitement that trembled beneath her touch. Her fingers worked their way slowly upwards, nearing the heated centre of Sam's sex. The stretched lips were flushed dark with excitement and the cleft was fringed with a neatly trimmed tuft of hair. As luxuriant in colour as the locks on her head, Sam's pubic bush was a burning fire of flaming red. Jo groaned and brushed her fingers through the hair. She felt the heat of Sam's passion wetting her and the two women sighed simultaneously. Jo pushed a finger inside easily and felt her digit engulfed by a tight slippery fire. Sam released a guttural cry of pleasure and stared wide-eyed at Jo.

Jo eased a second finger alongside the first. Both were coated with the slippery wetness of Sam's excitement and the musky scent of her arousal filled Jo's nostrils. As she began to slide the two fingers slowly in and out, Jo tried to contain the urgency of her own arousal.

Sam writhed from side to side on the top of the desk, raising her legs towards her chest in order to expose the desperate need of her sex more fully. Eagerly, she wrapped her arms around her legs, holding them high so Jo could do whatever she wanted.

Jo stared longingly at the sight. Her desire to taste Sam's succulent cleft was almost unbearable. Kneeling down on the cold wooden floor, she placed her head between Sam's legs and inhaled deeply, relishing the fragrant scent. Sliding her fingers slowly out, she moved her mouth hesitantly towards the glistening pussy.

Sam was sighing soft words of appreciation before Jo's mouth touched her, and when the wet tongue flicked gently over the urgent pulse of her clitoris, her murmurs became a hoarse lament, encouraging Jo to do more and more.

Jo brushed her tongue against the sensitive flesh of Sam's sex, holding the lips wide apart, allowing the tip to trace wetly against the slippery folds. Drawing a circle around the glistening wet hole, Jo heard Sam's delight increase. The cries shifted to moans of mounting enjoyment.

Jo allowed her tongue to rub firmly against Sam's perineum, stroking dangerously close to the puckered ring of her arsehole. When she pushed her tongue into Sam's eager pussy, she relished the glorious taste of the redhead's arousal.

Sam groaned loudly. The sound echoed eerily from the library walls but neither of the women noticed.

Jo felt a light spray of pussy juice sprinkle against her nose. She inhaled the climactic moisture with a triumphant air. Moving her hands away, she eased Sam's hands from her legs and smiled.

'More,' Sam begged. Her eyes were wild with delirious ecstasy. 'More,' she insisted, 'please.'

Jo grinned. 'Maybe later,' she conceded. 'We still

need to talk and I can't imagine that desk is comfortable for you.'

'I can put up with it if you carry on doing what you're doing.'

Smiling, Jo slapped her playfully on the leg and then began to straighten the exercise suit. 'We'll play later,' Jo assured her. 'But I think we should have a few things sorted before things get too much out of hand.'

Reluctantly, Sam sat up on the desk and slowly reached for her clothes. She graced Jo with a grudging expression that summed up her gratitude and annoyance. 'That was something else,' Sam breathed softly.

Jo nodded, not trusting herself to speak. She was trying not to look at Sam's body whilst she dressed. It had taken a determined effort to stop herself from licking the redhead's divine pussy for a second time. It had been even more of a struggle to refuse her plea for more.

Jo could not recall the last time she had enjoyed herself so much. Stopping that train of thought before it had fully evolved, aware that it would lead back to melancholy memories, Jo fixed her attention on the case. She picked up the notepad Sam had been writing in and studied the list. There were four names there and Sam had written a brief description of each girl's scandal.

'Do these girls have anything in common?' Jo asked crisply.

'Aside from them all being students here, no,' Sam told her. 'Melanie Solomon, Grace Smith and Becky Warren are all members of the Black Garter. Debbie Chalmers isn't, although I know she has wanted to be.'

'Has wanted to be?' Jo repeated. 'Has she given up on the idea?'

Sam shrugged. 'She seems to have cooled off a little, yes. Actually, she would have been my first choice if she hadn't been caught by the papers herself.'

Jo glanced at the notes Sam had made. 'Drunk in a pub,' she read. A frown crossed her brow. It seemed unreal that any newspaper would consider the story worth printing. 'How provincial is this newspaper?'

'That story came just before the video story,' Sam explained. 'I suppose they just wanted to print some story about the lapse of standards at the Kilgrimol. They photographed Debbie pissed out of her brains in the Royal Oak and in the same edition there's an editorial condemning the lack of morals in this once-great school.'

'What was the "video story" about?' Jo asked.

Sam snorted rudely. 'That was a set-up and a load of hype. Someone gave the *Clarion* a lesbian porn film and said it belonged to Becky Warren. The only proof they had was that the video box had a letter in it with Becky's name and address on it. I've spoken to Becky and she says it was her letter but it wasn't her film. She has no idea who set her up.'

Jo nodded and turned her attention back to the notepad.

'It would be a lot easier if you let the Black Garter deal with this,' Sam said quietly. 'Once we've found out who's leaking the stories, we can sort her out in our own way.'

Jo shook her head, her attention still fixed on the list of names. 'That's not going to happen. I wouldn't trust your girlfriends to do it properly.'

'What the hell's that supposed to mean,' Sam demanded.

Jo glanced up. 'When I spoke to Edwina Fairchild, she said things had already started to go too far. Last night, a girl was found stripped naked and blindfolded in the gym. The girl didn't say what had happened to her but there were signs of physical abuse.'

Sam blushed softly. 'That was just a standard punishment detail,' she explained. 'She'd already had a single red garter. She should have cleaned up her act and she wouldn't have received the pair.'

'Red garters? Pairs of garters?' Jo did not bother hiding her confusion. 'Are we talking punishment or freebies from an Anne Summers catalogue?'

Sam smiled. 'It's Black Garter protocol. A single red garter is given to a girl to let her know she's being watched. If she doesn't clean her act up then she gets a pair of red garters.'

'And?' Jo prompted.

Sam continued blushing. 'That's to let her know she's due for a punishment detail. Like I said . . .'

'I know,' Jo broke in. 'It's standard Black Garter protocol.' She shook her head wearily, unable to comprehend the bizarre intricacies of the group's ceremonies. 'Were you involved?'

Sam shrugged. 'All of the Black Garter were there.'

Jo nodded. 'And what was she being punished for?'

Sam studied the buttons on her blouse as she fastened them, rather than looking at Jo. 'Her grades had slipped. The Black Garter were just trying to show her she should be a little more diligent about her studies.'

Jo placed her fingers under Sam's chin and lifted her face up. They stared at one another in silence for a second, Jo's hard gaze dominating Sam's unhappy frown. 'If they'll strip and beat some poor cow dumb enough to score badly on a school test, what do you think they'll do to the school snitch?'

'What are you saying?' Sam asked quietly.

Jo moved her fingers away. Her gaze continued to hold Sam's. 'I'm saying that we have to keep this investigation between you and me. Regardless of whether or not you like it, it could be a matter of life and death.'

Five

Bunny stared hungrily at Steven's cock. He lay beside her, a half-smile resting on his lips. Glancing at the long, semi-hard length of flesh that lay against his belly she smiled and moved her head towards him. Her tongue reached out and she stroked it slowly over the soft flesh of his shaft. Almost instantly, she could feel him hardening. Her smile broadened.

Steven released a distant sigh of pleasure and, encouraged by the noise, Bunny continued to move her mouth over him.

She wondered what it would feel like to have Steven's cock between her legs. The previous evening had been a combination of wondrous excitement and agonising frustration. The joy she had received from wanking and being touched seemed immeasurable. It had almost been as satisfying as the thrill of sucking and tasting Steven's and Peter's cocks. The pair of them seemed blessed with endless erections and she remembered fondly how she had played with their lengths and allowed them to cover her body with their seed for most of the night.

But still she felt desperately frustrated. It was not that she hadn't climaxed: the sheer carnal indulgence of oral sex had been enough to make her come and the heady sensation of having a cock fill her mouth had been bewildering. She had adored the taste of the thick, creamy fluid of the two men and the knowledge of the climactic joy she was giving only added to her euphoria.

But it did not satisfy the urgent pulse that beat between her legs. She had a need to feel a cock inside her and sucking was not enough to satisfy that craving.

Steven's cock was fully erect now. Because she had been licking him so wetly, his foreskin had rolled back to reveal the swollen purple end of his cock. Bunny held it with delicate fingers and placed her mouth around the tip. She sucked gently on it, savouring the subtle flavour of his previously spent climaxes.

Her fingers traced through the curly hairs that covered his balls and she held the sac fondly in warm fingers and applied the softest pressure possible to the steadily pulsing rocks. Steven groaned a little louder, accepting the pleasure that Bunny offered.

It was difficult to stop herself from thinking how good the cock would feel between her legs. The urgency of her sex's fevered pulse was already beginning to beat again and the need for penetration began to well within her as it had throughout the previous evening.

She lifted his cock at the base, moving it slowly so the head never left her lips. Still sucking on the eager length, she pushed her mouth down towards her hand. She didn't stop until she felt the swollen glans press at the back of her throat.

Steven writhed beneath her touch, 'You really are savouring that, aren't you?' he said as he ran his fingers through her blonde tresses.

Her lips broke into a smile around his shaft and she traced her tongue around him. Squeezing his balls delicately, she began to work on him with more urgency. The need to taste his come was like an undeniable hunger and the thought of feeling his length pulse into her mouth inspired a burning arousal that she had to satisfy.

He continued to rock from side to side on the bed. His fingers toyed unconsciously with her hair and shoulders.

Bunny worked her lips wetly up and down his length then she teased the eager sac of his balls with her fingertips, aware that he was nearing the brink. With a final suck on his length she felt the throb of his climax. It started in his balls and shot furiously up his rock-hard shaft. A warm, thick spray of semen filled her mouth. The liquid jetted against the back of her throat and suddenly she was filled with the joy of tasting him. The sweet, salty taste of his cream spilt over her tongue and, so that she did not waste any of the fluid, Bunny swallowed greedily.

She could hear Steven groaning above her. His cries were a muted sound of joy. Bunny continued to suck him, determined to relish as much of his come as was possible. When she had licked the last droplet from his flailing penis, she lowered the length to his belly and turned to face him.

'How was that?' she asked quietly.

He was staring down at her, an expression of delight on his face. 'Wonderful. Just wonderful,' he replied. 'Normally I'm happy with a croissant and a fruit juice of a morning but that has to be the best wake-up call I've ever had.'

She smiled at him and moved carefully up the bed. 'I'm glad you enjoyed it.' She rubbed the aching swell of her hardening nipples and added, 'Perhaps you can do something for me now.'

His smile broadened. He glanced down at his flaccid cock and then turned the grin back to Bunny.

'It might take a while to rekindle my enthusiasm,' he told her, 'but you seem to have a knack for making that happen.' His hands reached for her breasts and pushing her fingers away he began to fondle the heaving orbs.

Bunny sighed softly, revelling in the perfection of his caress. Steven seemed to know exactly where to touch her. His thumbs caught the febrile nubs of her breasts and sparked a tingle of delight that coursed through her entire body. The pads of his fingertips gently massaged the sensitive swell of her large bosom, thrilling her with a thousand subtle pleasures she could never have imagined.

Using her breasts like handles, Steven tugged Bunny softly towards himself and kissed her on the mouth. Returning his kiss with a furious passion, her tongue explored him, her hands snaking eagerly across his smooth hairless chest. Not content with just kissing his mouth, she moved her lips over his face and neck, teasing his flesh with subtle pecks and bites.

'What did you want me to do for you?' he murmured quietly in her ear.

She moved closer to him and placed her breasts in front of his face. Wordlessly, Steven took a nipple in his mouth and suckled gently on the hard, thrusting tip. His tongue licked carefully against the areola as his teeth teased the sensitive, erectile flesh.

Bunny shivered and made a small sound of protest, but she did not make him stop. Considering the urgent pulse of her desire, she realised she could not have stopped him; she needed this sort of attention far too much and knew there were limits far greater than this for her to reach.

'I want to feel you inside me,' she whispered deliberately. 'I want to feel your cock between my legs.'

Steven stared awkwardly up at her. Releasing the nipple, he lay back on the bed and continued to tease her breasts with his fingers. 'I thought you were saving yourself,' he remarked dryly.

'I am,' she told him. She kept her position above him, not wanting to disturb his deft fingers as they stroked her breasts to the pinnacles of ecstasy.

He seemed not to have heard her. 'I thought you wanted to enter the sanctity of marriage, *virgo intacta*. You can hardly do that if I deflower you here and now.'

She grinned down at him, a dark twinkle lighting the corner of her eye. 'You can fuck me and leave me a virgin if you do it carefully,' she told him.

Puzzled, he stared uncertainly up at her. 'How?'

Bunny grinned. 'Fuck my arse,' she whispered.

He drew an urgent breath.

'Fuck me up the arse and let me feel your cock deep inside me,' she begged.

If she had been watching his cock when she spoke, Bunny would have seen it twitch eagerly at the suggestion. Steven's eyes shone with excitement and his fingers pressed tightly against the swell of her nipples. She gasped in response. He swallowed thickly, studying her face, as though he suspected she might be having a joke with him. 'You really want me to do that?'

She moved her mouth close to his ear, blowing warm breath against his neck when she spoke. 'I want you to bugger me,' she whispered. 'I need to feel your cock inside me and this is the only way I can think of doing it.' She considered telling him about the choice her father had given her, then rejected the idea. Now was neither the time nor the place for such a revelation. It would be bound to destroy his eager mood. 'Listen to me, Steven,' Bunny implored him. 'I want your cock up my arse.'

He nodded, licking his dry lips eagerly. 'OK,' he agreed. He sat up on the bed and pushed her face downward until her giggles of excitement were muffled by the pillow. Steven began to rub his hands over the beautiful moons of her arse cheeks. The cleft of her pussy lips glistened wetly with excitement but he ignored the delightful vision it presented. Instead, his gaze was fixed hungrily on the tight ring of her arse. Placing his mouth over the hole, he drew his tongue against her in a slick, wet circle.

Bunny groaned delightedly. She thrust her backside towards his face and wriggled the cheeks of her arse against him. Her nipples were rock-hard with desire and she quickly moved her fingers to them. Rolling the stiff nubs back and forth between thumbs and index fingers, she was swiftly transported by the exquisite sensations.

Steven allowed his tongue to circle her arsehole a second time before he moved his mouth away. He grinned down at her and stroked the stiffening length of his cock with eager fingers. 'Are you sure you want me to do this?'

'Hurry up and do it,' Bunny hissed urgently. 'If you don't fuck my arse now, I'll go and find Peter and get him to fuck it.' She reached a hand behind herself and teased the tip of one finger against her anus. Aware that he was watching intently, she slid it inside.

Her feverish desire for satisfaction welled more furiously when she felt the intrusion and her breathing deepened to a soft, ragged sigh as she gently teased the finger in and out.

'Are you going to fuck your own arsehole?' Steven asked quietly. 'Or did you want me to do it?'

Pulling the finger out, she smiled wickedly. She studied the tip of her index finger and her grin broadened as she realised where it had just been. The urgent pulse of her longing beat harder. She stared at the finger then a frown crossed her brow and she murmured, 'I'm not very wet, am I?'

'I know how to make you wet,' he said cheerfully.

She glanced back at him and watched him lower his mouth against the heated ring of her anus. This time he was not content with simply circumnavigating her arsehole. He pushed his tongue forcefully inside her. She could feel the delightful intrusion forcing her sphincter wide open. The slippery wetness sent a magnificent thrill through her body and she shivered with joy as she felt him pushing deeper into her.

Steven grasped her thighs in a warm embrace and she could feel him tugging her purposefully back to meet the intrusion of his tongue.

Delighted by the pleasure he was stimulating, Bunny allowed herself to be manoeuvred. This was just an appetiser, she reminded herself. He was only moistening her hole, ready for that huge, glorious cock he sported. The thought sent her head spinning with anticipation.

The previous evening had been a whole new experience for her. The caresses and attention of two eager young men had excited her but now she was going to have that excitement properly fulfilled. Distantly, she almost wished Peter was still at the flat. If he had been, she could have had his cock in her mouth when Steven began to penetrate her arse.

He moved his lips away from her and tested her wetness with a finger. Bunny squealed excitedly and raised herself on to him, shrieking as she felt the finger sink deeper and deeper into the tight hole. Joyous pinpricks of pleasure exploded throughout her body. Waves of debilitating delight swept over her. She blinked back a haze of mist that seemed to cloud across her vision and released a triumphant cry of elation. The orgasm ripped through her body with the force of a hurricane, leaving her giddy, shaking and breathless.

Steven was laughing softly. 'Are you sure you want me to carry on?' he asked. 'This is only my finger. My cock might make it a whole lot worse than that.'

She groaned, excited beyond all measure by the thought of having his length inside her. 'Fuck my arse,' she growled thickly. 'Do it now, Steven. Do it NOW!'

There was so much urgency in the command of her words that she knew he would not be able to refuse. His finger slid slowly from the velvety depths of her anus and the source of her enjoyment was replaced by the pressure of his cock, gently pushing against her.

She trembled excitedly, aware that she was about to feel proper penetration for the first time. The sensation was so intense, she had to focus on her breathing for fear of passing out. She tried not to think of how wonderful it was going to feel having a cock inside her but, no matter how hard she tried, her thoughts kept returning to it.

Steven held her thighs and tried pulling her on to him. Bunny could feel his cock pressing against her, then sliding away from the tight hole. She reached between her legs and her fingers casually encircled his length. She held his shaft firmly then placed the swollen tip against the rim of her anus and pushed. At the same time, Steven bucked his hips forward, forcing his length to enter her anus.

Bunny released a shriek. Before, with her own finger, the sensation had been intensely satisfying. When Steven slid his tongue, then his finger up there, she had reached orgasm with an ease that was almost casual. But this was totally different. She could feel the tight sphincter of her backside being pulled so wide open it felt as though it would split. A shriek of delight escaped her and a hard, brutal orgasm shook every nerve-ending in her body. Before she had a chance to recover from that experience, she could feel his length sliding deliberately inside the forbidden passage of her anal canal. The velvety depths of her anus were slowly opening themselves to his cock as he pushed ever deeper into her.

Groans of furious enjoyment, interspersed with heated words of passion, spilt from her lips. Orgasm after orgasm tore through her, leaving her hot and cold in the same instant. Her entire body was drenched with a glorious sweat and, as he began to slide slowly backwards, she dared to clench her inner muscles around him, inspiring another wave of undreamed pleasure to explode inside. She was desperate to experience more of him and at the same time she feared the actual indulgence. Her delight was so intense she wondered if it would be possible to die of pleasure.

Her hand was still behind her, even though she had already released Steven's cock from her fingers and idly, she toyed with his balls as he rode slowly in and out. She used her fingertips carefully, trying to gauge how close to climax he really was. As much as she wanted to feel it, she was reluctant to have him shoot come up her arse. His cock was already taking her to greater heights than she felt comfortable with and the thought of feeling his climactic pulse might be more than she could tolerate. Perhaps, she consoled herself, that would be a joy they could share on another day. As soon as she felt the orgasm rising in his balls, she squeezed the sac and started to pull him out of her.

Steven seemed to sense what she wanted and allowed her to guide his cock from the blissfully tight haven of her backside. His penis shivered with the mounting thrill of his climax but he did not allow her to hurry him as he withdrew. He moved slowly, seeming to concentrate on her comfort, rather than his own needs.

Unfortunately, Bunny realised, he was moving too slowly. She had already experienced more delight than she would have believed possible and the tip of his member was just on the point of slipping from her anus, when she felt it pulse unmistakably.

A furious cry of animal delight fell from her mouth. She pushed herself forward, collapsing on to the bed in a delighted heap. As she did, his cock slid from her, continuing to spray thick, wet globules on to her back and between the heated cleft of her legs.

Laughing happily as she rubbed herself against the quilt, Bunny whispered soft words of thanks. He collapsed on top of her, still shivering with the strength of his own climax.

'That felt . . .' She shook her head and stopped herself. 'Words can't do it justice,' she said.

'I think I should be thanking you,' Steven began.

Bunny did not allow him to get any further. She silenced him with a kiss then embraced him as they lay on the bed together, holding one another.

An hour later they had both showered and dressed and were working their way through breakfast. A local rock-music station whined from the radio, playing old but tolerable songs. Bunny smiled fondly at Steven whilst she sipped at her fruit juice.

'About last night,' he began carefully.

She grinned. 'It didn't happen last night,' she reminded him. 'It happened this morning.' A delicious warm glow seemed to have filled her. The experience of having his cock inside her had proved to be just as wonderful as she had imagined and, now she knew how good it felt, she was determined to enjoy it again. She dearly hoped he would want to see her again this evening. The thought of what they could do sent her pulse racing.

Steven grinned at her. 'Last night,' he began again, 'we were discussing the Kilgrimol school and the Black Garter.'

'Don't remind me of those things,' she said quietly. 'Can't you see I'm in a good mood. I don't need reminding about hell and those devilish bitches.'

He placed a reassuring hand on hers. 'So far,' he explained, 'you've helped me get some great stories about the school. I think I'm on to another one. I've already started working on it, I just need a few more pieces of information.'

Bunny frowned. 'What sort of information? What's the story?'

He smiled at her curiosity. 'I'll need copies of three yearbooks that I haven't been able to get hold of and a little background information that only you might be able to supply.'

She held his gaze, not committing herself to helping him just yet. 'What's the story?'

He nodded and made a gesture with his hand that said he would answer the question in his own time. 'Do you know how good a school the Kilgrimol is? It's actually responsible for the production of more successful career women than any other school in this country.'

Bunny shrugged. 'And so it should be. Daddy says the fees are three times that of some of the more well-known schools.'

Steven nodded. 'He's exaggerating a little, but not much. The fees are inordinate in comparison to most places.' He eased himself slowly from his chair and walked leisurely to the small study area of his flat. A computer dominated the desk but it was surrounded by books, papers and files in an organised shambles. Bunny watched him retrieve a large, battered once-black box binder. 'This,' he said, passing the binder to her. 'This is going to make my career in journalism.'

Bunny smiled curiously at him and took the box from his hands. 'Surely not,' she said with a measured degree of politeness in her voice. 'I wouldn't have thought the Kilgrimol would have interested anyone outside the area.'

He nodded agreement. 'No one outside Kilgrimol is interested in the school, with the exception of a few hundred parents each year. But once this story hits the papers, everyone will have heard of it.' His grin widened when he saw the disbelief in her smile. 'This piece isn't going to be for the *Kilgrimol Weekly Clarion*. I think I can get this story on to the front page of the nationals.'

Bunny grinned up at him, surprised by his sudden rush of self-confidence.

Leaning over her shoulder, he opened the box binder and showed her the jumble of papers inside. 'This is the list of the country's top one hundred achievers for last year,' he explained, pointing.

Bunny glanced at it curiously.

'It's divided sixty-forty between men and women.' A tight smile crossed his lips and he added, 'The women are the forty.'

Bunny nodded. 'That's no surprise.'

Ignoring her remark, he went on. 'I did a little research into each of those women. Thirty-two out of the forty went to the Kilgrimol.'

Bunny whistled, surprised by the degree of success.

'And that's nothing,' he went on quickly. He was

leaning over her, so close she could smell the subtle fragrance of the shower gel he had used. Hardly aware she was doing it, Bunny placed her fingers on his arm and stroked his muscular bicep.

Steven barely seemed to notice. He was lost in the exciting world of his own investigation. 'This is the list of the top one hundred women earners in the country,' he explained, pointing at another cutting from a magazine. 'You can't really include her,' he said, pointing at a picture of the Queen. 'But even without removing her, Kilgrimol girls make up eighty-six per cent of this list.'

Bunny whistled again. She began to understand why he thought there was a larger story involved. 'What do these mean?' she asked, noting he had drawn comments and symbols next to each name on the list.

He nodded and explained. 'The K stands for Kilgrimol, obviously,' he began.

'I'd worked that one out,' Bunny said patiently. 'And the other letters?'

He smiled and took the seat facing her, then shifted it around a little until he was sitting beside her. 'N stands for netball, CC stands for chess club. They're all abbreviations for the school activities that these women were involved in.' His finger pointed at name after name, resting just beneath the letters BG each time. 'As you can see, every Kilgrimol girl on this list has been a member of the Black Garter.'

'The Black Garter are supposed to be secret,' Bunny hissed, unconsciously lowering her voice as she explained this. 'I told you about them in confidence.'

He nodded reassuringly. 'I know you did,' he replied. 'But I've been researching them quite a lot since then. Those scandals you told me about seem to be just the tip of the iceberg. I've heard rumours about members of the Black Garter getting up to all kinds of things. It's the sort of thing that makes the video we watched last night look positively tame.'

Bunny raised her eyebrows, trying to conceal her eager interest.

'And not just scandals,' he went on. 'There seems to be something perverse about the whole set-up although I don't have anything definite yet.' He graced her with a winning smile. 'With your help, I'm sure it won't take long, but I think I'm on to the scandal of the century.'

Thinking of her own embarrassing liaison with the Black Garter, Bunny could not stop herself from nodding agreement. She glanced down at the list and frowned. 'No,' she said quickly. 'You're wrong about them all being in the Black Garter. Look here. This one and this one –' She pointed sharply to the first two names she saw. 'And this one,' she said quickly, spotting a third. 'There are no BG letters next to these.'

He smiled patiently. 'I think their names will be in those three yearbooks I asked you to get for me.'

She glanced up from the papers and studied him with newly earned respect. 'You've really stumbled on to something here, haven't you?'

He nodded, not bothering to hide his self-satisfied grin. 'I think it could be a major story, especially if the rumours I've heard are true. With a little more luck, I could scratch a book out of this.'

She nodded, grinning broadly. Already Bunny could see the part she had to play in his story and she smiled indulgently at him. 'I'll get the yearbooks,' she said, tracing a finger purposefully over his hand. 'I'll bring them around tomorrow night.'

Steven nodded. 'And can you give me any personal

information on the Black Garter? Do you know anything about them, or their secrets?'

She paused, frowning. A memory stirred in the back of her mind and she realised she still needed an apology from him. 'Last night,' she began, 'you called me a liar.'

He frowned as his thoughts chased back to the point. When recollection hit him, his cheeks coloured suitably. 'That was wrong of me,' he apologised. 'But you were lying about being horny, weren't you?'

'I've been telling you the truth about the Kilgrimol and the Black Garter,' she assured him. 'You do believe me about that, don't you?'

He nodded earnestly. His hands reached across the table and he held hers tightly. 'I'm sorry I called you a liar and I can now say, with all sincerity, I believe you,' he told her.

Bunny nodded. That was what she had wanted to hear. She had thought his idea for a news story about the Black Garter sounded quite lame to begin with. The only thing that would be likely to save it would be her own personal knowledge of the group's perverse pastimes and she thought how easy it would be to exaggerate some of their practices. 'Steven,' she said, squeezing his fingers with her own. 'Prepare to see your name in the nationals.'

Six

'What the hell are we doing, Hera?' Anna demanded.

'Shush!' hissed Hera, her voice an urgent whisper. 'He'll hear us.'

It was unsettlingly eerie in the equipment store. The forty-watt bulb threw more shadows than light across the cluttered array of vaulting horses, exercise mats and games paraphernalia. The light barely touched the bare plaster walls, shrouding the pair of them in gloom.

Outside, in the adjacent gym, Anna could hear the laughter and raucous catcalls of the senior girls preparing for a game of netball. The twenty young women outside the equipment store were making no attempt to be quiet and Anna saw no reason why she should. Nevertheless, she lowered her tone when she next spoke to Hera. 'Who'll hear us?'

Hera had her face pressed against a crack in the wall. 'I'm watching Guy,' she explained quietly. 'He's having a wank.'

'You're kidding!' said Anna. She pushed Hera away and placed her eye over the crack in the plaster. Staring eagerly through the hole, her gaze focused on the school's only male teacher, the gym instructor.

The equipment store was the first of three rooms that ran along the main wall of the gym; Guy's office was the middle one, next to the changing rooms and showers. Anna could see his familiar broad back, naked this morning, and rippling with well-honed muscles. His narrow waist and tight, pert buttocks had the aesthetic perfection of a professional body builder and a shiver of delight tickled between her legs as she studied his nudity. Like herself, he had his face pressed against a crack in one wall. Glancing at the urgent movement of his hand, Anna realised Hera had not been mistaken. The gym instructor really was tossing himself off. He rolled his thick, meaty cock swiftly back and forth with one hand.

She had heard rumours about him doing things like this in the past, but Anna had always treated those stories as nothing more than scurrilous gossip. Guy had a reputation for knowing everyone in the school and it was said he had intimate knowledge of many of the students. Watching him roll his length up and down, she could see how he had acquired some of this knowledge.

'He's masturbating,' Anna hissed. She placed a hand over her mouth to suppress the burst of laughter that threatened to erupt from within. She moved her face away from the wall and turned to see Hera grinning.

Hera placed her eye back to the crack. 'I'd always thought he was doing something like this,' she whispered. 'Melanie and Grace must have caught his eye.'

In the gloom of the equipment store, Anna frowned. 'What have Melanie and Grace got to do with this?'

'They're in the showers,' Hera explained. 'That's what Guy's watching. I told them both to play a little in there and he's watching the show that they're putting on.'

'Show?' Anna repeated, perplexed.

Hera moved, allowing Anna to take another look. 'You weren't this naïve last night,' she noted quietly.

Anna blushed.

'Mel and Grace are busy playing touchy-feely games in the shower,' Hera explained. 'I'd always thought Guy was perving off at us and I figured that if those two didn't catch his attention, nothing would.'

'You've set all this up?' Anna exclaimed. 'Why?'

Hera laughed softly. 'I've got less than a week before I relinquish control of the Black Garter and go out into the big wide world. I'm just trying to settle a few old scores before I go.'

'What old scores?' Anna asked curiously.

Instead of a reply, she heard the equipment-room door close softly behind her and, glancing over her shoulder, Anna realised she was alone. Shaking her head, trying not to think about Hera's enigmatic comment, she pushed her eye back to the crack for one last look at the scene.

Obligingly, Guy had half-turned as he continued to pull himself off. Anna was treated to a glimpse of his long, stiff length, tipped with its glistening, rounded end. His hand worked furiously, rubbing from the swollen top, down to the thick swatch of dark hairs covering his balls. As he wanked, he kept his eye pressed against the peephole in the shower wall.

It felt bizarre to be watching a watcher, Anna thought. She was aware of her own distant arousal as she studied him but she knew it was nowhere near as strong as his. His powerful, rigid body seemed to tremble with desire as he stared into the room beyond. Distantly, Anna wondered what Melanie and Grace could be doing to excite him so much. She stopped her thoughts from continuing in that direction. Last night with Hera had been enough of a revelation for that sort of activity. Aware of the tingling arousal that sparked as she watched Guy, Anna did not trust herself to entertain that particular memory right now. If she had given herself over to such thoughts, she knew that Guy would not be the only person in the Kilgrimol spending the morning pressed against a wall, wanking themselves to a climax. She would be following his example.

Remembering she was alone in the equipment store, Anna decided she should be trying to find out what Hera was planning. Regardless of how entertaining she found Guy, she realised that there were others things for her to be doing. As she was about to turn away, her attention was caught by a movement in the gym instructor's office. She saw the office door fall quietly open and a woman tiptoed into the room.

Guy continued to pull at his raging cock, oblivious to the fact that he was no longer alone.

Behind him, Hera grinned at Anna through the peephole and raised a thumb. In one hand she held a table-tennis paddle and she waggled it cheerfully in the air. Anna held her breath, not sure what to expect.

Hera stepped closer to Guy. Her pace was so measured and cautious Anna knew she would not be heard. Still, she held her breath, not daring to think what might happen next.

For the first time that morning, she found herself watching Hera without admiring her body. The gym skirt she wore was so short it barely covered her black garter. The entire expanse of her long, muscular legs was on display, providing an exciting, enticing view but Anna ignored it. She was not even concentrating on the delightful swell of Hera's beautifully rounded breasts, pushing against the thin, stretchy lycra of her top. Her attention was riveted by Hera's audacity.

Hera raised the paddle high in the air.

Anna cringed as though she was about to feel the impact herself. She could see the evil grin that split Hera's lips and realised the expression was mirrored on her own face. Guessing where the arc of the paddle would strike, she felt a moment's brief sympathy for Guy when she thought of the discomfort he would endure. The thought was soon quelled when she wondered how many times he had tugged himself off whilst watching her. Considering this, her sympathy evaporated and she willed Hera to put as much effort as possible into the blow.

Silence seemed to have fallen over the entire school, as though every girl was holding her breath. Only moments earlier the entire gym had been filled with the sounds of netball practice. Now there was only a thick, anticipatory hush.

Anna did not have time to consider the lack of noise. Her attention was fixed on what was about to happen.

Hera swung the paddle hard against Guy's backside. The resounding slap echoed hollowly in the room. To Anna, it sounded like the harsh snap of a twig. She snatched a short breath of surprise.

Guy howled with pain and turned to face Hera.

The leader of the Black Garter was already running out of the office and Anna watched as Guy chased after her. Not wanting to miss a moment of the action, Anna left her spy-hole and ran to the equipment-room door. It led directly on to the gym and she got there in time to see Hera burst from the room.

The naked gym instructor was only inches behind her, shouting and cursing threats of diabolical retribution. He seemed to have temporarily forgotten his nudity but Anna doubted that would last for long.

As soon as he appeared in the gym, a shriek of delighted excitement greeted his arrival.

All twenty girls had been waiting in silence and Anna guessed that Hera had quietened them before entering Guy's office. The woman had enough power to command such a thing without any effort.

As soon as he appeared, the girl nearest to the door quickly locked the office and threw the key to Hera. She caught it easily and stopped running from him. She turned to face Guy, her expression triumphant.

Guy was blushing furiously. His hands covered his erection and he kept twisting and turning, as though this would make his nudity less noticeable. 'Give me that fucking key,' he demanded. Risking one hand, he made a swipe for it as Hera held it teasingly in front of him.

'Consider this a warning,' she said, in a voice that carried easily over the chuckles filling the gymnasium. 'You'll have a plasterer plug that hole this afternoon, and we'll say no more about what a wanker you are.'

The glare he fixed her with was venomous but Hera was not intimidated.

Even from her place by the store door, Anna could see Guy had no other option. He nodded surly agreement and held his hand out for the key. His other hand was still trying to cover the enormous length of his shaft.

With a Machiavellian twinkle in her eye, Hera tossed the key over his head and behind him. Guy reached for it with both hands and turned to catch it as it went beyond his reach.

The netball team shrieked delightedly as they were treated to the sight of his full-frontal pose. Guy's crimson cheeks burnt a dull purple. He scoured the gym floor with his gaze, trying to see where the key had landed.

One of the netball team saw it shining dully. She placed her foot firmly over the key and as Guy lunged towards her, she kicked it sideways. It went skittering along the hardwood floor and he lurched in pursuit. A second girl, following her friend's lead, stopped the key and kicked it hard to a third girl.

Anna watched, a broad grin illuminating her face. She saw that a bright red circle had begun to flourish on Guy's backside and she heard herself chuckling indulgently. An unknown hand slapped the mark and Guy whirled angrily on the perpetrator. Before he could respond properly, a second, then a third, then a dozen hands were playfully slapping at his bare flesh.

Guy's entire demeanour, normally so composed and self-assured, evaporated in an instant. Anna saw panic light in his eyes and she stepped away from the equipment-store door, realising what his next move would be.

He rushed past her, into the sanctuary of the dark room, pursued by twenty laughing and jeering young women. A handful tried to follow him but he managed to keep them out. Anna guessed he was leaning against the door and she doubted he would let up until the gym was cleared.

Laughter shook her entire body.

Hera placed a friendly arm over her shoulders. 'Not a bad way to start the day,' she grinned. 'Fancy a coffee, whilst we discuss plans for tonight?'

Anna smiled up at her. 'Plans?'

They talked idly as they walked, leaving the gleeful chaos of the netball team behind them. The school's cafeteria was only a short walk from the gymnasium and, because the morning was not particularly cold, neither bothered changing out of their gym uniform.

Normally, Anna would have spent time admiring

the scenery that surrounded the Kilgrimol as she made this walk. The school enjoyed near-perfect isolation from the outside world. Acres of landscaped greenery stretched towards the horizon, spoilt only by the intrusion of the occasional tree. Beyond the horizon, she could see the dusty purple ripple of rugged hills and mountains but these seemed as far away as her own life beyond the school.

This morning the scenery went unnoticed. The brilliance of Hera's nearness seemed to eclipse even this breathtaking view.

Because no official break had begun yet, the canteen was virtually deserted. Hera got coffees for them both then led Anna to a large window table. It was a familiar enough seat to both of them. Everyone in the entire school knew this was Hera's table and it was an unwritten rule that only she, or her closest friends, were allowed to use it. Even though the Black Garter was a secret organisation, it went without saying that they would punish anyone who transcended this rule. Anna did not doubt that everyone in the school knew this.

She studied the view of the school from the canteen window, enjoying the moment's respite. Hera lived her life at a relentless pace and, whilst she adored being close to her, Anna always felt drained after spending the day in her company. She already seemed to have dismissed the morning's fun in the gym and was now looking for the next challenge. Watching her gaze flit in every direction, Anna knew Hera was planning something. The woman would reveal her thoughts in her own time; she knew this much and, patiently sipping her coffee, Anna waited for Hera to speak.

'Will you be all right to take Cassie into Kilgrimol this evening?' Hera asked casually.

Anna shrugged. 'I've got my car,' she said. 'It shouldn't be a problem. Why? What for?' Her eager curiosity was tinged with a note of caution. She enjoyed Hera's company and would happily do whatever the woman asked; however, she also knew that Hera had a dangerous side and her plans seldom followed the safest route.

Hera grinned, as though she had sensed her friend's nervousness. She placed a reassuring hand on Anna's. 'You know yourself that the Black Garter isn't just about punishing people, don't you.'

Anna nodded, enjoying the subtle touch of Hera's fingers. 'Of course. I think I learnt that much last night.'

Hera smiled, seeming to enjoy the memory herself. 'I think Cassie needs a bit of a confidence booster. She worked hard to get through her initiation. I think it took a lot out of her and I've organised a special little something for her this evening.'

Anna smiled, surprised by Hera's thoughtfulness. 'Beneath that steely exterior –'

'Beats an even steelier heart,' Hera broke in with a grin.

Anna sipped her coffee. 'So, what's the confidence booster?'

Hera stared at her levelly. 'I've organised for a couple of guys I know to meet you both in Kilgrimol,' she explained. 'You can let Cassie fuck the pair of them. That should bring her confidence back on line.'

Anna almost choked on her coffee. 'You are kidding!'

Hera shook her head. 'Relax. You'll enjoy it. Try them yourself. They're very good,' she grinned wickedly. 'Trust me, I know.'

Anna could think of a hundred and one reasons

why she couldn't do it and a hundred and one more why she wouldn't enjoy it. Ignoring the dull excitement Hera's suggestion inspired, she was about to state each one of them.

'You're a pair of fucking perverts,' a cold voice hissed next to them.

Anna whirled around to see who had spoken. She was not surprised to see her roommate, Debbie Chalmers, sitting at the adjacent table. She did not know how Debbie had seated herself so discreetly, without either of them noticing, but she was used to the woman creeping up on people like that. Debbie had a frustrating habit of appearing close to the most intimate conversations.

'Did you say something, Debbie?' Anna asked coldly.

Debbie met her gaze with surly defiance. Her hair was an untidy mop of tousled blonde curls. Her face was unremarkable and plain, save for the retroussé nose. If it had not been for her stupendously large breasts, Anna thought there would have been nothing attractive about the poor girl.

'Just talking to myself,' Debbie replied shortly. She lifted the can of Coke she was drinking and swallowed a mouthful.

'They used to put people away for doing that,' Hera replied sharply.

Debbie glanced hesitantly at her. She was brave enough to challenge Anna but Hera was obviously a far more intimidating prospect. Nevertheless, she seemed to steel herself and respond with suitable bluff and bravado. 'And what do they do nowadays?'

Hera smiled tightly. 'Nowadays, they just leave them to me.'

'You don't scare me,' Debbie said firmly, although the quiver of her voice seemed to undermine her words.

'I don't intend to scare you,' Hera replied. She shook her head sadly and said, 'You could have been a valuable asset to the Black Garter.'

'I don't need your girl-guide group. I don't need anyone.' She fixed Anna with a pitiful gaze. 'You're not really going to do what she's asked, are you?' Her obvious disgust was prevalent in each word.

Anna glared angrily at Debbie. She had thought of many reasons why she could not go out with Cassandra and the two unknown men but, staring into the contemptuous expression on Debbie's face, she abandoned them all. 'Not that it's any of your business,' she growled. 'But I'll be doing whatever I want tonight.'

'You're going?' Hera asked, mildly surprised.

Anna glanced at her and nodded simply. She glared at Debbie when she spoke. 'Of course I'm going.'

Debbie shook her head. 'A pair of fucking perverts,' she repeated wearily. Before Hera or Anna could say another word, she had taken her drink and rushed from the canteen.

'Do you want her marked for punishment detail?' Anna asked, turning back to Hera.

Hera shook her head. 'She'll wait.' A sad smile rested on her lips and she added, 'Debbie's been punished enough in the last few days.' Before Anna could get her to explain the remark, a movement by the canteen door caught her eye. Anna glanced in the direction Hera was looking and saw the bespectacled red-haired girl in the doorway.

'Come on,' Hera snapped, leaping from her chair. 'We have business.'

Ignoring her coffee, Anna rushed to follow. She had no idea why Hera wanted to talk to Sam, or why her mood seemed to have suddenly swung towards one of its darker aspects. She was used to the furious pace of being near Hera and with less than a week to enjoy it, she was determined not to miss a moment.

Sam sat scared and miserable in Hera's bedroom. Anna and Hera towered over her, and the air was thick with malice. Memories of the previous evening's pleasure were now forgotten.

For a while, as she shared the heady intimacy of knowing Jo, her inferior position in the Black Garter had been forgotten. Their lovemaking had been intense and wonderful and she had felt like a grown woman, independent and strong enough to make her own decisions and choices. Jo's intimate attention had made her feel truly special. Staring into Hera's cold, uncompromising face, Sam wished she could recall that feeling.

'Who's the leak?' Hera demanded.

'Give me a chance,' Sam began. 'I've only had a week to work on that.' Her voice trembled nervously.

'Who's the new bitch?' Hera snapped.

She could feel her cheeks colouring as she made the reply. Hera was shrewd enough to know a lie when she heard one and Sam knew that. She did not want to risk the wrath of Hera's anger – even Black Garter girls were not beyond being punished – but Jo had asked for her help. Nervously, Sam pushed her glasses to the bridge of her nose and blinked meekly at the woman. 'Do you mean the assistant gym instructor?' Sam asked with a frown.

Hera shook her head and released a heavy sigh. 'Sam,' she said wearily. 'I'm not happy with you.' Her hand struck hard across Sam's face and she pushed herself close to the redhead and glowered menacingly. 'Who's the leak?'

'I told you,' Sam repeated, holding her burning

cheek. 'I don't know. I'm still working on it.' She risked a fearful glance at Hera.

Hera grunted angrily. 'And who's the new bitch?'

Sam stifled a sob of exasperation. She was torn between her duty to the Black Garter and the promise she had made to Jo. 'Give me another day on the case,' she said quickly. 'I'll have all the answers you want tomorrow, honestly.'

The cold smile on Hera's lips was uncompromising. She grabbed a fistful of Sam's hair and pulled the redhead's face close to her own. 'You can have another day,' she said crisply 'But I want some answers first.' Her wicked smile was darkly threatening. 'I think we both know there's only one way I'm going to get the answers I want.'

Sam swallowed nervously. She could read the unspoken promise of merciless punishment in Hera's expression and the sight chilled her. 'There's no need,' she began quickly. 'I'll tell you everything you want to know tomorrow. Just give me –'

'Assume the position,' Hera snapped sharply, releasing Sam's hair.

'But –' Sam began. A second slap across the face stopped any argument she might have dared raise. She climbed from the bed and turned to face it. Bending forward, she placed a hand on each knee, thrusting her backside out for whatever punishment Hera cared to administer. Her face glowed crimson with embarrassment and shame.

Because she was dressed for the gym, in a short skirt and tight top, she felt decidedly vulnerable. Knowing Hera and her merciless idea of justice, Sam knew she had every right to be frightened. Behind her, she could feel her skirt being lifted. As if it wasn't embarrassing enough to be displayed in such a way, she felt her knickers being eased away from her arse and pulled down to her ankles.

'There's no need for this,' Sam said quickly. 'If you'd just let me –'

A hand slapped hard across her backside. Sam bit back a cry of surprise. The blow stung furiously and left a burning explosion in its wake.

'Don't talk,' Hera snapped. 'Just answer. Tell us who's been talking to the newspapers.'

Sam glared fiercely ahead. When she spoke, her words were choked raw with emotion. 'I've already told you. I have no idea.'

Hera chewed her lower lip thoughtfully. 'And you say this new woman is just a gym instructor's assistant?'

Sam was looking at the floor when she spoke. 'That's right,' she replied, her voice softer than before.

'You're lying,' Hera said flatly. The menace in her voice was gone. Instead, it was replaced by cold, business-like resignation. 'You know what happens to liars, don't you, Sam?'

Sam began to protest, then stopped herself. Hera had already warned her not to speak and she knew better than to defy the woman's orders. Trembling, and dreading the minutes that lay ahead, Sam stared at the plain quilt covering Hera's bed.

'Cane her,' Hera barked.

Sam stiffened, prepared for whatever blow Anna was about to deliver. She saw Hera walk into her field of vision and start to rummage through the drawers of her bedside cabinet.

'Who's the leak?' Anna asked.

Sam tried to compose her thoughts but fear made everything seem chaotic. Anna's voice was directly behind her and Sam knew what she could expect. 'I've already said,' Sam repeated wearily. 'I don't know.'

A welt of pain bit at her backside. The cheeks of her arse were suddenly aflame. As the exquisite fury of the ache made itself known, tears of shame welled on the lower lids of her eyes. She blinked them back quickly.

'Wrong answer,' Hera said simply for the bedside cabinet. 'Try again.'

'Who's the leak?' Anna repeated.

Sam drew a long breath, preparing herself for another blow. 'I don't know.'

Hera shook her head sadly as she rummaged through the drawers.

Anna delivered two more short, sharp strikes against Sam's arse. The pain was so intense, Sam wondered distantly what she was using; it felt like a razor was slicing into her flesh. Recalling Hera's initial command, Sam wondered if she really was being beaten with a cane. The thought was only in passing as the intense flare of pain in her backside made every other notion seem irrelevant.

Long, punishing minutes passed as Anna repeated the same question and Sam repeated the same answer. Each exchange was punctuated with a whistling blow of the cane to her buttocks and each blow seemed to renew the intolerable pain that erupted in the cheeks of her arse. Sam closed her eyes as she answered, trying to mentally escape from the room but the searing sting of the strikes did not allow her any reprieve.

When she opened her eyes, she saw that Hera was naked, save for the single black garter she always wore.

Sam swallowed nervously, wondering what she could expect now.

'You haven't given me the answer I want,' Hera said softly. 'I wish you'd cooperate.'

Sam did not dare answer. She watched as Hera reached for something from her drawer and stroked it lovingly. Her eyes widened with fear when she saw exactly what it was.

Hera smiled at her disquiet, carefully adjusted the straps on the implement and began to fasten it to herself. When she was finished, Hera was sporting a huge strap-on dildo. Her beautiful feminine curves were accentuated by the massive erection she now bore. Her fingers lovingly stroked the pink plastic length.

'What do I have to do to get an honest answer out of you?' Hera asked quietly.

'I told you,' Sam sobbed, 'I haven't found out who the leak is yet.'

Hera nodded. 'And I've told you, I don't believe you.' She walked behind the weeping girl and stroked her hand over the redhead's bruised backside.

The touch of her fingers was a cool balm after the burning pain and Sam could not stop herself from responding. She did not want to admit to herself how aroused she was by Hera's gentle caress. The punishment that lay ahead was already more than she could contemplate, although her treacherous body did not seem aware of this.

Between her legs, Sam felt the dull throb of desire begin to pulse. Tears welled on her lower lids again as the feeling of excitement brought with it a renewed sense of shame. She hated to submit to Hera's punishment but she could rationalise that as being part of her membership to the Black Garter. The thing she despised most of all was her eager response to the caning. The urgent throb of her pussy's longing made her feel sick with self-loathing, especially when she realised how much she was enjoying this degradation.

'One last time,' Hera began.

Her voice was directly behind Sam. She could feel the pressure of the dildo's head resting against her pussy lips, not an unpleasant or uncomfortable feeling but still she shivered at its touch. The strap-on was larger than anything she had ever had between her legs and Sam wondered how much it would hurt as it plunged inside. She barely entertained the notion of enjoying the ordeal. This was one of Hera's punishments and Sam knew from experience that the victims never enjoyed themselves.

'Who's the leak?' Hera asked.

Sam braced herself. 'I don't know,' she whispered.

Hera's cool hands fell to her sides, holding her still. Sam felt the tip of the strap-on push firmly against the soft lips of her labia. The rounded end penetrated her wetness and slid forcefully inside. Sam groaned softly as the entire length was pushed deeper and deeper. The experience was not as unpleasurable as she had anticipated but she did not doubt that Hera had more planned.

From the corner of her eye, she saw Anna take aim with the cane. She felt the impact before it actually happened. A burning shard of delight exploded across the top of her arse. Sam did not know how the woman had managed to avoid hitting Hera with the blow and, as the pain soared through her, she realised she did not care. Her thoughts were clouded with burning shame and the abhorrent urgency of her own desire.

Hera plunged the plastic cock in and out of Sam's tight pussy, stretching her and bruising her with scant regard for the redhead's feelings. Her fingernails bit into Sam's sides as she bucked her hips, forcing the phallus in and out.

As Hera fucked her, Sam was treated to blow after

blow from Anna's cane. Each bite of the wood against her backside seemed more painful than the last. Sam knew that the pleasure of Hera's strap-on would have been divine without the punishment; her pussy had ached to be satisfied after the initial stirrings of her arousal and the hard length of plastic was doing an excellent job. Her inner muscles were stretched to capacity and the sensation of fullness brought with it an almost orgasmic sensation of euphoria. Coupled with Hera's measured tempo, slow and languid as the cock pushed in, then out, Sam felt the climax building quickly.

Anna delivered a stinging blow to her backside. The tip of her cane landed unnervingly close to the puckered ring of Sam's anus and she groaned loudly, making the sound as she thought of the pain that might have been inflicted. Her cheeks were a burning pit of coals and Anna's cane was no longer inflicting pain, it was merely stoking the glowing embers.

The combination of pleasure and pain were becoming inextricably linked. The delight of Hera's strap-on cock should have contrasted with the agony of Anna's cane. Instead, the pair seemed to complement one another. The vicious bites of the cane made her ecstasy that much more satisfying.

Sam felt her body begin to erupt with a mounting orgasm. She tried to stifle the sounds of pleasure as they spilt from her lips – Hera was punishing her and Sam doubted she would be pleased if her victim started wailing with enjoyment – but the power of her delight was so strong that she could not suppress it and, as the cataclysmic waves of elation rushed through her, Sam released a triumphant roar of satisfaction.

Behind her, she heard Hera laughing softly. The sound was not cold or harsh but it still unsettled Sam.

'Did you enjoy that?' Hera asked quietly.

Sam could not trust herself to speak. She felt Hera's hand slap her backside playfully. It should only have been a light blow but because the cheeks had been striped so severely a welt of pain exploded in her buttocks. Sam sucked in her breath, thrown off guard by the flare of discomfort.

Hera's laugh darkened. 'I'll take that as a yes,' she grinned. The dildo was still between Sam's legs and she continued to rock back and forth inside the redhead. 'Now, why don't you save yourself the trouble of having all this turn nasty?' she suggested. 'You don't have to tell me who the leak is yet,' she went on. 'You can tell me that tomorrow when you've had the chance to investigate some more. I'd just like to know who the new woman is.'

Sam released a small groan. Prickles of pleasure were still shimmering dully throughout her body. The gentle to-and-fro motion of the strap-on was already rekindling the climactic delight she had succumbed to only moments earlier. The orgasm had been an intense experience and Sam realised that Hera had been deliberately showing her how much pleasure she could give. And, if Hera could invoke such satisfaction, Sam could see how easily she would be able to inflict suffering.

'Who's the new woman?' Hera repeated.

Sam braced herself and closed her eyes. 'She says she's the assistant gym instructor.'

The strap-on was pulled sharply from inside her. She felt a hand on her arse and then she was being pushed to the bed. Hera and Anna fell on top of her and began to tug her clothes from her body: the skirt was pulled from her hips; the top was pulled quickly over her head and the knickers were snatched from her ankles. Hera ripped Sam's bra from her body with an almost casual flick of her wrist. Within a matter of moments, Sam was left naked on the bed.

She considered defending herself and fighting against the two women but in her heart she knew it would be useless. Not only did Sam believe that the pair would overpower her, she also knew they would make her life at the school a living hell afterwards. She lay trembling on the bed, stripped of everything but for the black garter on her leg.

Anna and Hera loomed over her, wearing expressions of the darkest malice. Hera had taken the cane from Anna and she tested its arc, swiping it harshly through the air above Sam's naked body.

Sam flinched on the bed, terrified to stay where she was and fearful of moving. She watched as Hera tapped the tip against her bare breast and swallowed thickly. The nipple, like the rest of her treacherous body, responded to Hera's touch rather than her own heartfelt longing.

'I believe you when you say that you haven't discovered our leak,' Hera admitted calmly.

Sam stared into her face, wondering what Hera was leading up to.

'But I want to know more about this new woman,' she went on. 'I think you're hiding something from me.'

Sam shook her head. 'No,' she began.

Hera whipped the cane hard across Sam's bare breast. The tip landed squarely on the eager thrust of her erect nipple. The intensity of the pain was so severe, Sam felt a scream of anguish tear through her. All of the blows Anna had inflicted were merely a lover's caress compared to the debilitating agony of this blow. She sat up on the bed, her fingers protectively cupping the bruised tip of her pulsing nipple. The pain was so sharp she dared not even touch the nub. Her breath fell in fearful gasps and she realised that as well as the pain, she was experiencing the stirrings of another powerful arousal and, as much as that thought sickened her, she could not deny it had a dark, delicious attraction.

Hera pushed her back on the bed. 'Tell me now, Sam,' she whispered softly. 'Tell me now, or it starts to get a lot worse.'

Sam closed her eyes, trying to suppress the sting of tears that spilt from them. 'Her name is Jo Valentine,' she said, her voice thick with emotion. 'Her name is Jo Valentine and she's a private investigator.'

Anna and Hera exchanged a glance. 'A private investigator?' Hera repeated. She grinned down at Sam, tapping the tip of the cane gently against her chest until the redhead opened her eyes.

Sam glared at Hera with dull anger in her eyes. She knew that a shine of reluctant excitement was probably glimmering there as well but she felt beyond caring.

'You must tell me all about this private investigator when we've finished punishing you,' Hera said.

Sam's eyes widened with fear. 'Punishment?' she whispered, trying to sit up on the bed. 'But I thought . . .'

Hera shook her head and pushed her back down. 'Anna and I were just getting information out of you then,' she explained. 'Now we know you've been lying to us, it's only right that we punish you, wouldn't you agree?'

Sam closed her eyes, not daring to answer in case she said the wrong thing. She had let the Black Garter down, she had failed with her investigation and she had broken her promise to Jo. In a mood of bitter self-loathing, she supposed she deserved to be punished. It occurred to her that Hera would probably not be able to make her suffer as much as she deserved.

When she felt the stinging blow of the cane strike between her legs, Sam changed her mind about that thought. If anyone could make her suffer sufficiently, Hera would be the woman to do it.

Seven

Jo smiled warmly at Steven as she took the seat he offered. It was a tatty office, even by newsroom standards. A yellowing PC rested on one desk and in front of it sat a broken typist's chair, the crippled back hanging lazily to one side. Pens, pencils and sheaves of paper covered every available surface. A battered dictionary and a coverless thesaurus lay forgotten in one corner and Jo wondered cynically if she was staring at the *Clarion*'s reference library. Considering the numerous spelling errors she had seen in the most recent issue, it would not have surprised her.

Steven shook her hand and sat down. Behind him was a framed movie poster from *Citizen Kane* and a blown-up front page from that week's issue of the *Clarion*. Some wag had blanked out part of the masthead's lettering so it now read 'The Kilgrimol W C'. Jo had to smile at the appropriateness of the name change. Beneath the masthead, the banner headline read: 'KILGRIMOL SCHOOL PORN VIDEO SHOCK'.

'And what can I do for you this afternoon, Miss Valentine?' Steven asked.

'You seem to be doing a lot of stories about the Kilgrimol school,' Jo began, nodding at the front page behind him. 'Do you write them yourself?'

Steven nodded. 'Of course. Is that why you've come here? Have you got a story about the school?'

Jo laughed tightly. 'Who's your source?'

He grinned at her and shook his head. 'My source is confidential.'

'How confidential?' Jo asked.

He gave her a quizzical smile. 'What do you mean how confidential? Confidentiality doesn't come in degrees ranging from slightly to extremely. Confidential is confidential.'

Jo reached inside her jacket and withdrew a cheque book. Opening the cover, she leant forward in her chair and rested the cheque book on the desk. She could see that Steven was staring at the broad expanse of cleavage she revealed and his appreciative eyes warmed her. Writing a small amount on the cheque, Jo asked, 'Is it this confidential?'

Steven glanced at the figure and smiled. 'It's a lot more confidential than that.'

Jo nodded and tore the cheque from the book. After shredding it with her fingers, she tossed the scraps of paper towards his wastepaper bin where they fell on the floor like confetti. Still smiling, she began to write a second one.

'Save your cheques,' Steven said, placing a steadying hand on hers. 'I've said it's confidential and I meant it. You don't have enough money to get me to reveal my source for that story.'

Jo shrugged philosophically and put the pen and cheque book away. The money would have been added to her expenses and she already realised it would be a tooth-and-nail fight to get Mr Smith to reimburse her. There would be other, easier ways to get the information from Steven, she assured herself. 'Has it been the same source for all of the stories at the Kilgrimol?' she asked.

He frowned. 'I'm not going to talk about my stories until you tell me why you're here.'

Jo nodded ruefully and sat back in the chair. She crossed her legs, raising the hem of her skirt slightly as she did this, revealing the tops of her stockings to him. She could see the lascivious grin lighting his face and she knew he was already intrigued. His obvious appreciation of her was something she intended to use to her own advantage. 'I can't bribe you with money,' she said softly, reaching for the button on the front of her jacket. She teased it slowly from its hole, allowing the lapels to fall open. Beneath the jacket she was wearing a lacy basque. The midnight-blue colour was complemented by the darkness of her suit and it accentuated the wan tones of her flesh.

She could see Steven noting all of this, his smile widening eagerly.

'So, what can I bribe you with?' she asked coyly.

He shook his head, his broad smile crumbling sadly at the edges. 'Confidentiality is important to me,' he explained, 'but you have got me intrigued.' Studying her eyes, he asked, 'Why are you so interested?'

'That's confidential,' Jo told him.

He smiled. 'Stalemate.'

Jo folded her hands in her lap and stared thoughtfully at him. She couldn't tell him why she was interested in the school – he was a reporter and would make a story out of it, blowing her cover, and adding to the Kilgrimol's problems – and, because of his journalistic ethics, Steven could not reveal the name of his source.

'Stalemate,' she said softly.

He was comparatively young for a senior reporter she thought, and devilishly handsome. With his steel-grey eyes and dark mop of untidy hair she found his looks far more than appealing. She tried to decide who would confide in someone like this and realised it could be anyone.

'She's female, isn't she?' Jo guessed.

He grinned. 'That was a fairly safe bet for an all-girl school with only one male employee.'

'And she's one of the students, rather than a member of staff,' Jo went on.

He nodded, not committing his reply to words. 'Again, if you're playing the percentages, that was fairly easy to work out. I believe the school has two hundred students and twenty-some staff. The odds are, she's right-handed too.'

Jo scowled good-naturedly. 'That doesn't narrow it down a great deal. I'm now looking for a female student in an all-girl school who may or may not be right-handed.'

He shrugged. 'You can't say I haven't tried to help. Now, let's talk about you.'

Jo glanced around the untidy office. 'How do you work in an environment like this?' she asked. The place was so cramped and dingy it reminded her of her own office. 'Do you mind if I take my jacket off?' she continued and, without waiting for his reply, she stood up and slid the jacket from her shoulders. Revealed in all its glory, the basque accentuated the swell of her ample breasts and pulled the muscles of her flat stomach to their tightest.

Steven swallowed before continuing. He snatched his gaze from Jo's body. 'So, why would a professional investigator be interviewing me about the stories at the Kilgrimol? I don't think you're with the police, so someone wants to know who's giving me my information.'

Jo glanced at the poster of *Citizen Kane*, then turned her attention to the computer. 'That looks very high-tech,' she observed lightly. She actually thought it looked prehistoric, but it was something to talk about other than her involvement with the school investigation.

Steven glanced at the PC. His lips wrinkled into a soft frown of disgust. 'It's a crock,' he said shortly. Turning back to Jo, he said, 'Perhaps the school principal called you in, to find out about these scandals.' Just then the telephone started ringing and he lifted the receiver. Listening to the voice on the other end, he smiled and winked at Jo. 'Funnily enough,' he said into the mouthpiece, 'I was just talking about you. I'll switch you over to voice-mail so you can leave a message.' He pressed a button on the keypad and Jo heard the geriatric PC whirr noisily into life. An attached modem began to flash urgent red lights and whistle a high-pitched electronic sound.

Jo reached into the pocket of her skirt and produced her double-headed sovereign. Idly, she began flicking it into the air, then catching it. 'I could tell your editor that you've given me the name of your source,' Jo said thoughtfully. 'How do you think he'd react to that?'

Steven shrugged nonchalantly. 'You could try that,' he said generously. 'Our editor is retiring in a week's time and his interest in the *Clarion* is negligible to say the least, but if you think it's worth a shot . . .'

Jo cursed under breath. 'Would you care to toss for the information?' she suggested, spinning the coin high in the air. 'Heads, you tell me the name of your source. Tails I'll tell you what I'm investigating.' She caught the coin halfway through its descent and slapped it against the back of her hand.

He nodded. 'OK,' he said. 'But the other way around,' he added quickly.

She fixed him with a questioning expression.

'I'll tell you the name of my source if it's tails,' he explained.

Jo slid the sovereign back to her pocket. 'Perhaps this is too serious a matter to gamble with,' she told him. From the tight smile on his lips, Jo could see that he had guessed the coin was double-headed. She stood up and extended a hand across the desk. 'I'm sorry we weren't able to help one another, Steven.'

He shrugged. 'It really is a shame,' he agreed. 'I'm sure we could have worked well together.'

Jo tested an indifferent smile on him, then reached for her jacket. Before her fingers had touched the garment, she whispered theatrically, 'Oh! Blast.' Testing a plastic smile on Steven, she explained, 'My suspender belt has come loose; you don't mind if I adjust it, do you?'

She did not wait for his response and instead placed one high-heeled shoe on the chair and stroked her hands up the length of her leg. As a pretence of straightening the sheer fabric of her stocking, it was far from convincing. Nevertheless, by the time her fingers had reached the dark band of her stocking-top, Steven's interest was caught. He licked his lips as he watched her tease the suspender fastener back into the hosiery.

Jo glanced coyly up at him, aware that she was displaying a glimpse of pale inner thigh. Her fingers rested against the flesh. 'If we can't help one another,' she said softly, 'then I'd better leave.'

She could see his face twist with concentration as he tried to think of something he could offer her. If she had been blessed with a crueller nature, Jo would have gleaned enjoyment from his discomfort. She took her foot from the chair and straightened the line of her short skirt. Tossing the jacket casually over one shoulder, she took a step towards the door.

'Perhaps . . .' he started.

Jo paused and turned to grace him with an enquiring smile. Steven was out of his chair and standing up. The front of his trousers was contorted with an excited bulge that she could not fail to notice.

'Perhaps I could ask my contact if it's OK to divulge her name to you? Could you see that as a gesture of co-operation on my part?'

'It sounds like a start,' Jo allowed. She moved back towards his desk and leant over it. Placing her lips inches from his, she asked, 'Was it the sight of my stockings that made you change your mind?'

Nodding, he grinned.

'If I show you some more,' Jo whispered, 'might you tell me more about your contact?'

Their mouths were separated by a hair's breadth. She was aware of his nervous excitement and guessed he was anticipating the pleasure of having her. His sense of duty seemed to be struggling with his sense of desire and she could see the indecision twisting his face. 'I don't know much about her,' he confessed honestly. 'I don't even know her real name. Just a nickname.'

Jo kissed him. She pushed her mouth forward and pressed her lips hard against his; her tongue plunged inside him and she placed her hands against his face, holding him tightly.

Steven responded hungrily. His hands fell to her shoulders and he stroked the bare flesh of her arms. From there, his hands moved down to her narrow waist, softly caressing the tender skin through the tight basque. Deftly, he unfastened the buttons on her skirt, allowing it pool around her ankles.

As she continued to kiss him, she could feel the urgent warmth of desire beginning to spread through her body. She felt intoxicated by the combination of her arousal and Steven's obvious eagerness. 'What's the nickname?' she asked softly.

He shook his head. 'No, I'd better not say,' he told her quietly, his conscience pricking him slightly.

Jo beamed at him. 'I'm sure you can tell me,' she insisted. She stepped away from the desk, kicking away the skirt at her ankles. She was fully aware of how good she looked in just the basque and stockings. The high-heels forced her calves and thighs into a perfect shape, and the sheer black stockings clung to her legs. The basque emphasised the slenderness of her waist and the fullness of her breasts. Tossing her long dark hair over her shoulders with a casual flick of her head, she studied him thoughtfully.

'It would be wrong to tell you,' Steven said again.

Jo shook her head. 'There are lots of things in this world that are wrong,' she reminded him. Her face was illuminated by a broad smile. 'That doesn't stop us from doing them, does it?'

She reached her thumbs down to the waistband of her panties. Turning her back on him, she eased the knickers slowly over the swell of her arse and down her stocking-clad legs. She could hear his soft moan of appreciation as she removed the pants. It was a comforting sound. When he made the noise, Jo realised she had him exactly where she wanted him. 'You'll be telling me next that I shouldn't be standing in your office, dressed like this,' she remarked softly. Turning back to face him, she teased her fingers through the stubble of short hairs that covered her pubic mound.

'Bunny,' he whispered.

Jo raised a questioning eyebrow. 'Bunny?'

He nodded. 'That's the nickname you wanted. It's all the information I have, and it's all I'm going to give you.'

She took a step forward and climbed on to his desk. 'I hope it's not all you're going to give me,' she said, emphasising the lewd meaning of her words with a husky whisper. She kicked a pile of papers from the surface of the desk and stood with her legs apart.

Steven stared unbelievingly up at her, his face inches from the semi-shaved haven of her sex. The glistening wetness of her labia was revealed to him, so close he would barely have to move to touch it. Deliberately, he brushed his fingers over the silk-smooth fabric of her stockings.

Jo grinned down at him, then placed a hand between her legs and, with her manicured fingernails, spread the lips of her sex open. She allowed the tip of one finger to brush over the febrile nub of her clitoris and was gratified by the spark of electric passion.

The tremors returned when she felt Steven's tongue flick hesitantly against the exposed flesh of her pussy. His hands were softly caressing her legs, creating a warm friction over the silk then, with growing confidence, he pushed his tongue against her more forcefully. This time, he allowed the tip to push slightly inside the glistening wetness of her hole.

Jo drew breath, her excitement mounting. She took her fingers away from her sex, then placed both hands against the back of Steven's head. Pushing him further on to her heated desire, she could feel an impending explosion threatening to erupt inside her.

Steven teased the lips of her labia with his tongue, moving his hands slowly up her legs, to the tops of her stockings. Softly, he caressed the black band of stocking-top, brushing against the bare flesh of her inner thighs. Daringly, his fingers began to steal ever so slowly upward.

Jo found his touch was disturbingly exciting. She

suppressed a groan of delight, unwilling to lavish too much encouragement on him just yet. Her inner muscles were already clenching and unclenching in greedy anticipation of the pleasures to come.

Steven's hands went behind her, cupping the swell of her buttocks; his fingers stroked the peach-like orbs of her arse, tracing subtle circles that crept slowly closer to the cleft of her sex.

Jo shivered happily then released his head, happy to let him continue on his own course. He pushed his tongue in and out of her slippery hole, occasionally teasing the tip against the flesh of her inner lips and then suddenly he pushed his finger against the rim of her anus.

Jo heard herself gasp as his finger prodded softly into her backside and then she felt the orgasm course through her. It started with her knees trembling, then she could feel the urgent tremors rippling through the inner walls of her pussy until finally a groan escaped her lips and every muscle in her body seemed to ripple with ecstasy.

Beneath her, Steven shifted position. He sat on the desk, allowing his tongue to enter her from behind and stroked her thighs lovingly as he moved his mouth forward along the entire length of her cleft. His tongue touched the tip of her clitoris, then trailed back over the swell of her inner lips, pushing rudely at the puckered ring of her arsehole.

Jo pressed herself on to him, enjoying the heady intimacy of his cunnilingus. She could feel a second orgasm building inside and she rested on the plateau of anticipation. 'Undress,' she told him, her voice a husky whisper.

Steven needed no more prompting. Keeping his tongue pressed close to the musky source of her arousal, he began to unfasten his trousers and shirt as he lapped at her then kicked off his underwear and shoes before shrugging the shirt from his shoulders.

From her position above him, Jo smiled down. Since Stephanie's wedding, she had felt locked in a sexless world that no longer held any fascination for her. Last night, making love to Samantha, Jo had felt forgotten feelings being rekindled. The climaxes she enjoyed then had been the first since Stephanie and Nick announced their engagement and Samantha's touch had inspired a hunger that she desperately needed to satisfy. Staring at the eager length of Steven's huge cock, Jo realised she could start to satisfy those urges right now.

With the explosion of the second orgasm, she felt her pussy squirt climactic juices into his mouth. The thrill that coursed through her was intensified by Steven's greedy licking and his tongue did not stop lapping until it had removed every last trace of her climax.

Jo shivered, not daring to risk a third orgasm whilst standing on the desk. Her knees were beginning to ache from the earth-shaking pleasure she had already received and with another orgasm, she could see herself tumbling from the top of the desk and hurting herself as she struck the floor.

She lowered herself slowly downward, forcing her pussy lips to stay in contact with Steven's body as she moved. The swell of her sex stroked against his smooth chin, over his chest and down towards his hard, flat stomach. The thrust of his erection prodded at her and she slid the wet lips of her labia against his hardness.

He was well-built and his arrogant attitude implied he would have stamina. The prospect of having him inside her was so sweet she savoured it indulgently for a while, allowing him to kiss her neck and whisper gentle words into her ear.

Unable to resist him any longer, Jo circled her fingers around his cock and squeezed it softly. He moaned excitedly, his breath deepening. Jo rubbed the tip of his swollen member against the wet lips of her pussy and teased the end against her clitoris. Her urgency and desire were suddenly too strong to deny and she pushed herself on to him.

Steven growled happily as they fell together into his chair.

Jo released her own sigh of pent-up emotion. His length filled her, stretching the lips of her labia wide apart as he entered and the tip of his cock seemed to go further and further up as she took his entire length inside. When she felt the head pressed hard against the neck of her womb, Jo gasped for breath, fearful of the strength of her threatening climax. She pulled herself back, allowing him to ease out of her, then sat down quickly on to his length. His cock filled her, spreading her pussy lips wide open.

Steven gasped for breath, his pleasure obviously as intense as hers. He raised his fingers and began to brush at her breasts through the stiff fabric of her basque.

Jo shivered excitedly, the added stimulation heightening her arousal. She pulled away from his length, slowly and with deliberate care. Each millimetre's movement of its egress sent ripples of joy shimmering through her body. When she felt the tip resting against the lips of her eager hole, she sat heavily down on him again. The plunging motion sent furious explosions of joy to every nerve-ending in her body and this time the roar that escaped her was triumphant. Pushing herself against the huge length between her legs, she rocked happily backward and forward until pulses of pleasure swept through her thoughts, leaving her breathless and giddy as the orgasm finally overtook her.

'Wonderful,' she whispered, the word escaping her lips as a sob of gratitude.

'It gets better,' he assured her. His fingers moved from her breasts and held her waist. With surprising strength, he lifted her from his cock, eased himself from the chair and placed her on the desk. Holding her legs high in the air, he pushed her back against the surface, then nuzzled his length back between her legs.

Jo writhed eagerly against him. She felt the tip of his shaft probing the lips of her sex and held her breath. Then she felt him pushing forward. The cock entered her wetness easily, sliding deep into her.

Steven used his cock with arrogant skill. He was confident enough to know his own abilities and adept enough to know exactly what she wanted. He rode her slowly at first, forcing waves of pleasure to erupt inside her and holding her legs high, Jo felt her body's entire concentration focused on the satisfying rhythm of his pounding cock. As he pumped himself repeatedly into her, she was transported to a plane of bliss that she had not visited in a long time. The world, its problems, the Kilgrimol and the Black Garter ceased to matter; all that existed was the euphoric pleasure between her legs. Sighing happily, she allowed the waves of joy to wash over her.

Steven slid his penis from the tight confines of her pussy and turned Jo easily over. Her backside was on display to him and she pushed it against him as he entered her. Bent over his desk, her pussy filled by his broad girth, she could feel an animalistic fury rising inside. His hands gripped her hips as he pushed into her and she released urgent, loud growls of encouragement as he pounded his hard length into her tight, wet hole.

Her suspicions about his stamina were being proved correct, she realised. His shaft was hard and eager but she could feel none of the familiar tensing she had experienced in new cocks before. Steven seemed capable of riding her for as long as she wanted. As the pleasure continued, Jo let him.

He snatched her from the table and quickly turned her around to face him again. His length momentarily fell from her, only to be back a second later pressed hard, up to the hilt. Jo circled her hands around his neck and wrapped her ankles together behind his back. As he held her in the air, she rode slowly up and down his length. His strong arms held her tightly, enforcing a feeling of intimacy that she would not have imagined possible for such a casual liaison. He must have read her thoughts as he bent his head towards her and placed soft gentle kisses on her face.

Roaring with excitement, Jo returned his kisses, still sliding her wet pussy lips lithely against the stiffness of his manhood, every pore of her body shrieking with joy. The friction of her stocking-clad calves brushing against his waist was disturbingly erotic, increasing the fullness of her enjoyment.

Steven held her with one arm for a moment whilst his other hand went to the cheeks of her backside. Pulling her towards himself, Jo felt his cock pushing deeper than ever between her legs. Her ecstatic cries echoed around the dusty room and it occurred to her briefly that other people might be able to hear her, then she decided she didn't care. If someone wanted to listen, she figured they could listen. Considering the enthusiasm of her mood, she wouldn't have minded if someone else had wanted to join them. Her satisfaction went beyond anything she had experienced in months.

Orgasm after orgasm coursed through her. They did not come with the hectic, giddy rush of a multiple climax. Instead, she seemed to be having repeated single, powerful orgasms. Each seemed stronger and more debilitating than the last. Every time the euphoria of climax tore ferociously through her body, Jo felt herself given over to the intense elation of her joy. As each wave of delight ebbed away, she tried to caution herself about over-indulgence. However, the hard, consistent tempo of Steven's hammering length banished all thoughts of caution and within moments she could feel herself rushing eagerly towards the next triumphant orgasm.

He changed their position repeatedly, inspiring more and more rapture in her as she found different ways of enjoying his skill. Jo allowed him to take her up against the wall, laying on the floor and sitting in his swivel chair. Each time, her pussy seemed to explode with elation as she discovered a further way of enjoying him and each position was exploited until Jo had shrieked with the climactic force of her exultation.

When Steven eventually came, Jo was almost glad of the respite.

She felt his huge cock pulse between her legs and she knew his climax was imminent. Forcing herself fully on to his length, she squeezed her inner muscles tightly, extracting every last drop of his seed before she relented the pressure.

Steven groaned, his cries of joy matching those she had been making and even going beyond some of them. His hands pressed hard against her waist and she could feel every muscle in his body trembling with the enormity of his orgasm.

'Incredible,' he murmured softly.

She kissed him. 'You're not so bad yourself,' she told him. Easing herself off his prone body, Jo sat on the floor and smiled thoughtfully at him.

Steven returned the smile and pushed himself slowly from the floor. 'We're fortunate enough to have a shower in this building,' he said carefully. 'If you'd care to join me, I wouldn't object to the company.' His smile slanted to one side and he studied her carefully.

Jo shook her head. She inhaled deeply and revelled in the heady musky scent of their lovemaking. 'You go and shower,' she said. 'I'll just dress and leave.'

He nodded, his face creased with understanding. Jo watched him slip loosely into his clothes and then bend down to kiss her before leaving. 'Will you wait until I get back before you leave?' he asked.

She shrugged. 'Probably.'

He grinned at her and left the room.

Alone, Jo grabbed her panties and stepped quickly into them. She dressed in seconds, draping the jacket of her suit over her shoulders as she settled herself in front of Steven's PC. In the early days of the Valentine Investigation Agency, she had relied on Stephanie to operate computers. The damnable machines had never appealed to her and her understanding of the things was severely limited.

Aware that she did not have much time to try and become a hacker, Jo hit the space bar on the keyboard. The monitor lit up. A small box at the centre of the screen said: PLEASE ENTER YOUR PASSWORD, STEVEN.'

Jo frowned. She glanced around the untidy office for inspiration. She knew little about PCs and their mechanics but she had watched Stephanie trying to hack her way through password screens. From what she had seen it had nothing to do with knowing about computers, it was merely a matter of knowing about people.

In that field, Jo considered herself an expert. She glanced at the front cover of the *Kilgrimol Weekly Clarion* and wondered if that could provide any clues. He was a reporter and an arrogant bastard, she thought logically; perhaps that could combine to make a password. A thought occurred to her and she smiled quietly to herself. Typing with one finger, she entered the word 'superman'.

The screen blinked. A sour note of disapproval honked from the internal speaker and a white cross inside a red circle appeared in the box. The message now read: INCORRECT PASSWORD, PLEASE ENTER THE CORRECT PASSWORD, STEVEN.

Jo glared at the screen. Time was running out and she knew it would not be long before Steven returned, ready for the rest of his day. She slammed her hand against the keyboard in frustration.

The screen blinked. The sour note of disapproval sounded a second time and the message changed again. As well as the white cross inside the red circle and the previous statement, there was now a warning below the box.

FAILURE TO SUPPLY THE CORRECT PASSWORD ON THIS ATTEMPT WILL RESULT IN THE SHUTDOWN OF THIS STATION.

Jo grunted unhappily. 'Why don't they just put "last chance"?' she whispered tersely. She glared at the *Citizen Kane* poster and a smile illuminated her lips. Typing carefully, she entered the word 'rosebud'. She checked the spelling twice before she dared to press the enter key. When she felt sure it was correct she pressed the key firmly.

The computer screen blinked and the warning message disappeared.

Jo stared at the icons now displayed and struggled to remember what they actually meant. A picture of a telephone was flashing at the bottom of the screen and she reached for the mouse. Moving the pointer clumsily, she placed the arrow above the flashing picture and pressed the mouse's button. The screen changed and she saw she had accessed Steven's voice-mail.

'You have one new message,' the computer said with the voice of a sultry American female.

Jo blinked, surprised to hear the machine talking to her. She considered talking back to it, then stopped herself. A box had appeared on screen, asking her if she wanted to hear the new message. Jo clicked the 'yes' button. Instead of hearing the American woman speaking to her, Jo now heard a young, English girl's voice.

'Steven, it's Bunny. Two girls from the Black Garter are going into town tonight on a paid-for date. I don't know if you can make a story out of it, but I thought I'd let you know. Call me back if you need more information. Bye.'

Jo blinked. A message had appeared on screen, asking if she wanted to save the message or delete it. Without hesitating, Jo pressed the delete button.

She exited from the voice-mail screen and tried to make sense of the other icons. A picture of a pencil on a sheet of paper caught her eye and she clicked on that. After all, she reasoned, Steven was a reporter and if he had anything he considered important on the computer, it would be connected with his writing.

She was not surprised to see a list of file names appear on the screen. Even with her limited knowledge of computers she had half-expected that much. The thing that surprised her was the names of the files: BG94, BG93, BG92 and so on.

Assuming the BG stood for Black Garter, and the number was a year end, Jo realised she was looking at a list of files detailing information about Sam's secret society over the years. Some of the years were missing and she made a mental note of them but it looked to be a fairly comprehensive list even with those exceptions.

She clicked on one of the file names and the screen changed again. Now she was staring at a list of women's names. Jo recognised a couple of them as being modestly successful business women but the others were unknown to her. She checked a second file and found she had never heard of any of the names on that list.

'Why isn't there a fucking printer?' she demanded, barely aware she had spoken aloud. In every episode of *The X Files*, whenever Mulder or Scully accessed something they shouldn't on a computer screen, they always had the opportunity to print it out. Not only was there always a printer sat next to the PC but it was invariably loaded with enough paper to print the file they were looking at.

'Welcome back to reality, Valentine,' Jo reminded herself sourly. 'This isn't *The X Files* and you aren't Dana Scully!'

For an instant she wished she was still working with Stephanie. If Stephanie had accessed the files, Jo knew her former partner would have found a way of printing the files out. The chances were, Stephanie would have sent them to a printer in the newspaper's reception area and had them presented to her as she walked out of the building. But Stephanie wasn't with her and Jo knew that she never would be. Determined to solve the case without the help of her former partner, Jo's resolve hardened. She grunted unhappily and exited the computer back to the welcome screen. Wondering if she had learnt anything that she might be able to use, Jo slipped her arms into her jacket and made her way out of Steven's office.

Eight

Debbie replaced the telephone receiver, her heart beating fast. She did not like having to use the public telephone in the common room but her mobile was charging back in her dorm and she had needed to make the call quickly. The fear of being overheard had stayed with her as she talked and it was only when she finally severed the connection that she allowed herself to breathe easily again.

'Chalmers. I want a word with you.' A hand fell on her shoulder and the gentle tinkle of golden charms, rattling softly on a heavy bracelet, left Debbie in no doubt as to who had caught her.

She whirled around, startled to hear Hera's voice so close to her. She swallowed nervously when she saw that Hera was not alone. Standing on either side of her, arms folded and impatient scowls twisting their lips, were Melanie and Grace. The two women glared menacingly at Debbie.

'Hera?' Debbie said, her heart beating like a military tattoo. 'What do you want?'

Hera smiled. 'I think you know what I want,' she said coolly. 'It will be best if you and I talk in private.'

Debbie glanced around the empty common room, wishing there was someone she could turn to for help. The idea was ludicrous as she had few friends at the

Kilgrimol and, even if she had been adored by everyone, Debbie knew that she would still have been alone in a confrontation with Hera. 'I have a class,' she stammered nervously, snatching at the first excuse her frightened mind could think of.

Hera shook her head. 'All your classes have been cancelled for today.'

Debbie glanced from Hera to Melanie and Grace. She knew she had no choice other than to do as Hera commanded. The prospect of what might lie ahead left her cold.

'We'll talk in your room,' Hera said, turning her back on Debbie. 'Anna's going to be out for most of the evening so we should be afforded some privacy.'

Debbie watched the woman walking away and when she noticed Melanie and Grace still staring impassively at her, she knew she had to follow. As she fell into step behind Hera, the two women walked on either side of Debbie. Sullenly, she realised she had no hope of escape. Whatever Hera had in mind, there was no chance of avoiding it.

They walked along the empty corridors of the Kilgrimol's long halls, heading towards the east wing where the dormitories were situated. The sun had already fallen from these corridors and the building was held in the thrall of a still, grey light. Debbie glanced at the baize-covered cork-boards they passed with unseeing eyes. She was dreading whatever lay ahead and she knew she had every reason.

'I was a trifle hard on you the other evening,' Hera said quietly. She was still walking purposefully forward, the words thrown casually over her shoulder as she marched towards the dormitories.

Debbie frowned, not sure she had heard the woman correctly. 'When?' she asked.

Hera stopped and turned to face her. Her features

were contorted into a dark mask of anger and Debbie wanted to cower away from them, 'The other evening when I had you tied to a bed and I was dripping candle wax on your cunt lips,' Hera hissed sharply. She pressed her face close to Debbie's and said, 'Do you remember that, or do you need a reminder?'

Debbie's cheeks coloured darkly. She remembered the evening so vividly that when she closed her eyes, she could still feel the burning spatter of wax against her bare flesh.

Like the majority of girls at the Kilgrimol, Debbie had embraced the dream of becoming a Black Garter girl. The panache and flair of the women involved with the group was enviable and to be accepted by them would have meant she was part of an elite team.

The night had started with the usual air of menace and gloom that seemed to pervade all of Hera's ceremonies. The bedroom was dark save for the flickering glow of the candlelight; long, wavering shadows stretched along the walls of the bedroom. Naked, and frightened, Debbie had been tied to the bed. Before she had started to do anything, Hera had demanded Debbie remain silent throughout the initiation. It was the only condition she had insisted on. If Debbie managed to obey that condition, Hera explained that she would have earned her black garter.

Desperately wanting to join the group, Debbie had agreed to the condition. She had tried not to fidget restlessly as the woman undressed and she had tried to contain her rising panic when Hera had dripped molten candle wax across the taut buds of her bared nipples. She had stayed silent throughout the entire beauty of the punishing experience. The pleasure of submitting herself to such indignities was greater than she would have believed and she did not know if the promise of acceptance was the thing that excited her or if she had a submissive side that Hera had inadvertently discovered. Whatever the cause of her enjoyment, the fact was she had orgasmed twice whilst Hera punished her. The pleasure had been bitter and tinged with degrees of pain that should have made her scream. Aware that she was unable to make a sound, Debbie had stayed silent until the last moment. As Hera held the candle over the wanton lips of her pussy, Debbie had thrilled to the exquisite sensation of having her labia waxed. The searing sensation inspired an explosion of delight to rush through her body and she had barely managed to hold back her scream of joy.

And then Hera had blown the candle out. She had placed the base firmly against the lips of Debbie's sex, and was about to push it inside her when Debbie had screamed for her to stop. The words had come out before she knew she was making them. The initiation had ended abruptly. And so had her chances to join the Black Garter. She had allowed herself to be subjected to Hera's initiation ceremony and before it was over, she had failed. The memory of what she had lost was more unsettling than the pain could ever have been.

'I don't need a reminder,' Debbie whispered softly.

Hera nodded. She turned away and started back towards the dormitories. 'I was a trifle hard on you then,' Hera repeated, 'and I suppose I owe you some sort of an apology.'

Debbie stared uncertainly at the woman's back. She had been expecting a punishment of some sort, or worse. Because Hera had caught her concluding the telephone call, Debbie had thought her secret had been exposed and waves of relief washed over her.

'An apology?' Debbie whispered.

'Not that I'm going to apologise,' Hera went on, turning a corner and starting up a flight of stairs. 'But to try and rectify the situation, I thought you'd appreciate a second chance to join us.'

Debbie felt her heart beginning to soar. She glanced from Melanie to Grace, her eyes wide with disbelieving happiness. A sudden thought struck her and she felt a heavy storm cloud pass over the sunshine of her hopes. Placing a hand on Hera's shoulder, she stopped the leader and placed her mouth to the woman's ear.

Hera frowned. 'Initiates have no place dictating what will or won't happen.' A smile softened her face and she added, 'But because you had the guts to say that, I'll bear it in mind.'

Debbie followed the woman into the dormitory with a grateful smile on her lips. Melanie closed the door and Grace sat herself on the dusty chair next to the cluttered desk. Anna was continually complaining about the untidy, dishevelled appearance of the dorm but Debbie was quite fond of its homely charm. She stared at Hera, standing amongst the clutter and disarray of the room.

Before the woman had a chance to say anything, Debbie uncoupled her mobile phone from the battery charger, annoyed that it had already replenished its battery. The realisation of how much she could have lost through using the public telephone still weighed heavily on her mind. Aware that Hera was frowning at her, Debbie placed the phone in a drawer.

'You didn't do very well the other evening,' Hera said crisply. 'Silence doesn't seem to be your strong suit.'

Debbie blushed, her cheeks not just reddening at the memory of blowing her first chance of acceptance with the Black Garter. But before she had a chance to dwell on the other matter, she realised Hera was still talking.

'In the light of what you've just told me, I suppose I can understand your stopping me. I realise now that I was right to give you a second chance but be warned, this is the last one. You won't be given a third chance to join us.'

Swallowing nervously, Debbie nodded.

'Strip her,' Hera commanded crisply.

Before Debbie had a chance to respond, she felt Melanie and Grace grab hold of her. The two women tugged at her clothes and began to briskly remove them from her body. Not daring to protest, Debbie allowed them to do as they wanted.

'Before we get down to business,' Hera said tersely, 'I think we need to talk about your abominable behaviour this morning.'

Debbie swallowed unhappily. 'Yes,' she said quickly, remembering her outburst in the canteen. 'I'm sorry about that. I –'

Hera cut her words off. 'Assume the position,' she commanded crisply.

Debbie opened her mouth, about to make a protest, then stopped herself. The delight she felt at being given a second chance to join the Black Garter was stronger than her fear of Hera's punishment. The woman had said this was a matter to be dealt with before her initiation and that meant she could look forward to being allowed the chance of joining after she had earned her forgiveness. She turned her back to Hera and bent over, pushing the cheeks of her arse out.

A pair of hands, Hera's she assumed, caressed the peach-like skin of her backside. The touch was soft, almost loving, and Debbie suppressed a tremor of excitement.

'Nice arse,' Hera murmured.

Debbie felt the woman's fingers brush daringly close to the cleft of her sex and, unable to stop herself, she drew a sharp breath of surprise. The intimacy of Hera's touch had aroused her more than she had anticipated and she struggled against the emotion that welled within her.

A hand slapped hard across one cheek. The blow was hard and unexpected and left a stinging redness in its wake that had her shivering. She released a small groan of surprise, not wanting to give her discomfort greater voice for fear of being thought unworthy.

A second blow, harder than the first, slapped the other cheek.

This time it was harder to bite back the squeal of surprise as the stinging handprint on her arse burnt dully.

From the corner of her eye, she saw Melanie and Grace move behind her. Their hands were suddenly holding her legs and she could feel their fingers close to the tops of her thighs. Without any care or tenderness, she felt the cheeks of her arse being spread wide apart.

She held her breath, not daring to think what Hera had in store for her. The woman's intentions already seemed obvious enough but Debbie dared not dwell on them for too long. She was afraid that her nervousness would make her do, or say, the wrong thing.

She felt another stinging blow of pain on her backside and she grunted unhappily. This time the bite had been harder and crueller. This had been no slap from Hera's open palm, she realised. The blow had been too stiff and impersonal for that. Recalling the untidy clutter of papers, sweet wrappers and stationery on her desk, she wondered if Hera had taken something from there.

Her thoughts were confirmed a moment later when Hera asked softly, 'You don't mind my borrowing your ruler, do you?'

Debbie shook her head. Her thoughts were a turmoil of fear and excitement and she was dreading the sting of the ruler against her arse again. She dared not contemplate why Melanie and Grace were holding her in such a way as, although the proximity of the two women and the softness of their touch was exciting, Debbie still felt more apprehension than she was comfortable with.

Repeatedly, Hera slapped the ruler hard against Debbie's arse. The tip bit like acid into the hot flesh and it took every ounce of willpower she possessed to stop herself from shrieking. Each blow seemed to get closer and closer to the ultra-sensitive flesh of her sex and the effort of self-restraint became greater with each resounding thwack of the plastic against her exposed skin.

The hardest stroke, as she had feared it would, landed squarely against the puckered ring of her arsehole. In spite of all her efforts to contain her cries, Debbie heard herself shriek as a bolt of pain shot from her backside, filling her body with a tingling explosion. The sensation felt so close to pleasure she wondered briefly how she should be able to tell the difference.

A second blow, lighter but just as accurate, sparked a second eruption of fire throughout her. The ruler's tip felt suddenly sharp against her anus and instantly she could differentiate between these feelings and true pleasure. Pleasure, she could endure. The intolerable explosion that now inflamed her body was something she could not endure for a moment longer.

As though she had read Debbie's thoughts, Hera commanded her aides to let go and turn Debbie around. 'Do you consider yourself punished?' Hera asked crisply.

Blushing and unwilling to meet the woman's eyes, Debbie nodded.

Hera smiled softly. 'I suppose that will do for the moment,' she conceded. 'I'll allow you to speak during this initiation,' Hera went on magnanimously. 'You may say yes, or no. Just remember if you do say any other word, your last chance will be over. Do you understand?'

Debbie nodded. 'Yes,' she whispered.

'That's good.' She glanced around the untidy room and her eyes fell on a collection of sweets on the corner of Debbie's desk. Hera picked up an M & M and placed it in her mouth. As she teased the sweet with her tongue she appraised Debbie's large breasts. 'I love your tits,' she said in a matter-of-fact tone.

Debbie blushed. She was about to mumble a thank-you when she remembered the condition Hera had given – the words 'thank you' were neither a yes or a no. Smiling with embarrassment, she tried not to meet Hera's lascivious gaze. When she felt Hera's finger tracing softly against the dark brown flesh of her areola, she forced herself to stay still and endure the woman's touch.

'Do you like Debbie's tits?' Hera asked.

Debbie glanced up to see the question had been directed at Melanie. The mousy-blonde girl smiled and nodded. Without any encouragement, she placed her hand over one of Debbie's orbs and squeezed the mound fondly.

Debbie inhaled deeply.

Melanie's fingers stroked and caressed the bare flesh, her long manicured fingernails teasing the taut tip of Debbie's nipple and rolling the hard little bud between her finger and thumb.

Still fearing Hera's retribution, Debbie resisted the urge to sigh.

Hera was smiling at her. 'I want to test your obedience,' she explained carefully. 'Is that acceptable to you, Debbie?' As she asked the question, she slipped a second M & M into her mouth.

'Yes,' Debbie replied nervously. To get into the Black Garter she was prepared to do almost anything.

Hera made a show of enjoying the sweet and reached for a third. 'Do you like these sweeties, Debbie?'

Puzzled by the sudden distraction, Debbie frowned and nodded. Aware that she was able to respond properly, she said quickly, 'Yes.'

Hera placed the third sweet between her teeth and moved her mouth close to Debbie's. 'Take this one,' she commanded.

Debbie moved her mouth close to Hera's, morbidly aware of what she was being asked to do. Her lips touched Hera's and she reached for the small round sweet with a hesitant tongue. She felt the sweet fall into her mouth and before she could move her head away, she was being kissed. Hera's tongue plunged into her mouth, tasting her, exploring and exciting her.

The tight buds of her nipples, still enjoying the gentle caresses of Melanie's fingertips, stood harder than before and then a second pair of hands began to stroke her body and she realised that Grace was touching her as well. The multiple stimulation was delightfully unanticipated and a light film of excited sweat rose across her forehead.

Hera broke the kiss and grinned at Debbie who

was still enjoying the attention of the two other women. She swallowed the untasted sweet whole and fixed Hera with an expectant expression.

'Did you enjoy that?' Hera asked coolly.

'Yes,' Debbie replied.

Hera grabbed the packet of sweets and passed one each to Melanie and Grace. They both seemed to know what was expected of them. Melanie placed an M & M between her teeth and placed her mouth mere inches away from Debbie's.

With a sigh of excitement, Debbie found herself kissing another woman within seconds of having kissed her first. On the night of her initiation, even though they had both been naked and Hera had been exciting and aroused her, there had been no real intimacy. Then, there had just been the flickering threat of the candle and the exquisite delight of the molten wax. Admittedly, she had climaxed and each orgasm had been a rich, satisfying experience but they had not been warmed by the pleasure of intimacy.

This was different and, although she felt just as frightened, not all of the excitement could properly have been called unpleasant. Her breasts were still being expertly fondled by Hera's colleagues and shivers of delight were erupting inside her body. When her kiss with Melanie had ended, she felt her head being twisted to meet Grace's mouth.

Grace virtually spat the sweet into Debbie's mouth before greedily pressing her lips against the blonde's. The fury of her animal passion was so intense it was frightening and Debbie felt overwhelmed by the woman's urgent command of her. Grace's tongue filled her mouth and, as she kissed, her fingers pressed mercilessly hard against the soft flesh of Debbie's eager breast.

When their kiss finally ended, Debbie dared to

swallow the sweet. She glanced meekly at Hera to see if she was still meeting with the woman's approval.

Hera was smiling at her.

'You do like those sweets, don't you,' Hera observed lightly. 'I can't recall the last time I saw someone enjoying chocolate so much.'

Debbie grinned softly, not daring to look away.

'Perhaps you'd care to take another from me?' Hera suggested. She waited for Debbie to nod acceptance before reaching for the packet. Settling herself on the chair, Hera raised the hem of her short skirt and parted her legs so that the lips of her half-shaven pussy were on bold display. With elegant fingers, she placed the M & M against the lips of her labia and then moved them away. Smiling excitedly up at Debbie, she said quietly, 'Take your sweet.'

Debbie could feel her heart beating fast with excitement. The woman was breathtakingly beautiful and Debbie had always found herself drawn to her. She had not considered her feelings to be sexual before, but now that the chance was being offered she saw no reason to deny herself. She was already enjoying stimulation from Melanie's and Grace's caress and if her mind considered that to be acceptable, then she saw no reason not to take the sweet that Hera was offering.

She licked her lips as she moved her mouth close to the warmth of Hera's sex. The sight of Hera's black garter circumnavigating her leg reminded Debbie of the reward she would receive for going through with this. It was inspiration enough to make her move her mouth quickly downwards.

More than anything she wanted to join the Black Garter. If this was what she had to do to join then Debbie was more than willing. The thoughts of atonement and revenge were now gone from her mind. She knew she had wronged the group over the last few weeks but she believed she could end all of that whenever she wanted. No one knew what she had done and, if she had her way, no one was going to know. If Hera deigned to accept her into the Black Garter, then Debbie was prepared to work hard to make up for the wrong she had done the group. If it involved doing things like this, then she believed she could honestly look forward to making amends.

She placed her mouth gently against the soft folds of Hera's sex and licked the sweet away from her. Without thinking, even after she had swallowed the confectionery, Debbie traced her tongue against the flesh a second, then a third time. The heady taste of Hera's musky pussy juice filled her nostrils. The fragrance was so rich and erotic, she could feel her own excitement mounting quickly.

Melanie and Grace had followed her to the floor as she knelt before the group's leader. Relentlessly, they still teased and caressed her. Grace nibbled playfully at her ear, exciting the sensitive flesh of her lobe, whilst Melanie had daringly moved her mouth over one of Debbie's nipples and was rubbing the tip with her tongue. Sparks of pure delight erupted from the sensitive tips of her breasts. Exhilarating waves of delicious pleasure had begun to rush over her, filling her with warmth. Debbie tried to ignore the distractions they were giving her. Both women were exciting and glamorous creatures and whilst neither of them compared to Hera she would still have been happy to entertain their individual attention. Having them both touch and caress her was so exquisite it was almost intolerable.

'Eat my cunt,' Hera whispered softly.

Debbie held her breath, not daring to believe what she had heard Hera command. Her nose was a kiss away from the lips of Hera's sex and, although she had already brushed the woman's labia with her tongue, the thought of being commanded to perform oral sex still unnerved her. She gazed at Hera's nether lips, trying to inhale the intoxicating fragrance of pussy honey that glistened against the darkly flushed folds of flesh.

'Prove your obedience and eat my cunt,' Hera whispered.

Debbie glanced up from her silent appraisal of Hera's cleft and realised the woman was staring at her darkly. A smile twisted her lips but there was a subtle air of menace lighting her eyes and Debbie feared the retribution that lurked at the back of them. Without delay she pushed her tongue into Hera's depths. Her mouth and nostrils were suddenly filled with the heady scent of the woman's desire. The delicate pink lips of her sex seemed to kiss Debbie's mouth as she rubbed her tongue deep inside and the musky bouquet and the rich flavour of her arousal seemed to envelop and possess her.

Aware of the pleasure she was deriving from the act, Debbie stopped, realising she was on the brink of an orgasm. She was baffled. She knew that Melanie and Grace were stimulating her sexually and she could not deny that they were highly skilled, but they could not have inspired this magnitude of arousal; their touch was so soft and subtle her body was simply enjoying it, not revelling in it. The climactic thrill that filled her was far greater than anything either of those two could arouse. Smiling up at Hera, Debbie realised what the source of her excitement was.

Considering her great beauty and magnificent charms, Debbie knew that Hera was the one who was affecting her this way and, when she saw the smile being returned, Debbie moved her mouth back to the cleft between Hera's legs. She plunged her tongue deep inside Hera, guzzling pussy juices that filled her mouth and made her feel dizzy with the delight of being allowed such a privilege. Then she flicked the tip of her tongue against the hardening swell of Hera's clitoris, surprised to see the nub pulse beneath the slick touch of her tongue.

Hera's fingers brushed through her hair, tugging softly at the blonde tresses and urging her to lift, then lower her face. For a moment Debbie felt as though she were a machine that Hera was using just to perform cunnilingus. It was not unpleasant and Debbie realised distantly she did not mind being used in such a way. She could have lapped at Hera's pussy for the rest of the evening.

'Enough,' Hera snapped abruptly. She spoke as though she had read Debbie's thoughts and knew she was enjoying her initiation too much. Pulling Debbie's hair sharply, Hera moved herself away from the deft ministrations of the blonde's eager tongue. 'I want to see how obedient you are,' Hera reminded her, standing.

Debbie nodded, trying to hide her disappointment at not being allowed to continue using her tongue. She realised Hera was studying the untidy clutter of her desk and she saw the frown of disapproval crease her forehead before she spoke.

'This place is a fucking dump,' she murmured softly. 'No wonder Anna despises this place and calls it a hovel.'

Debbie drew breath as though she had been slapped. She needed Hera's praise and encouragement; the woman's reassurance and support were like a drug that she suddenly craved. Words like this hurt worse than the fiercest blow she had received from the ruler.

'You'll tidy your act up if you're allowed into the Black Garter, do you understand?' Hera growled, running her fingertips through the scattered papers.

Debbie nodded earnestly. 'Yes,' she whispered. The word was not simply an agreement. It was a pledge.

Hera nodded, seemingly satisfied. Her fingers found something on the desk and she picked it up. Dangling between her finger and thumb, she held a long chain of paper clips high. She grinned happily at them as though an idea had just occurred to her. A cruel smile thinned her lips and she stared at Melanie and Grace.

'Take the seat, Mel,' Hera commanded generously. 'Let Debbie have another sweetie while you sit there.'

Melanie reached beneath the hem of her short skirt and pulled her panties off in one lithe, well-practised motion. She settled herself in the chair that Hera had vacated, smiling gratefully at the leader, then slowly turned her attention to Debbie. She raised the hem of her skirt to reveal the thick swatch of dark curly hairs that covered her sex and took two M & Ms. She placed one against the lips of her vagina then licked the second one, wetting the crisp sugar shell so that it was slightly sticky. With a careful finger, she touched the sweet against her anus. She held it with a fingernail for a moment, then moved her hand away. The M & M remained against her arsehole, waiting for Debbie to remove it with her mouth.

Hera grinned when she saw this. 'Eat your sweeties, Debbie,' she insisted gently.

Swallowing nervously, wishing the thought of what she had to do was not so disturbingly arousing, Debbie placed her mouth between Melanie's legs. She licked the first sweet easily, her tongue tracing lightly against Melanie's pouting labia. Before she even dared to contemplate the second one, she moved her mouth away and tried to pluck up the necessary courage. The sweet rested against the forbidden flesh of Melanie's anus and Debbie knew that if she wanted to join the Black Garter, she had to take it from there. The scent of Melanie's sex was drawn into her with each nervous inhalation. Perhaps the woman's fragrance was not as intoxicating or as divine as Hera's, but Debbie found she was still excited by the subtle aroma. The pulse of her desire was beating a strong, urgent staccato. As she moved closer, her eyes seemed to close involuntarily. She felt her nose brush against the folds of skin. The tip was suddenly wet with the glistening dew of Melanie's honey and her nostrils were plunged into the warm, moist haven of her sex.

Daringly, holding her breath with excited anticipation, Debbie flicked her tongue out and touched the M & M. The hard, pill-like sweet stayed where it was, and Debbie realised it was not simply going to jump into her mouth. She opened her eyes and stared at it, poignantly aware of Melanie's nearness. She realised that to get the sweet in her mouth, she had to put her lips against the flesh of Melanie's arsehole. The realisation brought with it a shiver of nervousness that was not wholly unpleasant.

Placing her tongue below Melanie's backside, Debbie gently drew the tip upwards, keeping it placed against the hot flesh. She felt herself touching the sweet, then it fell into her mouth. In that instant, she realised she had her tongue pressed firmly against the tight ring of Melanie's anus. The sensations of excitement and sheer humiliation were so thrilling she wondered if she was going to orgasm merely from licking someone. She swallowed the sweet and with a bold thrust of her tongue, she entered Melanie's backside. The woman's squeals of delight from above were encouragement enough for Debbie to continue and she prodded her tongue as far into the dark canal as she possibly could.

'You're enjoying that too much,' Hera barked suddenly.

Debbie felt Melanie flinch away from her. In the same instant she heard a slap and wondered what had happened. When she glanced up she saw Melanie holding a bruised cheek and staring miserably at Hera. The scene explained itself. She stared warily at Hera, wondering if she too was due for another bout of punishment. The thought brought mixed feelings of excitement and trepidation.

'You're not here to cream your fucking knickers,' Hera growled in Melanie's ear. 'You're here to help me with an initiation.'

Melanie mumbled an apology, still rubbing her face. From the corner of her eye, Debbie saw that Grace was staring at Hera with a certain degree of wariness and she sympathised with the emotion. She barely knew Hera and although she revered the woman, she still regarded her with a great amount of caution.

'Do you make these chains?' Hera asked, holding up the string of paper clips.

Debbie nodded quickly.

Hera grinned and allowed the string of clips to dangle purposefully between her fingers. She placed her hands on either side of the centre and tugged hard. The central paper clip gave and bounced against a wall with a gentle clink. Hera held the two freshly made lengths of chain in her hands and grinned down at Debbie. 'Stand up,' she commanded.

Debbie hurried from the floor, eager to do everything Hera commanded. She watched as Hera took one of the chains and moved towards her breast.

The thin sliver of metal glinted dully between her fingers and, as she reached for her nipple, Debbie saw exactly what the woman had in mind.

Words of protest rushed to her lips but she had promised to obey the rule of silence and maintained control despite the fear of what Hera was planning.

'Relax,' Hera snapped coldly. 'You'll only make it hurt more. Melanie could tell you that much.' A wicked glimmer illuminated her face and she smiled at the sullen Melanie. 'Let me show Debbie what I mean.' Her hands moved towards Melanie. Debbie heaved a soft sigh of relief. She knew the moment's reprieve was bound to be short-lived but she was prepared to enjoy any diversion that did not cause her too much discomfort.

Reluctantly, Melanie stood up. On Hera's command she removed the top she was wearing and stood there meek but defiant with her pert breasts exposed to the room.

Debbie snatched a quick look at the small, softly rounded orbs and tried not to stare. In the hedonism of the afternoon's events she felt as though she had lost all sense of decency and proportion. A voice at the back of her mind still insisted that what she was doing was wrong and that she was immoral for enjoying the embarrassment and humiliation of this initiation but, as she gazed at the perfect splendour of Melanie's naked breasts, Debbie could not find it in herself to listen to that voice. The throbbing pulse of her own arousal was too strong to allow her to listen.

As she watched, Hera took the end of the paper-clip chain and fastened one piece of wire against the tip of Melanie's exposed nipple. The metal pressed cruelly hard against the sensitive flesh, making the nub stand awkwardly.

A pained expression flitted across Melanie's face,

quickly replaced by a smile of surprised excitement. Melanie drew a deep breath and stared curiously down at the source of this new-found pleasure and her grin broadening, she glanced up at Hera.

Debbie could see the slap coming before it hit Melanie. The mousy-blonde released a soft growl of annoyance but there was no hint of retaliation in her voice or her manner. She met the challenge of Hera's gaze with sultry defiance.

'Stop creaming yourself,' Hera repeated sharply. 'Next time, I won't tell you in such a nice way,' she added menacingly.

Melanie nodded.

Watching, Debbie realised Melanie was manfully resisting the urge to stare at her own nipple. She admired the woman's composure and if she had not been suffering the brunt of Hera's wrath, Debbie knew she would have envied her.

'Doesn't that look good?' Hera murmured, stroking her fingertip softly against the rose-tinted flesh of Melanie's tightly clipped areola.

Debbie nodded and whispered her agreement.

Hera reached artlessly for Debbie's breast and grasped the nipple between her finger and thumb. She rolled the pliant flesh gently, stimulating her with the subtle pressure of her touch. Debbie could feel a groan of delight welling inside her but she suppressed the sound, aware that Hera was likely to punish her for it. She held the woman's gaze, hoping that she was doing exactly what was expected of her.

With deft fingers, Hera slipped the cruel wire of the paper clip over the tip of Debbie's teat. The metal pressed hard against the flesh and Debbie wondered how the biting pain could feel so exquisite. She coughed back a groan of joy and fixed her eye determinedly on Hera, awaiting her next instruction.

Nodding, Hera smiled silent approval.

Debbie could see that her nipple was on the end of the same chain that was attached to Melanie. The length of ineffectual links bowed into a U between them. When Hera accidentally caught the chain with her fingertips, its gentle sway caused delicate waves of delight to ripple through Debbie's breast. Her eyes opened wide as the unexpected pleasure took over her body and filled her with joy. Unconsciously, she realised she was staring at Melanie who seemed to be feeling the same excitement.

Hera took the second length of chain and with quick fingers, she fastened one end to Melanie's other breast. Melanie closed her eyes. Her lips were pressed tight together in a silent grimace that did not look totally pained.

Hera snatched at Debbie's nipple and again rolled the nub between her thumb and forefinger. She seemed to be watching Debbie, as though she was waiting for hesitancy or reluctance. Debbie met her gaze coolly. The expression was rewarded with a smile.

This time, when Hera had fastened the clip against her nipple, she pressed the metal hard against the sensitive flesh. Debbie drew a slow breath, not sure if she was struggling against a moan of despair or a cry of delight.

'And there we have you both,' Hera observed. 'The pair of you are linked.' Her smile tightened cruelly and she moved her mouth close to Debbie's ear. 'Take a step back,' she whispered.

Without any hesitancy, Debbie did as she was instructed. She could see the chain pulling against her nipples but that did not stop her from obeying. Melanie released a soft growl of surprise, her breasts being tugged sharply by Debbie's movement.

A furious passion stole over Debbie and this time she could not suppress the sigh of excitement from escaping. Prickles of pleasure erupted inside her breasts, igniting explosions of delight that seemed to traverse her entire body.

'Kneel down,' Hera commanded.

When she saw the expression of horror that filled Melanie's face her grin broadened. 'I did mean both of you,' Hera explained patiently. She turned her attention to Grace and spoke softly into the woman's ear.

With a reluctant expression and a nervous glance in Melanie's direction, Grace nodded assent to Hera's whispered command. She helped her friend into a kneeling position as Debbie lowered herself to the floor. They both managed to make the movement without experiencing any great measure of discomfort from the chains that linked them.

Hera stepped between them, her legs straddling the chain easily. She smiled down at Debbie and raised her skirt. 'This is your last test of obedience,' she explained quietly. 'All you have to do is lick my cunt, and keep those clips on your tits.'

Debbie nodded her acceptance. She saw Grace move behind Hera and realised that Melanie was going to have to do the same thing for her. The chain between their breasts was already stretched taut. With the two women between them, the links felt as though they were being stretched to biting point and Debbie could feel her breasts being gently pulled and tugged by the merciless clip that bit into her nipple.

Trying not to think of the discomfort or the pleasure it aroused, Debbie raised her head to Hera's sex. She pushed her tongue into the moist hole and licked greedily at the slick wetness that waited for her. The pain in her nipples was already thrilling her beyond belief and with the added excitement of drinking Hera's pussy honey she could feel herself hurtling madly towards a powerful orgasm. Her body ached with the pounding pulse of her joy and as she lapped furiously at the delicate folds of Hera's sex, she could feel the euphoria of divine bliss sweeping over her like an all-encompassing blanket. Her entire body seemed to have been filled with the delight of orgasm and she wondered distantly if such an act was permissible in the middle of an initiation. She was unable to see Hera's face from her position below her but she was determined to stall her climax until she felt sure it was allowed.

Gradually, as the biting in her breasts seemed to increase in intensity, she realised she was being pushed backwards. She could just make out the delicious mounds of Grace's backside and noted the woman had moved slightly away from Hera. With a soft smile of realisation, Debbie saw that the two women were deliberately forcing her and Melanie backwards. Each careful step was placing more and more pressure on the links of the chain that connected them.

Hera's hand, pulling her hair sharply, yanked Debbie's head back into the proper position. She knew she should not have needed reminding about the task at hand and eagerly plunged her tongue back against the warm, succulent flesh of Hera's sex.

A soft growl escaped the leader. Debbie felt the noise rather than heard it but she could not stop herself from smiling when she realised she had been the instigator of the woman's pleasure. Her smile disappeared when Hera stepped forward, thrusting the lips of her demanding pussy into Debbie's face.

Pushed backwards, Debbie felt the pressure on her nipples reach an unbearable pitch. The delicate pleasure they had given her at first was now replaced by a constant pulse that was an almost an ache. Her body was screaming for the release of an orgasm and she did not know if she could contain the explosion of delight much longer.

Grace and Melanie were making sounds of enjoyment and she tried not to think of the things they might be doing to one another. Instead, she tried to channel her thoughts away from her own enjoyment and into the task of pleasing Hera. Her concentration was focused on Hera's pussy. Both the scent and the taste were totally exhilarating.

'Yes,' Hera growled, her voice rich with triumphant elation. Her fingers still rested on Debbie's hair and she tugged hard as she enjoyed the explosion of her orgasm.

Debbie could feel her face being pressed into the dark swatch of pubic curls and a fine spray of pussy juice spattered against her cheeks and nose, exciting her with their warmth and intimacy. Too late, she realised the excitement of Hera's climax had proved too much. As the leader orgasmed, she had bucked her hips forward with the force of the pleasure and the pressure on the paper clips had finally grown too strong. Her breasts were suddenly aflame with the exquisite joy of such torturous punishment when the clips delivered their final bite before departing.

She screamed happily as a powerful climax overwhelmed her. Unable to stop herself, she toppled backwards, away from Hera. She fell heavily to the floor, too lost in the rapture of her delight to note the bruises she sustained to her forearm and elbow. The waves of bliss that swept over her were so great she did not even realise Hera had tugged a handful of hairs from her head as she fell.

When her mind finally cleared and she was ready

to face reality after the thrill of her climax, she opened her eyes to see Hera smiling benignly down at her.

Behind her, Grace was helping Melanie to dress. The two women seemed to share an intimacy that went beyond their membership of the Black Garter and in her mood of sublime satisfaction, Debbie found herself wishing them well.

'Congratulations,' Hera said, kneeling on the floor next to Debbie. She leant forward and placed a soft kiss on Debbie's lips. Moving back slightly, she reached for Debbie's ankle and moved her hands over it.

Debbie's heart was beating with excitement as she realised what Hera was doing. An inane grin split her lips and she smiled giddily at the woman.

Hera fastened the garter at the top of Debbie's leg and, after sliding her hands from beneath it, she allowed her fingertips to tickle gently against the subsiding pulse of Debbie's labia. 'Welcome to the Black Garter,' Hera whispered.

Debbie wished she could find words that summed up her gratitude properly.

'I wish we could stay and talk,' Hera said, stretching herself as she moved from the floor. 'But I still have a lot to do. I'll want to talk with you in the next couple of days though,' she went on. 'So, I trust you'll make yourself available to me.'

Eagerly, Debbie nodded. She heard the muted ring of her telephone from its drawer. Hesitantly, she glanced at Hera, wondering if she had to ask permission before she could use it.

Hera nodded. 'Take your call,' she told her, 'we're leaving now.'

Debbie watched the three of them leave before going for the telephone. She was warmed by their parting words of farewell and touched by the new look of respect they graced her with. Smiling, she realised it was not truly respect, they were simply looking at her now as though she was an equal.

The telephone continued to ring. Taking it into the bedroom, Debbie lay wearily on the bed and pressed the receive button.

'Bunny? Is that you?'

Debbie recognised Steven's voice straight away.

'Yes, it's me,' she replied quickly. A sudden wave of horror stole over her as she realised how close she had come to destroying her chance of joining the Black Garter. The stories she had told Steven, the information she had given him, it could all have worked so badly against her.

As she held the phone in one hand, she teased the fabric of her new black garter with the other. The sense of accomplishment and belonging that the black garter embodied made her tremble.

'Did you leave a message on my voice-mail?' Steven asked sharply. 'I don't know if my PC's playing up, or if I've had someone snooping through my records.'

Debbie frowned. 'Yes, I left a message,' she assured him. She repeated the words she had left on the recording, though the prickle of her conscience weighted the words with regret as she spoke.

'Where are they meeting, Bunny?'

Debbie hesitated. 'I'm not sure.' It suddenly seemed so wrong to be betraying the Black Garter that she found it difficult to talk to Steven. 'Listen, perhaps I've been wrong to go telling tales on these girls,' she suggested suddenly.

Even over the telephone she could sense the iron in Steven's voice. 'You'll go on telling me about them if you know what's good for you.'

Debbie caught a frightened breath. 'Are you threatening me?'

'That's as good a word as any,' he agreed boldly. 'Now speak, Bunny. I want to know about these two girls tonight, and I want those three yearbooks you promised me. You'll tell me what I want to know, or I'll make your life at that school a living hell.'

Unhappily, Debbie realised he was in just the right position to make good with the threat. Closing her eyes, and hating herself as she did it, Debbie told him about Anna and Cassie's planned night out.

'But just that and the yearbooks,' she said abruptly.

His sinister laugh was chilling.

'I mean it,' Debbie insisted, unable to keep the rising panic from her voice. 'I've given you enough already. You should be happy with what you've had.'

'Just carry on making me happy and neither of us will have a problem, Bunny,' he said easily. 'Do you follow my meaning?'

Miserably, Debbie realised that she did.

Nine

Jo pushed the apartment door open and stepped tentatively inside. A snake of fear unfurled itself in the pit of her stomach. Her heart was an arrhythmic pulse and her nerves were stretched kettle-drum tight.

There were two things Jo liked about being a private investigator, aside from the regular payments. The main one was solving cases. Finding all the pieces and fitting them together was like working on a complex human jigsaw. After the hard work came the thrill of success and finally being able to see the picture as a whole invariably gave Jo a feeling of total satisfaction. She had already realised that the more demanding the case, the greater her personal sense of triumph seemed to be. With a case as complicated as this one, Jo expected the rush to be almost orgasmic.

The second part of the job that she adored was the thrill of doing something a little bit dangerous. Admittedly, there was nothing truly perilous about breaking and entering but Jo knew if she was caught in Steven's apartment the repercussions would be far-reaching. She could kiss her investigator's licence goodbye – that was a foregone conclusion. She also knew that if caught, unless she found a sympathetic judge, a short spell in prison was not out of the question.

It was an invidious situation, fraught with

unsettling jeopardy and Jo relished every nervous tremor that tingled in her gut. The fear of being caught had to be the most powerful aphrodisiac she had ever known. Before, when she had been working with Stephanie, Jo had fantasised about her in moments like this. Now she realised her thoughts had turned to Sam. The image occurred unbidden and Jo had to struggle to get the bespectacled redhead from her mind.

She walked stealthily through the apartment, drawing the lounge curtains before turning the light on. Her critical eye scoured the unremarkable room noting only two things of potential interest. The first was a PC sitting on a desk in one corner. The second was, more importantly, a bottle of Jack Daniels standing alone on the mantelpiece.

As she reached for the bottle, Jo caught sight of her reflection in the mirror above the mantelpiece. It came as no surprise when she realised the reflection was grinning at her. 'Mad bitch,' Jo told herself, mock disapproval apparent in her whispered voice. Still smiling, she picked up the bottle with one black-gloved hand and twisted the cap open. Slowly, she inhaled the heady aroma of slightly soured whisky. 'This job is just full of bonuses,' she remarked. She switched the PC on and went to find herself a glass.

Glancing at her watch as she poured herself a drink, a momentary frown slipped across her brow. Time was against her. Because her car had picked this evening to collapse and die, Jo found she was more than an hour and a half behind schedule. She had allowed herself two-and-a-half hours to look around Steven's apartment which seemed insufficient, now she realised she didn't know what she was looking for. She had less than an hour to spare before Steven was due to return. She expected him to be back at ten o'clock and it was almost nine now. She cursed the fates that had robbed the time from her.

She took her drink to the PC, sat down and stared at the screen. A password prompt was waiting for her and she typed the word 'rosebud' without giving it a second thought. The prompt disappeared and a welcoming screen greeted her. Silently, Jo toasted the PC with her glass. As she tried to decide where to begin, she wondered if Steven was having as much luck with his investigation.

Anna sat alone in the front of the car, listening to the cheerful grunts and squeals of delight that were coming from the back. She smiled and made a mental note to thank Hera when she returned to the Kilgrimol.

It had been Hera's intention that this evening should be used to help build Cassandra's confidence up and, listening to the woman's shrieks of pleasure and her lurid exclamations, Anna realised that part of the plan had been accomplished already.

But something else was happening too and Anna wondered if that was part of Hera's plan. Since Hera had offered her the leadership of the Black Garter, Anna had thought of nothing else. It was a great responsibility and she was not prepared to accept the burden lightly. Over the past twenty-four hours she had considered every aspect of the role, trying to decide if she was worthy and capable. Now, as she drove through the fading sunset on the highlands, Anna realised she was close to making a decision.

'Where are we going?'

The question came from Tony, a swarthy local with an easy grin and mischievous eyes. He was supposed to be her date for the evening, Anna remembered ruefully. Considering that Cassandra had his cock in her mouth, she supposed that the pairing-off arrangements might have changed since she last took note. She was not even sure if that left her with the strong and silent Paul. By glancing occasionally in the rear-view mirror, Anna had already seen him fingering Cassandra's tight hole whilst she sucked Tony.

'I thought we could go to Kilgrimol forest,' Anna explained. 'I've been told it's quite secluded up there.'

'The necking woods,' Tony chuckled. 'Do you think we need seclusion?'

'I think you need a bucket of cold water,' Anna laughed, 'but let's see what happens when we get up there.' She passed him a reassuring grin through the rear-view mirror, then frowned. Behind the car, so far back in the distance that its sidelights were little more than specks, she saw the vehicle again. She did not think it really was the same one that had followed them discreetly through Kilgrimol's town centre but a cautious voice in the back of her mind insisted that it could be.

Without realising she was doing it, Anna pressed harder on the accelerator.

Jo glared angrily at the computer screen and contemplated throwing her glass at it. She resisted the urge, not wanting to add criminal damage to the mounting catalogue of crimes she already had under her belt. Breaking and entering, theft and unauthorised access to electronically stored data were more than enough for one evening.

So far, she had learnt nothing that was of any use and she wondered if she was searching in the wrong place. It had occurred to her that Sam might be a useful person to take with her on this case but she had not been able to find the redhead before leaving. Not that she would have wanted to introduce a naïve schoolgirl to the gentle art of lock-picking and unlawful entry.

She switched the PC off, not bothering with the correct shut-down procedures. Staring angrily at the books, files and folders that cluttered the desk, Jo picked up an unlabelled box file and began to glance at the contents. As she realised what she was reading, a broad grin suffused her face. 'Jackpot,' Jo whispered excitedly and, without even looking at what she was doing, Jo poured herself a second drink.

Her gaze was fixed on the contents of the file and she read it with a meticulous eye for detail. The importance of what she was reading made a thrill course through her. If she had been able to see her own reflection at that moment, Jo would have recognised the light of excitement that sparked in her eyes. The expression was so ecstatic it was almost sexual. 'Jackpot,' she whispered a second time.

'Jackpot,' Steven echoed, as he saw the car's taillights disappear over the hillock. There was only one route the car could possibly be following and from personal experience he knew it well. The bitch who was driving had tried to lose him; it had taken a hell of an effort to catch up with her but Steven's lunatic driving had finally paid off. Now, he knew without a doubt that they were going to the necking woods. There was nowhere else within fifty miles along this road.

The idea for a non-fiction book had come to him as he drove and the thought had stayed at the forefront of his mind as he followed the vehicle. The exposé of the Black Garter had to be worth more than a few articles in the national papers, he told himself. He would be revealing the raunchy background of dozens of successful names from all walks of life and that had to be worth more than a two-page spread in a colour supplement. The idea excited him and, as he drove, he made mental outlines for the book. The first section could detail the base and carnal habits of the Black Garter; the second part would reveal the names of the wealthy and successful women who had been former members. He could imagine some of the 'no comments' and other non-quotes that he could use to qualify the use of their photographs. The thought brought a thin smile to his lips. The final chapter, Steven decided, would be about the current members of the Black Garter. If he got the photographs he was hoping for this evening, he knew that they would make the book a worldwide best-seller.

As a cloak of trees covered the car in pale grey shadows, he killed the engine and tightened the handbrake. He was familiar enough with the necking woods to know that they could not travel far down this road. Taking the camera from the passenger seat, Steven crept stealthily into the forest.

Anna stepped from the vehicle and stretched her arms. She suddenly felt silly for having driven so quickly to the forest. Obviously no one was following them. She was simply suffering from the effects of paranoia, probably brought on by all those stupid stories that had been appearing in the *Kilgrimol Weekly Clarion*.

Shaking her head at her own foolishness, she wondered if this should affect her decision about leading the Black Garter. Hera should not be handing over her leadership to someone who ran from shadows.

The rear door of the car burst open and Anna

could hear the sighs of contentment breaking the silence of the dusk.

'Are you coming in to join us?' Paul asked, his broad Scots accent lilting cheerfully.

Anna inhaled the heather-scented air and shook her head. 'Why don't you come out and join me?' she suggested slyly. She reached for the top button of her blouse and unfastened it slowly. The bra she wore beneath it accentuated the swell of her breasts and the deep line of cleavage she displayed was more than alluring.

Paul's tranquil blue eyes shone excitedly. Needing no further prompting, he began to step from the car.

'Paul!' Cassandra's voice sounded hurt and petulant. 'I thought you were my date for the evening.'

Anna glanced into the car and saw that the strawberry-blonde's head had moved away slightly from Tony's cock so she could call out, although her mouth was still close enough to his length to flick her tongue against him without having to move. In the dull glow of the car's courtesy light Anna could see his cock was glistening slickly with her saliva.

'Join us,' Anna suggested. 'I might let you have both of them.'

Cassandra's eyes brightened and she began to shuffle out of the car. She tugged Tony's hand, encouraging him to follow. 'Where are we going?'

Anna smiled broadly. She took hold of Cassandra's hand and made her let go of Tony. 'We're going into the woods,' she told Tony and Paul. 'Catch me, and you can have me.'

Both men grinned and exchanged a knowing wink.

'Catch Cassandra,' Anna went on, 'and you can have her.' A meaningful expression filled her eyes and she said, 'Catch the pair of us, and you can have something really special.' As if to add emphasis to her words, Anna teased another button loose from the front of her blouse. The lacy fabric of her bra was now on full display to the two men. The honest lechery of their appraisal warmed her and with a lithe step backwards, she moved out of their reach.

'What makes you think we can't catch you?' Tony asked, buttoning up his fly.

Anna grinned at him. 'I want you to catch me,' she said. Tracing one hand up the length of bare leg, she raised her skirt a little. The top of her black garter was revealed and she moved her hand higher, allowing the two men to see the panties she wore. With a brisk motion she snatched them down and pulled them to her ankles. Stepping daintily out of them, she threw the pants to Paul.

He caught them defly and, with no hint of embarrassment, raised the pants to his nostrils and inhaled the warm scent she had left there. 'If I catch you, are you mine for the night?'

'Catch both of us,' Anna told him. 'Together, I think we can blow your mind.'

Cassandra was staring at her with wild-eyed excitement.

'Count to twenty, then follow,' Anna said carefully. She continued to smile, even as she caught sight of a furtive movement beyond the car, hidden amongst the nearby trees. She dismissed the movement as being nothing more than a recurrence of her earlier paranoia. They were alone in the necking woods, she reminded herself. No one was watching or following; that was just silliness.

'One . . . two . . . three . . .'

Paul's slow counting brought her attention back to the more important matters of the moment. He was watching her with lewd intent as he counted and

Anna knew he was mentally undressing her. She grinned at him, not bothering to disguise her obvious desire.

Steven ducked down, certain that the taller blonde woman had seen him. He heard the leaves around him rustle and tried to dismiss the notion that the sound had given him away. He had barely been able to hear their conversation and the rational part of his mind knew they wouldn't have heard him at that distance. Still his heart raced.

For an instant he forgot his professional composure. He could not tell what the other couple had been doing but he did not doubt it was sexual. The lustre of their smiles and their blatant appreciation for one another had made it obvious. The sight of Anna taking her knickers off had been darkly disturbing and Steven's arousal had been instantaneous. As he tried to will his erection away he reminded himself he had a job to do. He pushed his thoughts beyond the urgency of his desires and risked a wary glance through the undergrowth.

The two women were running into the forest, discarding items of clothing as they went. He watched as Anna cast her blouse free and allowed it to rest on the breeze for a moment and before it had fallen to the bracken-littered path, he saw she was unfastening her bra. The thrill of his excitement began to build.

Willing himself to act like a professional, Steven checked his camera one last time. The film was loaded, the lens cap was uncoupled and the settings were attuned to the most suitable for this sort of light. During an earlier discussion with Peter he had considered the idea of using a flash and then discounted it for not being discreet enough. Now, he glanced at the flashbulb he had brought 'just in case', and wondered if it might be worth using. He had no idea what the four intended to get up to but, as he watched Anna and Cassandra shedding their clothes, his vivid imagination was able to postulate a handful of theories.

Anxiously, he tried to decide if it would be worth the risk to take one definitive photograph or attempt to take twenty-four potentially unsuccessful ones. He decided to hedge his bets. He would take twenty-three unassisted photographs in the darkening twilight gloom and for the twenty-fourth he would use the flash.

He risked another glance through the undergrowth. The two women were almost naked now and disappearing into the forest. The two men were preparing to follow them. Grinning, Steven followed all four.

Completely naked, save for her shoes and garter, Anna danced happily through the forest. The light was quickly fading from the sky and within the confines of the dense trees she realised darkness was imminent. The thrill of the controlled excitement held her like an addiction. The occasional intimate touch of a tree's branch was like the reassuring caress of a lover. The feelings of excitement and elation that welled within her had mixed into a heady cocktail.

She felt like a mystical princess from some surreal myth or magic fantasy and the quickening twilight did nothing to dispel this image. Trees and bushes passed in a hectic blur as she danced lithely between the towering pillars of their broad trunks. The emerald canopy above her head diffused the fading light into a stage setting of dusty viridity scented by the forest's foliage. She felt healthy and invigorated. Behind her, the heavy footfalls and excited breath of her pursuers sounded closer and out of the corner of her eye she could see Cassandra throwing her pants behind her, giggling.

'You've done this before, haven't you?' Cassandra remarked, running alongside her for a moment.

Anna smiled, encouraged by the girl's confidence. Adventures like this were as alien to her as they were to Cassandra but she felt warmed by the thought that she looked experienced in such matters. Instead of answering, she asked, 'Are you enjoying yourself?'

Cassandra nodded. 'This is just what I'd imagined the Black Garter to be like,' she confided. 'It's so exciting.'

Grinning, Anna noticed that even though Cassandra had undressed, she too still wore her black garter. For both of them, the accessory was more than a simple item of clothing; it was a mark of who they were. 'I doubt it will be this exciting once Hera's left,' Anna said calmly.

As she ran, Cassandra studied Anna uncertainly. 'Will you be leader when Hera's gone?'

Anna nodded. The honest appreciation in Cassandra's smile was warming. 'I bet it will be even better with you as leader,' she said encouragingly.

Anna grinned and she was about to reply with some glib dismissal of the flattery when she felt the arms fall around her.

'Gotcha!'

It was Tony's voice, close to her ear. His strong hands cupped her naked breasts and she shivered happily beneath his touch. Sliding easily from his reach, Anna turned to him with a smile. Paul was coming up quickly behind him.

'Catch both of us,' she insisted. She reached for Cassandra's hand and pulled her away from the two men.

'You vixen,' Tony shouted.

Anna laughed. She hurried along to a small clearing of the woods that she remembered from her last visit. Then, the place had been busy with picnickers and noisy children. Now, the clearing was deserted save for the oak-hewn tables and benches. The only thing that broke the idyllic splendour was the presence of a bright red waste-bin but Anna chose to ignore it. Her fantasy of being a mystical princess could accommodate that.

She pulled Cassandra on to one of the picnic benches and they stood there side by side. Hardly aware that she was doing it, Anna placed her arm around Cassandra's slender waist. Her flesh was cool to the touch and she shivered when Anna touched her. For a moment, Anna thought she heard an uncharacteristic click. The sound was not the sort of thing she would normally have associated with a forest. There were plenty of things to hear in the woods, she thought, but this had sounded mechanical and out of place. It was more like the snap of the shutter on a camera than the sound of breaking twigs or bending branches.

Before she had time to dwell on the noise, Tony and Paul burst into the clearing. The pair of them stared up at the two women, eager anticipation apparent in their smiles. 'Now we've caught you,' Tony gasped, his voice only slightly breathless with exertion.

Anna shook her head. 'No, we've surrendered,' she corrected. She turned to Cassandra and placed a kiss on the shorter woman's mouth. She could feel her own excitement mounting and she could taste the erotic breath of desire that came from Cassandra. Behind her, she could hear both Tony and Paul gasp softly and congratulated herself for organising things so well. She pushed Cassandra down on to the picnic table, then straddled the woman, placing her pussy lips over Cassandra's face. She placed her own mouth near the heat of Cassandra's sex, then turned to Paul and Tony. 'Let's see if you were worth surrendering to,' she called cheerfully.

The two men ginned broadly. They could see what was expected of them and hurried to join the two women. As they ran, they started to step out of their clothes.

Whilst she waited for them, Anna nuzzled softly at the flesh of Cassandra's sex. She could taste the warm flavour of her arousal. The musky scent of her desire sent a warm tingle rushing through Anna's body. Beneath her, Cassandra giggled excitedly.

Anna glanced up as the two men neared. She saw that Paul was moving close to her face, his huge, rigid cock just about at eye level for her and she studied it with a broad grin. She watched him run his fingers along the shaft, brandishing the weapon towards her.

'What are you wanting to do with that?' she asked coyly.

'What do you think?' he grunted.

Anna studied him with a knowing grin. 'I couldn't begin to guess,' she said arrogantly. 'It looks like you're spoilt for choice here.' As if to demonstrate exactly what she meant, she teased the tip of one finger around the tight ring of Cassandra's anus then slowly she moved the finger up, and drew a line along the glistening lips of the woman's pussy. Aware that Paul was staring hungrily at the glut of pleasure before him, she licked her lips.

His smile widened and she realised he had not missed the subtle intimation of her gesture. He moved his cock forward, holding it millimetres from her face. 'You decide,' he told her.

Anna reached her hand out and guided his length towards her mouth. She sucked gently on the end, allowing her tongue to trace around the bulbous tip. Paul released a soft sigh of pleasure.

Behind her, Anna could hear Tony and Cassandra making similar noises. She guessed that Cassandra had taken Tony's cock in her mouth as the cleft between her own legs remained untouched. Not that she need stimulation like that at the moment, she reminded herself. The excitement of pressing herself against Cassandra's naked body and sucking on Paul's cock were providing more thrills than she could have imagined. The salty taste of his arousal and Cassandra's animal scent were intoxicating aphrodisiacs.

Something brushed against the lips of her pussy. She was not in the right position to see what was happening but the lips of her sex were highly sensitive and she quickly realised they were being spread by a pair of delicate hands. The soft, subtle touch of the fingertips against her labia was too tender to be anything other than the touch of another woman and her suspicions were confirmed a moment later when Cassandra teased her tongue against the delicate warm folds of Anna's sex.

Happily, Anna released her own sigh of elation. She sucked harder on Paul's cock, trying to communicate her intense pleasure to him through the tip of his shaft and, considering the way his length twitched and jerked inside her mouth, she guessed she had managed to convey something.

The end of Tony's cock was now rubbing against the eager wet folds of her sex. The urgency of his tip seemed to pulsate against her and Anna could feel the fury of his need. She sucked harder on Paul's length, trying to cover up the sounds of excitement that grew within her.

As Cassandra guided the cock between Anna's legs, she placed her tongue against the folds of flesh and lapped softly. The thrill was so great that Anna did not bother trying to mute her delight. Her groan of excitement carried powerfully beyond the trees and into the forest. Tremors of excitement had begun to shiver through her body.

She allowed Paul's cock to fall from her mouth and pushed the end artlessly against Cassandra's welcoming labia. With a gentle push, he was inside. Cassandra cried out softly, her words muffled between Anna's thighs.

Anna watched the man ride his length into the sopping hole for a moment. He had a decent sized prick, she thought, and whilst it was not the largest she had ever seen, she didn't doubt it was big enough for someone with Cassandra's lack of experience. As she watched him sliding back and forth, she realised his shaft was glistening with the slick wetness of Cassandra's pussy honey.

The fragrance was so sweet and succulent, Anna felt an overwhelming urge to taste the woman again. She buried her nose against Cassandra's pussy, licking and sucking, unmindful of the intrusion of Paul's cock. When she realised she was unable to get her tongue properly close to the source of Cassandra's juice, she pulled Paul's penis from the tight hole and drew her tongue greedily against the girl's sweet sex. Realising his length was sodden with the wetness of her arousal, Anna pushed her mouth against his cock and began to lick him clean.

Behind her, she could feel Tony pounding his length inside her with a quickening pace, while Cassandra was teasing her tongue over the eager nub of her clit with deft flicks. Occasionally her mouth would break away and Anna suspected that at these intervals she was probably using her tongue to tease Tony's cock.

With a soft moan of delight, Anna placed Paul's shaft back inside Cassandra's pussy and watched as the man rode purposefully into her.

Steven stared at the scene, unable to believe he was witnessing such torrid events. His camera's film was all but spent and he offered prayer after prayer to the god of cameras that the exposure would not be too dark. Even if he had not been planning to do an exposé of the Black Garter, he would still have wanted photographs like this for his own private collection.

Both of the women seemed so eager to be fucked it was difficult for him to believe. Their easy acceptance of each other's tongues and the two men's cocks left him feeling desperately excited. He did not know what the two women normally got up to and he didn't dare to contemplate it. The erection in his pants stood furiously hard and he wished he had the time to do something about it. As he stared at the two eager women on the picnic table he wondered if they would mind a third man joining in, then discounted the idea. It was not that he thought they might behave in a prudish manner if he turned up, but he did realise his presence would spoil the atmosphere. He also guessed that they might object to him carrying the camera and asking them all to smile and say 'cheese'.

Reminding himself of his professional obligations, he watched the scene for a moment longer and raised the camera to his eye. The light had now faded so much, it was little more than a visible memory falling beyond the horizon. He squinted at the frame counter and saw that he was already up to picture number twenty-two.

'Might as well make this the important one,' he told himself in a whisper-soft voice. With meticulous care, he attached the flashbulb to the camera's hot-shoe. As he watched the indicator light, waiting for it to say when it was safe to take the photograph, he tried to brush all thoughts of sexual excitement from his mind. It was not easy. Here he was trying to photograph two nubile young women who were getting screwed by two attractive young men; the thought kept recurring as he waited.

Regardless, he managed to gain control over his excitement and when the indicator lamp shone green, he dared to break his cover for an instant.

Anna could feel the mountainous excitement of her climax welling inside. She rode Tony's cock at a furious pace, his length filling her again and again as he pushed the tip of his prick hard against the neck of her womb. The lips of her labia were being spread wide apart by his thick girth. As he drove deep inside, she could feel Cassandra's fingers spreading the lips wider, so that her tongue had easier access.

Not that Cassandra's tongue was doing much worth mentioning, she thought ruefully. The girl was lost in an ecstatic haze of joy that seemed to have distracted her from her task. Cunnilingus was forgotten as she screamed words of praise and thanks for the joy she was receiving. Immersed in a maelstrom of pleasure, Cassandra writhed from side to side beneath Anna. The friction between their naked bodies, as flesh brushed against flesh, was exhilarating.

Remembering that Hera had instigated this evening for the benefit of Cassandra's confidence, Anna had to grade the whole episode as a complete success. She realised that it was not just Cassandra who had received a boost to her confidence; Anna could feel that her own sense of self-worth had grown as well.

Paul's cock was still ploughing rigorously into Cassandra and Anna darted her tongue against him as he fucked her. The intimacy and excitement of the moment were too intense and before she realised it was happening, another orgasm rippled through her body. Her inner muscles clenched hard and a groan of ecstatic joy screamed from her lips. In the same instant she felt Tony's cock stiffen and his pulse beat furiously inside her. The strength of his climax was enough to push her orgasm on to a greater plane of pleasure. Untold joy seemed to sing from the darkest recesses of her erogenous zones and, for a while, she was lost in a bliss-filled haven that transcended any delight she had known before. As the climax rushed through her she realised that these feelings of power, control and pleasure were the things she craved most in the world. When she got back to the Kilgrimol this evening, Anna knew she was going to accept Hera's offer to lead the Black Garter.

She could see the concentration in Paul's smile and knew he was on the point of his own climax. Grinning wickedly, she pulled his cock from Cassandra's wet hole and sucked on the end of his pussy-flavoured length. She had anticipated the moment perfectly. Her mouth was filled with the explosion of his seed so that, as well as the heady taste of Cassandra's sweet musky flavour, Anna was treated to the copious flow of Paul's climax. She swallowed his come greedily, amazed by the arousal she experienced from simply sucking him. Her heart was beating quickly and she glanced coyly up at him, his pulsing length still between her lips.

Darkness was now falling heavily around them and his features were little more than a grey etching on a silhouette. She released his cock from her mouth and was about to say something when the flashbulb exploded.

With the photograph taken, Steven turned and fled through the forest. If that picture managed to convey a tenth of the excitement he had sensed whilst taking it, the damned thing would go down in history as the most erotic photograph of all time. Stuffing the camera deep into one pocket of his jacket, he ran swiftly through the forest, remembering the tracks he had made with clinical precision.

Behind him, he could hear their startled cries and exclamations but they were already fading into the distance as he ran away from them. For one moment he wondered if either, or both of the men might be pursuing him. He had gambled on the hope that they wouldn't. Both were undressed and even the bravest of men would be reluctant to give chase to someone when they had no clothes on.

The idea had seemed logical before he took the photograph but now, as he ran ever faster through the forest, it did not seem as convincing. Even though his heart was racing too fast to allow him to hear properly, he felt sure that his ears could detect their footfalls as they chased after him. The sound seemed so real he did not even dare to glance back over his shoulder and instead kept his head down and ran. Several times he came close to tripping and tumbling headlong in the treacherous undergrowth but good luck seemed to be on his side.

When he finally caught sight of his own car, relief washed over him and he ran quickly to it, fearful that either of the men could catch up with him at any second. It was not that he was afraid of them; he simply knew how irate the pair were likely to be if they did manage to catch up with him. He had once seen Peter take a beating for photographing football violence and it had not been a pretty sight. Steven was determined to avoid any encounter like that.

He jumped into the front seat of his car and slammed his key into the ignition. At the same time, he dropped his elbow on the central locking, securing his own private sanctuary, then gunned the engine into noisy, spluttering life, daring to risk a glance in the rear-view mirror.

He was slightly disappointed when he saw that neither of the men had been chasing him. It would have been more heroic if he had managed to outrun someone but he did not dwell on the image for too long. As soon as he had flicked the car's headlights on, he pushed the car into first and sped away from the necking woods.

Feeling safe for the first time since he had taken the picture, Steven reached into his pocket to retrieve the camera. For an instant, he thought he had lost it. All his hard work and earnest endeavours were held over a chasm for a moment and he hovered over it with eyes widened by growing panic until his fingers finally fell on the camera, and he allowed himself to breathe again, unaware he had even been holding his breath.

'This,' he declared, 'is fame and fortune.' Driving with one hand, he initiated the camera's automatic-rewind button. The machine whirred noisily for a minute, vibrating gently between his fingers. As soon as the precious film inside was completely rewound, he removed it from the back of the camera and placed it safely in his jacket pocket. Peter had loaned the camera to him after extracting a promise from Steven that he would be 'ultra-careful' with it. 'It's worth about a grand,' Peter had told him. 'It's a vital part

of my kit and I can't afford to replace it if you drop
it down a crapper or something.'

Remembering his own earnest assurance, Steven
tossed the borrowed camera casually on to the
passenger seat where it bounced before settling. The
camera may have been worth a lot of money but the
picture it had just taken was worth a damned sigh
more. He glanced at the dashboard clock and his gri
widened. He had managed to secure the picture of hi
life and he would still be able to get home and b
tucked up in bed for ten-thirty.

'What the fuck happened there?' Tony demande
unhappily.

Paul shrugged.

Anna had her own thoughts about the matter bu
she stayed silent. She remembered the paranoia sh
had experienced earlier about the car following the
and the uncharacteristic sounds of the forest. Wi
hindsight it made perfect sense and she could ha
kicked herself for not doing something about th
situation when she had first suspected it. The blaste
reporter from the *Kilgrimol Weekly Clarion* had don
it again, she realised. This time he would have
scandal and a half to report, she thought ruefull
The only hope she dared to allow herself was that
had been too far away to get a decent shot. It was n
much of a hope but she clung to it fervently.

'Do you want us to go after him?' Paul venture
'Tony and I could get the dirty bastard's camera a
shove it up his arse for him.'

Anna shook her head, turning her thoughts aw
from the reporter and back to the two men. 'If you
in a mood to do something brave and exciting, w
don't you let Cassandra and I take full advantage
it?'

Paul's face was illuminated by his broad grin. He watched her fondle his spent cock, lovingly rekindling the life back to it. 'Don't you have to be back at your dorm by eleven?' he asked.

Anna grinned. 'We still have plenty of time for fun,' she assured him. 'And I'm sure it won't matter if we're a few minutes late.'

Cassandra placed a fond arm around her, nodding agreement. 'It won't matter one bit what time we turn up,' she said firmly. Fixing Anna with a knowing gaze, she said, 'As of next week, Anna here will be in charge of the school.'

As she returned the smile, Anna couldn't help but think Cassandra was right. Whatever the outcome of the photograph that had just been taken, she felt sure she could ride the embarrassment. After that, the leadership of the Black Garter would be hers for the taking.

Jo was on her fourth Jack Daniels and thoroughly immersed in the research material she had found. After an initial flick through the pages she had forced herself to slow down and study the pages more critically. As she did, she began to see the exact direction that Steven's research had followed. He had made copious notes in the margins of the photocopied pages and she learnt more from these than she did from the actual subject matter. It was only when she heard the heavy slam of a door in the building that she finally deigned to glance at her wristwatch. It was ten-forty-five.

Her eyes widened in horror. 'Shit!' she exclaimed hotly. She rushed to the kitchenette and considered pouring her drink down the sink but loath to waste the golden liquid, she drained the contents of her glass and swallowed it quickly before placing it with the rest of the untouched washing-up. The whisky burnt the back of her throat but she enjoyed the kick it gave her. The box folder was easy to file away and she slid it back into place, hoping fervently that Steven was not the type who remembered exactly where he had left things. She supposed that was unlikely given the state of his apartment but the doubt still niggled her.

With no time to consider niceties such as the drawn curtains and the half-eaten packet of chocolate biscuits, Jo rushed to the apartment door and turned all the lights off. She opened the door carefully and seeing the corridor was empty, stepped out into the safety of the hall. As she closed the door behind her, she released a soft sigh of relief.

'Jo? What the hell are you doing here?'

She turned on hearing Steven's voice and graced him with the most innocent smile she could manage. Her mind quickly searched for an appropriate response and she quickly asked, 'Where the hell have you been? I've been waiting here for an hour.'

He frowned and pushed past her to open his apartment door. 'What do you want from me that's so important?'

In response, Jo placed her arms around him and pressed her lips over his mouth. Her hands went down to his waist and whilst one slid into the pocket of his jacket, the other rubbed purposefully against the swelling in the front of his pants. 'I wanted to see you,' she whispered softly, adding obvious meaning to her words.

He frowned and stepped away from her. 'Perhaps we shouldn't,' he began hesitantly. She saw him glance awkwardly into his apartment, as though he feared her being near the information he had stored there.

Jo exercised her own frown, not wanting him to think she was too eager to get away after appearing so delighted to see him. 'But I thought you liked me,' she told him in a slightly hurt tone.

He shrugged, his smile sympathetic but set beneath resolute eyes. 'It's been a long day for me, Jo,' he said carefully. 'Maybe we could do this some other night?'

Jo grinned and kissed him again. 'I'll call you,' she assured him.

She heard the apartment door close as she was halfway down the stairs. Staring at the roll of film she had retrieved from his jacket pocket, Jo wondered if she was holding the results of his day's work. Considering the things she had read this evening, she dearly hoped so. She remembered the voice-mail she had intercepted earlier and that memory was enough to give her an insight into what had happened. Her grip on the film tightened as she realised what she was holding.

As a lover, Steven was more than acceptable but he was ethically bankrupt. The story he had planned was so lurid and fantastic the word 'sensational' did not do it proper justice. Perhaps it was based on truth but Jo could recognise a bastardised version of true events when she read one. If her act of petty theft was going to hurt him severely, then Jo felt very pleased with her evening's work. As she started to walk back to the Kilgrimol, she whistled cheerfully.

Ten

By the time she reached the Kilgrimol Jo had stopped whistling. The four-mile walk from the town to the school's grounds had taken its toll on her. The two-mile walk to Steven's apartment, from the spot where her car died, had seemed like a marathon. The four-mile trek home felt like some round-the-world charity event.

As she fought against the pain of a stitch brought on by walking, Jo wondered how she had thought she could convince anyone she was an assistant gym instructor. She would have been better off trying to pass herself off as a Japanese language tutor. She only knew the word *saki* and a handful of lyrics from *Madam Butterfly* but it was more than she knew about exercise and keeping fit.

She nodded at the prefect by the staff dorms, hoping she could avoid conversation. The combination of her laboured breathing and bad mood was likely to turn her words into an unpleasant rasp.

'You've been out late,' the prefect noted.

'Do I lose a house point for that?' Jo asked tartly.

The prefect shrugged, surprised by the sullen tone of Jo's voice. She held the door open, and even turned the hall lights on for her, as Jo made her way up the stairs. Her perfect manners and quiet acceptance of Jo's truculent mood made the investigator feel worse than if the girl had snapped at her.

Grudgingly, Jo thanked her before starting up the steps to her room.

The prefect grinned. 'Saying thank you won't get you your house point back.'

Jo smiled at her. 'I'll live without it.'

She climbed the steps slowly, each one stretching the overused muscles of her legs to an interminable degree. Her dorm was on the third floor and each step was a lesson in pain that she hadn't endured in a long time.

By the time she reached the door of her room, Jo was sweating. In her mind she planned a scalding hot bath filled with bubbles, all set beside a cool glass of Scotch. The image was so vivid that she could hear the tinkle of the ice cubes in the tumbler and see the bath's steam evaporating against the glass as she placed her key in the lock.

'Good evening, Jo Valentine. You've had us waiting.'

The voice startled Jo and she glanced hesitantly up from her thoughts. Waiting in the small dormitory were four women. She recognised Sam instantly. The bespectacled redhead sat meekly between two other girls whom Jo did not know. Sitting alone in a chair and smiling broadly at Jo was a tall, commanding brunette. She had been the one who spoke and, from her dominant attitude, Jo was able to guess that this was Hera, the leader of the Black Garter. She ignored the woman.

Speaking to Sam, Jo said cheerfully, 'It's good to see you. I see you've brought a couple of friends around for a pyjama party. What do we do first? Drink cocoa or talk about boys?'

Hera's smile slipped a little as she studied the

investigator. Jo slid her jacket off and threw it carelessly to the floor. The room was embarrassingly small with barely enough room for the furniture, let alone four visitors. Without bothering to acknowledge any of the other women present she made her way to the dorm's fridge and opened the door. 'We're all out of milk, girls,' she called. With a frown of annoyance she added, 'The ice-cube situation seems a little on the disappointing side as well.' Her imagined drink with ice cubes, beside a relaxing bath, disappeared when she saw the empty freezer compartment.

'We made ourselves free with your hospitality,' Hera said coolly. 'We didn't think you'd mind.'

'Not at all,' Jo replied tightly. 'I've left my cheque book lying around somewhere; would you like to take some of those whilst you're here?'

'I can sense a degree of hostility,' Hera said, sounding concerned. 'That's not how I wanted this evening to go. You and I have a lot to talk about and we shouldn't be arguing. Mel, organise a drink for our host.'

Jo watched the mouse-blonde hurry to obey the instruction. She took the seat the woman had vacated, placing herself against Sam's comforting warmth. To reassure the redhead, and for her own secret pleasure, Jo squeezed Sam's knee.

'Did you say you wanted milk?' Melanie asked curiously.

Jo shook her head. 'No. I heard a rumour about where that comes from. It's always sickened me since then.' Her joke was met with a sea of puzzled faces, making Jo realise her sense of humour was more mature than her audience. 'Just a Scotch on the rocks and hold the rocks.'

Melanie nodded and went about the laborious task of pouring a drink.

'How's your case progressing?' Hera asked.

Jo slid a quiet glance at Sam.

'Sam's told me everything,' Hera explained patiently. 'And you mustn't be angry with her. That's just how things work in this school. Everyone here answers to me.'

Jo remained silent, not trusting herself to make a response. She accepted her drink from Melanie and allowed the girl to stand awkwardly at the side of the room.

'Have you been very clever and found out who our leak is?' Hera asked.

Jo studied the woman thoughtfully. 'I work to a code that's called client confidentiality,' she explained. 'Just as you expect the members of your gang to be honourable and report back to you, I offer a promise of discretion to the people I work for.'

'But surely,' Hera broke in, 'you can see that this is different.'

Jo sipped her drink and raised her eyebrows. 'How?'

'Your information would have been given to me once you'd given it to your client,' Hera explained. 'I'm just trying to cut out the middleman.'

Jo drained her glass and shook it in Melanie's direction. 'You pour a very good neat Scotch,' she remarked solemnly. 'Would you care to prove it's a skill you've been blessed with, rather than just beginner's luck?'

Sullenly, seeming to resent the role of waitress that she had been forced into, Melanie took Jo's glass and replenished it.

'So,' Hera began again, her voice stiffening slightly with annoyance. 'Do you have a name for our spy?'

Jo laughed and shook her head. Shaping her words carefully, she said, 'I've already told you, I couldn't divulge a name, even if I had one.' She fixed her gaze on Hera and found herself held by the woman's commanding stare.

'Don't cross me,' Hera breathed softly. 'You could find out I'm a little like Doctor Jekyll if you cross me.'

Jo frowned, showing playful defiance in the face of the woman's threat. 'Do you mean, you've written a dictionary?'

Hera stared at her, slightly puzzled at first. When realisation struck her, an annoyed scowl creased her forehead. 'That was Doctor Johnson,' she explained tersely. 'Doctor Jekyll was Robert Louis Stevenson's creation in *The Strange Case of Doctor Jekyll and Mr Hyde*.'

Jo smiled. 'I'm sure you're just like her,' she agreed blithely. She sipped at her drink, smiling broadly. She could feel the woman's antagonism mounting and she realised she may be pushing her too far. Since entering the room, Jo had sensed an uncomfortable degree of animosity and although it was only to be expected under the circumstances, she had been happy to challenge it at first. Now as Hera's mood darkened she realised the time for caution had edged closer.

'I thought Doctor Jekyll was a man,' Melanie said quietly.

'She was,' Grace supplied quickly.

Jo was startled by the woman's words, having forgotten she was sitting on the other side of Sam. She glanced slyly at her, not sure if her words had been spoken with wry humour or rank stupidity. The indifferent mask of Grace's smile made it difficult to tell.

'To get back to my earlier point,' Hera began again softly. 'You can either see a nice side of me, or an unpleasant one. I don't like making threats but if that's the way you want me to play . . .'

Jo waved a silencing hand at the woman. She stepped away from her chair and reached into the pocket of the jacket she had discarded. Retrieving the stolen film she tossed it towards Hera.

Hera caught the roll in one hand. 'What's this?'

Jo grinned. 'It's as much as you're getting off me,' she said flatly. 'Consider it a token of goodwill, just to show you that I'm really on your side.'

Hera was still frowning. 'I don't understand.'

'Tomorrow, that would have been front-page news. In the newspapers, that could have been the scandal that ruined the lives of two of your friends. Tonight, it's proof that I'm on your side. I found it in the pocket of the *Clarion*'s reporter,' Jo explained. 'He'd been tipped off that two of your girls were out tonight and that's his proof of what they were doing.'

Hera breathed a soft sigh of disgust. 'The despicable bastard.'

Jo nodded. 'If he wasn't such a good fuck, he'd be useless,' she agreed. Realising Hera was staring at her, Jo grinned amiably at the woman. 'Do whatever the hell you want with that,' she said generously. 'Burn it, expose it to light or get it developed and prove that I'm not lying, but it's yours to keep. Just remember what I said: you're not getting anything else off me. I mean that, and like you, I don't want to see you get nasty.' She reached a hand out and touched Hera's leg. 'I wouldn't want to see someone as pretty as you turn nasty.'

'I'll have Grace develop this,' Hera said, holding up the roll of film and smiling excitedly into Jo's face. 'Melanie, Grace, Sam,' she snapped absently, still staring at Jo. 'We're leaving.'

'May I stay for a while?' Sam's voice was a meek whisper that startled all four of them.

Jo glanced at her, not sure if she was asking permission from her or Hera.

'I need to apologise to Jo and sort a couple of things out,' Sam explained to the Black Garter's leader.

'If Jo wants you here,' Hera conceded, 'then you may stay.' She studied Jo thoughtfully, toying idly with the roll of film. 'I'm prepared to accept this token of goodwill in the spirit that it's been given. I would like to know who the leak is but I wouldn't want to force information out of you that you don't want to give.' Her thoughtful smile broke into a broad grin and she added, 'If you'd been one of my girls, then that wouldn't have been an issue.' She stood up and gestured for Melanie and Grace to leave the room. Fixing Jo with a warm expression, Hera rubbed her fingers softly against Jo's cheek. 'If the Black Garter can be of any assistance to you in your investigations, you only have to ask.'

Jo could sense an underlying sexual invitation in Hera's words and she tried to ignore it. The woman was beautiful and powerful but Jo could perceive a dangerous side to her that was positively chilling. She willed herself to remain indifferent to the woman's touch. 'If there's anything you can do, I'll let you know,' Jo assured her, with no intention of asking for Hera's help.

Hera nodded and walked to the door. She called a soft goodnight to Sam before leaving the room.

Jo held her breath until she heard Hera's footfalls echoing softly down the corridor. 'What the hell does she want to be when she leaves school? A South American dictator?'

'Her parents are big names in the media industry,' Sam explained quietly. 'Her father wants her to work on one of his newspapers.'

Jo raised her eyebrows and considered the thought for a moment. She glanced at Sam and saw the redhead was staring miserably up at her. 'So what did you want to apologise for?' she asked kindly. 'Were you sorry you lied to me? Or were you sorry that you sold me out?' A thought occurred to her and she frowned. 'Or do I have some other nasty surprise waiting for me?'

'I didn't want to sell you out,' Sam whispered miserably. Her words were so softly spoken Jo could not stop herself from glancing at the girl. She felt a wave of self-loathing as she realised Samantha had started crying. It was not a bad evening's work, she reflected. In the space of one night she had managed to become a petty criminal, a thief and now she was making a schoolgirl cry. She thought it fortunate she had not been given the chance to rob from a poor box.

Sitting next to Sam, Jo placed her hand on the young woman's leg and squeezed reassuringly. 'I'm sorry,' she began, 'I didn't mean to say that.'

Sam sniffed back tears, shaking her head. 'You had every right to say that. I sold you out and it was wrong of me and I hate myself for it.' She glared angrily at her feet and added, 'I didn't want to.'

Jo stopped herself from saying something nasty and out of place. Instead, she placed a comforting arm around the girl's shoulders. 'Of course you didn't want to,' she agreed.

'I didn't,' Sam assured her vehemently. She dared to risk a glance into the disbelieving depths of Jo's dark brown eyes. 'Hera made me tell her and I've got the bruises to prove it.'

Jo frowned unhappily. 'Bruises?' she repeated.

'I'll show you.' Sam pulled away from her and raised the hem of her skirt. She stepped quickly and unaffectedly out of her pants and thrust her bum out for Jo's inspection. 'See,' she declared, pointing.

The cheeks of her backside were still a dull red from the slapping they had endured. Welts of a darker red marked the flesh in long, cruel lines and Jo could see faint blisters of white where candle wax had been dripped on to the girl's flesh. She raised a tentative finger and traced the horizontal path of one burning red weal with a careful finger.

Sam winced softly, struggling to contain the sound and Jo moved her finger quickly away, murmuring an apology.

'And here,' Sam said, turning around quickly.

The hem of her skirt fell down as she moved the cheeks of her backside away from Jo's reach. Sam quickly unfastened her blouse and released her bare breasts from the garment. She pushed her breasts close to Jo's face and urged her to look at them. 'I haven't been able to wear a bra since they did this to me,' she whispered softly. 'My nipples still hurt.'

Jo stared at the naked breasts with a sullen frown. The nipples, hard and thrusting, were a dark, uncomfortable red. Halfway along the nubs, tiny indents forced the flesh inwards. She reached a careful finger to the breast and gently touched the sore nipple. Sam made a small sound and Jo tried to convince herself it was mainly discomfort she was hearing. 'Nipple clamps?' she asked.

Sam shook her head. 'One of Hera's home-made contraptions. She filched some crocodile clips from the physics lab.'

'I'm going to kill her,' Jo said decidedly. She rose from the seat and reached to the floor for her jacket. 'I'm going to fucking kill her,' she declared angrily.

Sam restrained her with a touch. 'Don't make it worse for me,' she said miserably. 'You didn't notice the worst thing, did you?'

Jo dropped the jacket to the floor. 'The worst thing? What else has the bitch done to you?'

Sam allowed her blouse to fall closed over the swell of her aching breasts and she raised the hem of her skirt again. This time she faced Jo, revealing the luxuriant flaming red warmth of her pubic hairs. The mound looked as delectable and inviting as ever and, even with close scrutiny, Jo could not see any marks or blemishes. She moved her face closer, trying not to get excited by the delightful scent of Sam's musky warmth.

'What am I looking for?' Jo asked. 'And where? What did the bitch do to you?'

'Here,' Sam said, indicating. Her words were choked with the volume of her distress. The tip of her finger rested on the bare flesh of her upper thigh. 'Can't you see?'

For a moment, Jo was mesmerised by the gorgeous sight of Sam's bare leg. There was no mark or sign of any injury; all she could see was one beautiful, long coltish leg that went up to a sweet-scented paradise. When the realisation finally struck her, Jo found it difficult to believe the cause of the girl's upset.

'You're not wearing a garter,' Jo observed quietly.

Sam groaned miserably, as though the words had caused physical pain. 'I'm not allowed to,' she sobbed. 'Hera took it off me and said I had to earn it again.' Her entire body quivered with the misery of this declaration.

Jo reached out and embraced her. She could feel Sam's deep unhappiness and wanted to comfort and soothe her. The memory of the previous evening's intimacy was still fresh in her mind; the pleasure they had shared had been more than satisfying. For Jo, still recovering from Stephanie's rejection, the experience had been cathartic and she had been reminded that life went on. Considering the blackness of her mood then, it had been a revelation. Now, she needed to pay Sam back by consoling and reassuring her.

Sam placed her arms around Jo and held her tightly. Her bare breasts rocked slightly with muffled sobs and she placed her mouth close to Jo's neck. Slowly, she delivered a series of soft kisses to the smooth expanse of the investigator's neck. 'I'm sorry I sold you out,' she whispered meekly. 'I tried to lie to her but . . .'

Jo silenced her words with a finger on Sam's lips. She shook her head, assuring Sam that no more apologies were necessary. For her own part, Jo did not know if she could have tolerated Hera's punishment. She had withstood a lot of discomfort in the past, and remained silent throughout it; however, whilst she had been enduring that, she had always known how close she was to breaking her silence. She could have tolerated Hera trying to get information from her but she felt outraged that the woman had bullied Sam into talking.

Determinedly, she tried to concentrate on that anger, aware that it was quelling the other emotion that rose within her. Sam's nearness was inspiring unprecedented arousal and Jo did not believe the feelings were particularly appropriate. The redhead had been subjected to a painful and humiliating experience and, in spite of her own needs and desires, Jo did not think she needed to be seduced right now.

As though she had read Jo's thoughts, Sam pulled away a little. She still had her arms around the investigator but now she was able to stare into her face. Her eyes with shiny with a combination of tears and excitement. A hesitant frown creased her lips and she asked, 'Do you still find me attractive?'

Jo tried not to think about how attractive she found Sam. 'You won't be scarred for life,' she assured her. 'The marks will fade over the next couple of days and you'll forget all about them.'

Sam shook her head. 'Do you still find me attractive without the garter?'

Jo paused, not sure if she had heard correctly.

'I'm an outcast now,' Sam pointed out sullenly. 'I'm no longer one of the elite. Now, I'm just another shitty student from the Kilgrimol.'

Her words of self-pity seemed so misplaced Jo had to make a physical effort to stop herself from laughing aloud. 'How can you even think that?' she exclaimed quietly. She placed a kiss against Sam's mouth, tightening her embrace. As before, she had not wanted to do anything but reassure Sam in a warm but platonic way and the kiss was meant to help restore her lost self-esteem and remind her that she was still attractive, in spite of being ostracised from the Black Garter.

As their tongues met and intertwined, Jo realised the kiss was doing a lot more than that. She felt Sam's hands reach carefully for her breasts. The subtle touch of the redhead's fingers evoked long-forgotten feelings and she considered trying to fight against her desires one final time, then discounted the idea.

She did not think Sam could cope with any form of rejection at the moment, regardless of how well phrased it was, as any rebuff would appear personal rather than circumstantial. However, Jo's main reason for allowing her to continue was far more selfish; she desperately wanted Sam. The idea of having the nubile body pressed shamelessly against hers was so exciting it left her breathless. Sam was not just young and exciting; she was divine. Jo's desire for her was a strong, relentless tidal wave of passion.

The ardour of their kiss overwhelmed the pair of them. Jo could feel her heart pounding wildly, beating the exact same tempo that throbbed between her legs. The pulse of her arousal was furious in its intensity and she quickly tugged the open blouse from Sam's shoulders. Sam sighed excitedly and stared into Jo's face, a daring smile of anticipation resting on her lips.

Jo gently moved her mouth to the redhead's breast. She allowed her tongue to touch gently on the sensitive flesh of the areola, cooling the burning heat with the wetness of her mouth. When her tongue moved close to the bruised tip of the woman's nipple, she employed the utmost delicacy and the hard nub responded keenly to the intimate attention.

Sam caught her breath, making a sound that bordered between delight and discomfort. Jo risked a hesitant glance towards her face and was reassured by the eager smile she saw there. Needing no further encouragement, she pressed her lips around the excited tip of Sam's breast and sucked tenderly. The responsive bud stiffened inside her mouth.

Sam seemed torn between the delights of the current pleasure and the memory of discomfort that it inspired. Her cries of rapture became bolder as Jo turned her attention to the other breast and by the time her tongue had teased that tip into a frenzy of desire, Sam was panting excitedly.

Jo guided Sam into the chair and knelt down before her. She kissed her passionately, not wanting to destroy the precious intimacy of the moment. Sam's tongue responded eagerly. Her fingers reached towards Jo's body but the investigator kept moving away from her. Jo was determined that this evening would be devoted to Sam's pleasure with no thought for her own salacious appetite. She moved her head down Sam's body, kissing softly at the breasts, then the flat expanse of her slender stomach. Jo only paused when she reached the swatch of vibrant red curls and indulgently, she inhaled the heady scent of Sam's natural perfume.

She kissed at Sam's inner thighs, conscious of how close she was to the warm, succulent haven of the redhead's delightful pussy. Finally she succumbed to the lure of tasting Sam's excitement and, as her tongue probed gently against the soft flesh of her labia, she tasted the wonderful, tantalising flavour of Sam's pussy juice. Both women groaned in unison.

Jo dared to plunge her tongue against the sensitive flesh for a second time and she felt the inner lips unfolding to welcome her. The subtle movement of the inner flesh against her mouth was disturbingly exciting. Sam's responsive body was the perfect vessel for her desires. Moving her mouth up and down the warm, honey-soaked cleft, Jo lapped furiously at the eager lips, savouring the sweet taste of the intimacy.

Sam's moans of joy were quickly becoming more urgent. Her breathing had deepened to a ragged pant, each gasp torn from her throat amid guttural cries of excitement. Her words of praise and encouragement rang musically in Jo's ears and the sound inspired her to lick harder and more furiously. When the explosion finally erupted, her shrieks of delight descended into a groan of absolute ecstasy. Her entire body seemed to tremble with the force of her orgasm, shivers rippling through each muscle. She sat up suddenly in the chair and then collapsed back into it, panting and elated.

Jo continued to use her tongue, teasing the pulsing lips and drinking up the remnants of Sam's excited climax. Sam groaned and tried to push her away but the efforts were half-hearted. The struggle between her enjoyment and her weariness was short-lived and she nestled herself comfortably into the chair.

Eagerly, Jo pushed her face forward and stroked her tongue against Sam's tingling labia. The redhead groaned and sat up again, her hands against the sides of Jo's face.

'Is there something wrong?' Jo asked.

Sam shook her head, grinning. 'My turn,' she whispered, placing her mouth over Jo's. As they kissed, Sam pushed herself out of the chair and pushed Jo backwards. They fell lightly to the floor, Sam on top, stroking and caressing Jo eagerly.

The excitement of her touch was too great for Jo to argue with. It had been a delight to watch the joy of climax wash over the redhead but she had her own needs as well. After seeing Sam's explosive orgasm, Jo's own desires had taken on an urgency that demanded satisfaction and she willingly allowed Sam to continue kissing her, revelling in her attention.

The redhead's hands cupped and kneaded her breasts, awakening myriad pleasures in the sensitive orbs. Jo contained her groan of delight by kissing harder, teasing her own fingers gently against the recently punished tips of Sam's nipples, forcing the redhead to sigh.

Sam ignored Jo's ministrations, and pressed her mouth against the swell of Jo's breast, rubbing her tongue over the fabric of the blouse. Jo groaned excitedly. She eased her buttons open, allowing Sam's mouth the closeness that they both craved. The sensation of Sam's warm lips against the cool flesh of her breast was tremendous. Shivers of pleasure thrilled through her responsive body and the promise of a heady orgasm began to rise inside. Her entire body throbbed with the need for the redhead and using her hands to guide her face, Jo moved Sam from one breast to the other. She allowed her to suck and tease one nipple until she could take no more. Then she encouraged her to move on to the other. She repeated the process until both breasts were a tingling explosion of joy that craved Sam's mouth, yet shrank from the pleasure she inspired.

Aware that Jo was on the point of orgasm, Sam seemed to stop deliberately. She removed her own skirt, before helping Jo out of the jeans she had been wearing, then guided Jo's panties down her long, smooth legs. Her finger brushed against the short stubble of pubic hairs that covered her sex and Jo shivered. Her excitement had been close to euphoric as Sam licked her breasts. Now, with their naked bodies touching, warming and cooling one another simultaneously, she felt close to experiencing a cataclysmic orgasm from the simple pleasure of Sam's nearness.

The redhead teased a finger into Jo's pubic mound, allowing the tip to brush against the soft folds of her sex. The lips were moist with excitement and parted easily. The pulse of Jo's erect clitoris was apparent to both of them.

Jo felt the fingers slide inside as Sam's mouth rekindled the fire in her breast. She could feel the redhead's eager touch daring to penetrate her burning intimacy and Jo pushed herself on to the intruding hand, a triumphant grin of elation splitting her face. The thrill of a long anticipated orgasm began to sweep through her with the majestic force of a conquering army. Pleasure and delight plundered every nerve-ending, leaving her body aching and satisfied. She was about to grin into Sam's face when she saw her mouth moving down towards the source of the joy.

For an instant, Jo considered stopping her to allow

the pair of them time to embrace one another and share the intimacy of the moment. When she felt Sam's tongue touch inquisitively against the heated flesh of her sex, Jo changed her mind. Her body craved more of the delights Sam was administering and she knew she was powerless against the needs of her own carnal appetite.

She allowed Sam to lick and suck at the eager lips of her vagina, enjoying wave after wave of pleasure. The redhead kept her fingers inside the slippery warmth of Sam's tight hole, the friction of their entry and egress deliciously slow. Each tiny movement inspired unprecedented waves of excitement and the inner muscles of her pussy began to clutch furiously against the fingers once more, heightening the fervour of the feelings. Before she realised it was happening, Jo felt a second orgasm being wrenched from her. This time the joy had a divine edge to it that went beyond anything the evening had offered so far. She screamed her ecstasy, unmindful of the neighbouring dorms and the late hour. Her euphoria was so complete she did not care for these things. Her body was on fire with joy and she jerked spasmodically as the climax swept over her.

She blinked her eyes open, hardly aware she had closed them. Sam was smiling down at her. A curious expression rested on her lips.

Jo grinned. 'Did I make you feel better?'

The sound of soft laughter escaped Sam's lips. 'A little,' she allowed. 'How do you feel?' She traced her fingers against Jo's breast as she asked the question, evoking the memory of a pleasure too painful to be tolerated just yet.

'You don't want to know how I feel,' Jo said, moving Sam's hand away and kissing it tenderly. 'Come on, it's time to talk.' With every muscle in her body aching, Jo eased herself from the floor and led Sam towards the single bed.

An hour later, they were still entwined together. Jo could feel the comforting warmth of Sam's naked body pressed against her beneath the quilt. She desperately wanted to possess Sam again and enjoy the skill of her lovemaking but there was only so much her body could take in one evening and she felt sure she had reached her limit. 'That black garter meant a lot to you, didn't it?' Jo whispered.

She could feel the pressure of Sam's head nodding against her body. 'It was a sign of accomplishment. Now I no longer have it, I feel as though I'm a failure.'

Jo placed a reassuring kiss on the redhead's forehead. 'You're no failure,' she said comfortingly. Her fingers combed unconsciously through Sam's mane of red hair.

'Without a black garter I feel like one,' Sam said miserably.

Jo smiled at her. 'Is every woman in this school a failure if she doesn't have a black garter?'

Sam shrugged. 'Most of them,' she conceded.

'Am I a failure?' Jo asked. Sam's horrified denial of this suggestion would have been comical under other circumstances. Jo smiled kindly at her and silenced her with a kiss. 'How long do you have to go before you leave the Kilgrimol?'

Sam shrugged. 'It's moving towards the end of my last term now. Some girls will be leaving in the next few months. Hera leaves at the end of this week because her parents want her working for them.'

Jo thought of saying good riddance to the bitch, then stopped herself, aware that the words would spoil the mood. An irrational idea occurred to her, a notion so ludicrous and spur-of-the-moment it was insane and the more she thought about it, the wilder and stupider it seemed. As much as the rational part of her mind fought against it, Jo could still think of no real reason to stop herself from making the suggestion. 'Why don't you leave the school and come work for me?'

Sam studied her, an expression of disbelief on her face. Her eyes were wide with incredulous excitement. 'Do you mean it?'

Jo swallowed, suddenly unsure if she meant it or not. 'Of course,' she declared boldly.

Sam wrapped her arms around Jo and embraced her tightly. The feel of the redhead's naked body was no longer the stimulant it had been before, now Jo could feel responsibility weighing her down. She toyed with the idea of retracting her offer before Sam went and did something foolish like accepting it.

'Of course I'd want to work with you,' Sam enthused cheerfully. 'We'd be great together.'

Jo was already beginning to have her doubts about this but did not bother voicing them. She mentally chastised herself for deciding this was the right moment to speak without thinking. Fixing a warm smile on her face, she nodded agreement with Sam. She eased herself from Sam's grasp and sat up in the bed. 'Perhaps we can start being a success together if you help me solve this case?' Jo suggested.

Sam nodded eagerly. 'Of course. Where are we up to with the investigation?'

Jo tried to ignore her quick use of the word 'we' and swallowing thickly, she focused her thoughts on the facts she had managed to collate. 'We're looking for a woman who uses the nickname Bunny,' Jo said eventually. 'She's a student at this school and she has her ear to the ground. I don't have any other details, except that she may be blonde.'

Sam was frowning. 'How do you know she might be blonde?'

Jo shrugged. 'The reporter had blonde hairs on his coat,' she explained. 'Either he keeps an odour-free Labrador or he's been bumping uglies with a blonde. Even if the latter situation is the case, it might not be the Bunny who we're looking for, but it's always a consideration.'

'And you're sure her nickname is Bunny?'

Jo nodded. 'The reporter actually told me that, and I had it confirmed on his voice-mail. Do you know anyone?'

Frowning heavily, Sam shook her head. 'I'll ask around tomorrow and see.'

Jo gripped her arm tightly, shaking her head in adamant refusal. 'You won't ask anything,' she said firmly. 'This stays between you and I, do you understand?'

With a frightened expression in her eyes, Sam nodded meekly. 'Whatever you say.'

Jo nodded and released Sam's arm, feeling guilty for leaving red marks in the whey-coloured flesh. 'We have to keep this to ourselves,' she said calmly. 'I need to find out who Bunny is and get her out of the school before Hera can get her hands on the poor girl.' She shook her head unhappily as she thought about this. 'Christ knows what would happen if that psychotic bitch got hold of her first.'

Outside the door of Jo's dorm, Melanie smiled wickedly in the darkness. She had heard all she needed to hear. It had taken a long time but she felt sure Hera would be proud of her. Now they knew exactly who they were looking for.

Walking briskly but silently along the deserted corridor, Melanie started towards Hera's room. It was late, later than either of them had anticipated, but she didn't doubt the leader would be delighted to hear her news.

Eleven

'What the fuck do you want?'

Anna closed the door of Guy's office carefully behind herself. Remembering Hera's instructions, she pulled at the hem of her short gym skirt and tried to act bashful and awkward. A few days earlier she would not have needed to act the role. Then she had been a shy, gauche young woman. Hera's leadership had changed all that. After the events of the last forty-eight hours, Anna felt capable of putting in an Oscar winning performance.

She remembered the scenario Hera had suggested and tried not to grin as she thought how it easy it was to manipulate someone like Guy. Even with his unpleasant welcome, she knew he would do exactly as she said.

'It's sort of embarrassing,' Anna explained, smiling alluringly at the young gym instructor.

He stared at her with a scowl.

'Some of the girls and I were messing about in the changing rooms,' Anna explained. 'We were throwing clothes around, that sort of thing.'

Guy continued to stare at her in sullen silence.

'An item of my clothing got thrown about and it's stuck, on a nail near the ceiling.'

Guy shrugged. 'So, what do you want me to do about it?'

Anna rolled her eyes impatiently. 'You're taller than I am,' she explained. 'I was wondering if you could get it for me.'

He sniffed dourly and turned his attention back to the copy of the *Kilgrimol Weekly Clarion* he had been reading. 'I'll get it later,' he said, not bothering to look at her. 'I'm busy now.'

'Please,' Anna implored him. 'I can't go to the rest of my classes if I'm not properly dressed, and I can't go back to my dorm because one of the prefects will give me a demerit for being late.'

He glanced up at her, then turned back to his newspaper. 'You look suitably dressed,' he assured her. 'I'll put whatever it is in the lost property and you can pick it up tomorrow.'

'I can't go to my next class without my knickers,' Anna declared impatiently.

The words had the expected effect on him. He put his newspaper down and smiled broadly at her. 'You've got your knickers stuck to the ceiling?' He grinned. 'That's kind of embarrassing, isn't it?'

'To say the least,' Anna agreed. 'So, please can you help me?'

He was already climbing from behind his desk. Halfway to the door he stopped and frowned at her. 'This isn't another one of your games, is it?'

Anna tried to frown as though she had no idea what he was talking about. 'Games? I told you, we were messing about. The other girls have gone to their classes now and I'm stuck without my knickers.'

'I mean, like yesterday,' Guy continued, 'when that dark-haired bitch swiped my arse with a table-tennis paddle. This isn't another set-up, is it?'

Anna shook her head, feigning innocence. 'Come into the changing rooms,' she encouraged him. 'I'll show you where they are and you can see I'm telling the truth.' She started swiftly towards the door of his office but his hand on her arm stopped her.

'There is another way you can prove it to me,' Guy told her, his porcine eyes studying her excitedly. His gaze fell to the short hem of her skirt and his lecherous grin widened. 'If you're wearing knickers now, I'll know you were trying to set me up.'

'That's insane,' Anna declared hotly. 'How could you even think I'd . . .'

Guy started back towards his desk. 'If you don't want to prove it to me, then you can pick them up from lost property tomorrow.'

Anna glared dully at the top of his head as he settled himself back behind his desk. It was almost impossible to believe the audacity of his request and even though Hera had warned her, Anna had not really expected it to come to this. Yesterday she had felt a twinge of sympathy when Hera had so deftly humiliated him. Now, realising just how deplorable the man was, Anna felt she could enjoy herself a lot more with him. His suffering would be all the more gratifying now that she knew how much he deserved it.

'All right then,' she decided eventually. Guy glanced up from his desk.

Anna could feel herself blushing and she didn't know if it was acting or true nervousness. Whatever the cause, she knew it was adding to the reality of the role she was performing. 'You want me to prove it?' she demanded. She reached her hands to the side of her skirt and began to show him one bare hip. The smooth expanse of one milky white thigh was exposed for him to view. 'There,' she declared. 'Does that prove it?'

He shook his head. 'You could be wearing those high-cut pants,' he told her. 'I know what a devious bunch of bitches you lot are.'

Anna shook her head. 'What else can I do?' she asked. 'Do you want me to show you my cunny? Would that prove my knickers are stuck in the changing room?'

His lecherous grin widened. He leant forward in his chair. 'It would help,' he said coolly.

Anna tried to look shocked. She had expected him to say something like this and she glanced around the empty office to add conviction to her performance. 'Do you promise not to tell anyone?' she asked in a half-whisper.

'My lips are sealed,' he assured her. His eyes were sparkling with anticipation. He was no longer staring at her face when he spoke. His gaze was fixed on the front panel of her gym skirt.

From Anna's position, it looked as though he had x-ray vision and could already see the mound of blonde pubic curls beneath the grey linen. With his attention diverted so purposefully, she could have scowled or spat at him but she resisted the temptation. Instead, she teased the hem of her skirt slowly upward.

Guy licked his lips, his gaze fixed unfailingly on the tops of her legs.

Still blushing, Anna inched the skirt slightly higher. 'I don't know why you won't believe me?' she whispered.

He ignored her words, his attention fixed on the expanse of flesh she was revealing. His eyes were like saucers as she lifted the edge of the skirt higher. Again, he licked his lips and watched as she finally displayed the bare mound of her pubic curls.

The light, downy hairs were so pale they almost looked fluffy and she could understand his leering admiration. Arrogantly, she believed that if she were in his position, she would be smiling in exactly the same way. Her thoughts were brought quickly back to the room when she saw his hand disappear under the desk. Incredulously, she realised he was toying with his cock as he looked at her. The depth of his conceit seemed boundless.

Angrily, Anna snatched the hem of her skirt down, covering herself from his view. 'I've proved what you asked,' she told him sternly. 'Now I think it's time you helped me.'

He chuckled darkly. 'After that little peepshow, I'd help you to do anything.'

Anna ignored his remark and stepped out into the deserted gym. Guy was quick behind her, his hand finding its way to her backside with predictable ease. She tried to move away from his touch but his fingers had squirmed beneath her skirt and touched her before she could stop him.

'Sorry.' He grinned into her outraged expression. 'I forgot you weren't properly clad down there.'

Anna did not need to look at his lewd smile to know that he was lying; there was more chance of him forgetting his own name. She could see the slick wetness of her pussy juice on his fingers and watched as he rubbed the fluid absently with his thumb. The sense of outrage that welled inside her was tremendous. Revenge was going to be such a joy that she tried not to contemplate it and, not trusting herself to speak, Anna marched quickly towards the changing room.

Grinning, Guy followed her. He saw the knickers as soon as he entered the room. They were on the opposite wall, stuck to a nail he had been meaning to remove since the beginning of last term. His smile broadened as he saw Anna pointing up at them and trying to reach for the scanty piece of fabric. The posture made her skirt raise up and she was revealing a tantalising glimpse of her bare backside. 'So, you'd like me to pull your knickers down,' he chuckled. 'That's a rare invitation.'

Anna glared furiously at him. 'Can you get up there for me?'

'Can I get up there for you?' he repeated. 'Haven't they told you not to make invitations like that to men when you're knickerless and all alone?'

Hera cleared her throat and closed the door firmly shut. 'But you're not alone, Guy,' she said softly.

He whirled around to face her. His malevolent smile was quickly replaced by an expression of cold panic. 'You!' he exclaimed, glaring angrily at Hera. He turned to Anna and raised his hand in a half-hearted fist. 'I knew you were up to something, you conniving little bitch.' He took a step towards her and Anna backed away.

'Hit her and you'll really be sorry,' Hera assured him confidently.

He snorted with mirthless laughter. 'You think I can't handle myself against two fucking schoolgirls?' he demanded. 'I'll have the pair of you begging me to service you once I've finished.'

Hera studied him with an unintimidated smile. 'I'd like to have seen that,' she said quietly. 'What a shame it isn't just the three of us in here.' She snapped her fingers three times. The clicks echoed like breaking bones in the hollow confines of the changing room.

Guy stared at her, puzzled at first, then realisation dawned on him as he saw movement from the adjacent showers. A line of Kilgrimol girls began to walk out of the shower room. A handful of them were dressed for gym class but the majority were wearing the standard school uniform of dark skirt, white blouse and blue tie. Each one of them fixed Guy with a knowing smile.

Prudently, Anna took a step away from him. The girls were staring at Guy with barely concealed malice and she could understand their loathing. She also knew that if Guy was going to make a stand, to either escape or defend himself, now would be the time. She took comfort from Hera's warm smile of triumph by the door.

Guy watched the women surround him. His eyes widened with fear. 'I don't know what you've got planned,' he whispered tersely, 'but you won't get away with it. You know that, don't you?'

Now it was Hera's turn to laugh darkly. 'Relax, Guy,' she cooed softly. 'What makes you think we're planning anything?' Her laughter echoed cheerfully against the concrete walls of the changing rooms.

Debbie listened miserably to Steven's tirade. She had turned her telephone off yesterday evening, trying to hide from his calls by simply not answering them but unfortunately, her father had chosen that evening to call and she had found his irate message on her answering service, telling her he would call back. Her father's recording had been one of twelve. The other eleven messages had been left by Steven. He was threatening severe retribution if she did not talk to him, and now, because she had thought it might be her father on the phone, Bunny found herself listening to Steven's tirade.

As Steven spouted an outraged torrent of abuse at her, she began to wish she could just hang up, but the threats he had made on her answering service were severe enough to make her forget it. He would publicise her part in the scandals if she did not talk to him, and that was just the beginning. Trying not to think of the other intimidating suggestions he had made, she listened to his relentless verbal abuse. A part of her mind wished she could find some way out of the nightmare she had created for herself but all she could do now was to try and deal with it.

'Did you just phone to swear at me, Steven?' she broke in suddenly. 'You're only swearing so much because you know I despise coarseness.'

She held the phone away from her face for a moment, his outraged voice still audible as he shouted his expletive-filled response to her.

'See!' she pointed out sharply. 'And don't call me Bunny either. I only let close friends call me by that name. I don't count you as a friend any more. What do you want?'

She listened, still not sure she fully understood him. He was trying to make some point about having a picture stolen but his anger and her own ignorance of the topic made it difficult to comprehend.

'I haven't stolen anything,' she said firmly. 'And I'm not sure I'm happy with the intimation.'

As he continued to shout down the phone, an idea came to Bunny and she wondered if she might be able to appease him. She felt uncomfortable betraying her new friends in the Black Garter but if this was a chance to finally sever ties with the reporter then she had to take it. A message she had received over breakfast came flooding back to her and she thought it might be just the right thing to satisfy Steven.

'If you want more from me, you have to realise this is the last time I'm going to help you. I mean it too, Steven,' she added firmly. 'You've bullied me enough and this really will be the last time you make me do something against my will.'

She paused and listened to his assurance. She knew it was worthless but after she had spoken to her father, she would ask him to change the number on her telephone. After that, Steven would be unable to contact her and she hoped he would not make good his threats under those circumstances. She supposed it was a slim hope but in the situation, it was all she had to cling to.

'I've been told there's to be a punishment detail tonight,' she began carefully. 'No, I don't know who, or why. The girl I spoke to said that sometimes they're done without any reason. Anyway, I'll ask around and find out a bit more but if you want to see one of the Black Garter's meetings, you'll be in the school's gym tonight at ten o'clock.'

She listened to him a moment longer and unconsciously shook her head. 'I told you, I don't know who the punishment is for, or why. I'm not even sure if they know yet. You'll be able to find out all about it if you turn up tonight.'

She severed the connection without bothering to say goodbye. Placing the phone in her pocket, she sighed heavily. She doubted he would give up so easily, but it was something to hope for, she told herself. If she had only known who the victim was going to be, she thought that might have gone some way to appeasing him.

Unfortunately, Bunny had no idea who they planned to humiliate. She only knew that Hera had something particularly cruel planned for tonight's victim. As she thought about this, she had to admit that the idea excited her. It was comforting to be a member of the Black Garter.

Guy looked as though he was about to be crucified. On Hera's command, the Black Garter had stripped him completely despite his struggles and protestations. A series of coat hooks circumnavigated the changing-room's walls at eye level. His arms had been outstretched and his wrists had been secured to two of these.

When the girls stepped away from him, Guy was revealed to Anna in all his naked glory. His muscular sun-bronzed body looked pallid with nerves but she could not stop herself from admiring its aesthetic perfection. He had a broad chest, flat stomach and lean frame. It seemed a shame that so nice a body was wrapped around such a contemptible person.

His long thick cock stood defiantly erect. The foreskin had peeled back to reveal his swollen purple end and a pearl of pre-come glistened against the black hole at its tip. Anna knew she had caused his excitement initially but she wondered what had sustained it whilst he was being secured. A couple of the girls had been giggling as he struggled but she couldn't believe he would find excitement from the treatment they had given.

'If you do this the easy way, I'll have you released straight away,' Hera assured him. 'I simply want some information.' As she spoke, she played idly with a large bath sheet. Holding one corner, she twisted the towel in the air, wrapping its long folds around itself.

Anna held her breath as she watched this. She had seen the other girls doing something similar in the past: this was how you prepared for towel flicking. She glanced from Hera's confident smile to Guy's nervous look of defiance. If the man had not been so loathsome, she would have felt pity.

'You seem to take great pleasure in knowing more about us girls than we're comfortable with,' Hera went on. 'So I want you to tell me who Bunny is.'

'Fuck off!' he snapped irritably. 'You don't scare me.'

Hera flicked the towel at him. Anna could tell the leader had not been aiming for Guy's balls because the towel did not strike there.

There was a deafening whip-crack that echoed loudly in the changing rooms and Guy flinched, and gasped dully. He glared angrily at Hera, the fury of his expression matched only by the red welt appearing at the top of his leg. His erection began to fail.

'Just one name, Guy,' Hera said softly. 'Then you can go back to your wanking, or whatever it is you do of a morning.'

'Fuck you!' he declared boldly.

Hera shook her head. Instead of flicking the towel at him a second time, she nodded at Melanie. The girl rushed to Guy's side and began to tease her fingers over his chest, then she pressed her mouth over one of his nipples and sucked hard. The pressure of her lips had an instantaneous response and Anna saw Guy's cock twitch back to a state of full arousal. His face still expressed hard defiance but his body's response gave away his true feelings. She smiled at his length, unable to fight the rising appetite that grew within her. As despicable as she believed him to be, she could not deny that his body held a certain allure. Studying the perfection of his muscular frame, she came to a sudden decision.

Anna walked to Hera's side and whispered in her ear. With the leader's consenting nod, she moved towards Guy and took a firm hold of his cock with one hand. Melanie was still sucking roughly on his nipple. His length was hard and pulsing to her touch as she stroked the foreskin forward, then backward, rolling the palm of her hand over the bulbous dome. She watched his face as she did this, an inscrutable mask concealing her own emotions.

Guy stared at her, licking his lips and snatching faltering breaths of excitement. 'What do you want?'

Instead of replying, Anna simply smiled. She knelt

down on the floor in front of him and moved her mouth close to the swollen tip of his cock. Staring eagerly up at him, she dared to flick her tongue against the purple flesh. She tasted the pearl of pre-come that had grown on the end of his length; and the salty flavour made her smile broadly.

The rest of the Black Garter girls filling the changing rooms made soft sounds of surprise and delight. Their mood seemed cheerfully diabolical and Anna knew they would be willing to assist in any way they were asked. It would not matter if it was her own brand of teasing, or Hera's cruel style of punishment. The Black Garter were completely behind their leaders.

Without hesitating, Anna rubbed her tongue up and down his cock, then took his entire length in her mouth. Guy groaned softly as she sucked his erection.

Reluctantly, Anna moved her mouth away from him and wiped her lips with the back of her hand. She stood up and grinned. 'Would you like me to continue?' she asked.

He nodded enthusiastically. 'Of course.'

'You've been told what we want,' Anna explained. Her hand began to work quickly up and down his length as she spoke. The wetness of her saliva added a silky friction to the motion of her hand. 'Who's Bunny?'

He tried to shrug, a gesture too awkward in his current position. 'I have no idea,' he admitted eventually.

Anna shook her head sadly.

Hera frowned. 'Wrong answer,' she said crisply. 'Stand back, ladies.'

Melanie and Anna moved away, leaving Guy open and exposed to whatever the leader had in mind. The tip of the towel snapped sharply against his balls.

One of the watching girls released a sigh of sympathy but the noise was drowned out by Guy's cry of anguish. He pulled forward against the coat hooks but the bindings held him in position.

'Perhaps he's telling the truth?' Anna suggested.

Hera shook her head. 'He's so twisted, he couldn't tell the truth,' she replied. 'Guy knows everything about every one of us in this school. Isn't that right, Guy?'

'I don't know anyone called Bunny,' he gasped sharply. 'Don't you think I'd have told you by now if I knew?'

Anna and Hera exchanged a glance. 'You still think he knows?' Anna asked.

'I'd have bet money on it,' Hera said glumly. She flicked the towel idly in the air.

From the corner of her eye, Anna saw Guy flinch.

'Do you think I can whip it out of him?' Hera asked coolly.

'I don't know anyone called Bunny,' Guy insisted. His forehead was covered with nervous beads of sweat. 'I'd tell you if I did.'

The two women were ignoring him.

'I think I can get the information out of him if he does know something,' Anna declared confidently.

Hera raised her eyebrows. 'If you think you can do something that will work, then go ahead,' she allowed. She gestured with her arm in Guy's direction.

Smiling, Anna stepped back towards the bound gym instructor. She snapped her fingers at Melanie and pointed towards the formidable length of Guy's raging erection. 'Suck that,' she commanded stiffly.

Melanie obeyed without hesitation. She knelt in front of the man and placed her mouth around the purple end of his erection. Sliding her lips up and down the length of his shaft, she moaned softly, obviously enjoying the taste and feel of the man.

Anna placed her mouth close to Guy's ear and kissed his neck gently. She nibbled at his lobe for a second before whispering quietly into his ear. 'Remember in your office, when you saw my cunny,' she prompted him.

His nervousness was still apparent but Anna guessed his laboured breathing was due more to the impending explosion of an orgasm than any fear he might be experiencing.

'Did you like the look of my sex?' she asked. She made the question hotter by breathing the words in a husky voice. 'Did you want to push that beautiful, long cock of yours into my hole, and fuck me?'

Guy groaned loudly.

From the corner of her eye, Anna could see that Hera was grinning. Melanie still worked her mouth furiously up and down Guy's shaft, slurping noisily on the length of pink flesh.

'I haven't put my panties back on yet,' Anna told Guy. 'My cunny is still naked if you want it,' she went on. 'All you have to do is give us a name. That's not a lot to ask is it? Not when you think about what I'll be giving you?'

He shivered, the confines of his bindings making the movement stilted. 'I wish I knew,' he whispered. 'If I knew, don't you think I'd tell you?'

'But I think you do know,' Anna repeated. 'Don't you want to feel the tightness of my wet little pussy wrapped around that rock-hard length of yours? I think it would feel divine, don't you?'

'Yes,' he agreed sharply. 'But I can't tell you what I don't know. Do you want me to make up a name?'

Anna put her hand on Melanie's head and moved her from Guy's cock. She stepped away from him, shaking her head sadly. Turning to Hera, she said, 'he doesn't know. We're wasting our time.'

'Bastard!' Hera snapped angrily. She flicked the towel against Guy's stomach, winding him with the blow. 'So what the fuck do we do now?' she demanded impatiently.

Anna was about to shrug but the sound of the changing-room door bursting open stopped her from replying. A brief moment's fear of being caught was replaced by a wave of relief as she realised it was only Samantha Flowers storming into the room. The scowl of annoyance on Sam's face should have warned her that something was wrong. Before she could enjoy her relief, she realised the redhead was in a foul mood.

'How the fuck did you find out?' Sam barked, walking defiantly up to Hera. 'I want to know, and I want you to tell me. How the fuck did you find out?'

Hera smiled down at the redhead, unintimidated by her irate manner. 'You shouldn't be here, Sam,' she said flatly. 'This is Black Garter business and, as I recall, you're not a member of the Black Garter anymore, are you?'

'Fuck you, and fuck your black garter,' Sam screamed angrily. 'I want to know how you found out.'

Hera's smile widened maliciously. The glint in her eyes was dark and malevolent. 'I'm not sure,' she said mischievously. 'Wasn't it you who told me? You screwed that dopey private investigator for the information then came running to tell me we were looking for a girl called Bunny.'

Sam's scowl turned into a look of abject fury. With an animal roar of annoyance, she lunged at Hera. Her fingers were curled into wicked talons. If Anna had not made a particularly fast intervention, she knew the fight would have been vicious and bloody. Hera was already preparing to defend herself but Anna knew the leader would have suffered some bruises and scratching given Sam's vile mood.

'Calm down, Sam,' Anna insisted, struggling to hold the redhead's arms by her sides. 'Fighting won't solve anything.'

Sam glared at her but the pinnacle of her fury was gone. 'I want to know how she found out we were looking for a girl named Bunny,' Sam said stiffly. 'I want to know, and I want someone to go and tell Jo before she gets the idea that I betrayed her.'

Anna glanced at Hera.

The leader's smile was a sneer of contempt. 'Fuck off away from me, Sam,' she breathed coolly. 'Fuck off away from me, and I'll think about it.'

Sam struggled against Anna's grip but the blonde held her tightly.

'I could have got my information from you becaus you're so desperate to get back in the Black Garter Hera said thoughtfully. 'Or I could have received i from Melanie who was listening outside Jo's door las night.' Her wicked smile now looked positively evi 'I'm going to have to think about which version I te your friend.'

'You bitch,' Sam breathed angrily.

Hera sniffed derisively. 'Are you trying to help m make up my mind?'

'You wouldn't,' Sam said quietly.

Hera continued to smile. 'Do you want to put yo faith to the test?' She turned her attention away fro Sam and caught Melanie's eye. 'Untie him and sen him back to his office for the wank he so desperate needs,' she barked. 'You and you,' she growle snapping her fingers at two other girls. 'Tal Samantha here and get her out of my sight. The re of you, I want you to go out and find me a Bunny.' Her voice was rising with mounting anger and a scowl of the darkest fury creased her forehead. Her cheeks were burning the dull red colour of a furious passion. Anna regarded her with nervous apprehension.

'I don't care who you have to hurt, or what you have to do. I want the bitch who's been leaking to the press, and I'm going to have her,' Hera explained emphatically. 'Do I make myself clear?'

In the nervous aftermath of her outburst, no one dared to respond. Anna watched Melanie untying Guy from the coat hooks and she released Sam into the strong arms of the two girls whom Hera had summoned. The rest of the Black Garter filed out of the changing room, whispering amongst themselves with animated excitement.

'Wait!' Hera barked suddenly. She directed the words at Melanie who had just finished unfastening Guy. The pair of them turned to face her, fearful of whatever retribution she intended. 'Melanie, leave,' Hera snapped.

Obedient as ever, Melanie rushed from the changing rooms.

'You're going to go and tug yourself off now, aren't you?' Hera sneered.

Guy's cock was still rock-hard and Anna could see the silver slickness that covered his shaft. 'I don't have to answer to you,' he said gruffly.

'You don't have to answer to anyone,' Hera agreed. 'But you and I have a hold over one another and I was just wanting to make sure you were aware of it.'

He studied her uncertainly.

'If you chose to go to the principal and tell her about what just happened here, I can imagine my time in this school would be marred by the event. It could blacken my otherwise flawless record,' she explained.

He shrugged, searching around to try and find his pants. 'You don't sound that concerned about it.'

'I'm not,' Hera agreed. 'We both know that the principal would want to get rid of the pair of us if we started talking. You'd tell her how naughty I was yesterday, and just now. I'd tell her about the way you spied on us all in the shower rooms. We'd be out of here that quickly we could help one another pack.'

'What's your point?' he asked defiantly.

Anna closed her eyes. She did not understand why people insisted on being so foolish as to intimidate Hera. No one but Hera ever won.

'Tug yourself off,' Hera said shortly. 'I want you to do it whilst I watch. Whilst Anna and I watch,' she amended. 'Tug yourself off.'

He was studying her thoughtfully. 'Why should I?'

'I'm trying to be nice to you here, Guy. Start wanking, or you'll find out I'm not just a pleasant smile. You'll either do this, or I'll go to the principal.'

He grunted disbelief. 'You've just told me that it would mean your name got blackened,' he reminded her.

'And now I'm telling you that I don't fucking care,' Hera hissed angrily.

The menace in her voice was so clear, Guy's hand shifted to his cock instantaneously. He began to work his hand up and down the length, glaring sullenly at Hera as he did it. His fingers encircled his girth and he rubbed his fist furiously up and down his stiff shaft.

'Kneel down,' Hera commanded.

Guy did as he was told. All the time his hand was working up and down his length.

'Did you get a good look at Anna's cunt before?' she asked crisply.

Anna felt the leader's hand on her arm and moved to her side, standing before Guy. She watched Hera raise the hem of her skirt and felt the woman's fingers toying with the exposed lips of her pussy. The intimate touch inspired a shiver of delight.

She glanced at Guy and saw he was leering at the lips of her sex with tangible lust. His hand worked faster on his cock and she could hear his breathing coming in short, urgent rasps.

'Wouldn't you have loved to have felt your cock in this tight hole?' Hera asked curiously. 'What a shame you fucked it up for yourself.'

'I've told you,' Guy panted. 'I don't know who Bunny is.'

Hera spat contemptuously. 'Shut up and wank,' she growled. 'I don't want to hear you talking. It pisses me off.' As she spoke, she continued to stroke her fingers idly against Anna's sex.

The sensitivity of her fingers and the gentle caresses they were administering filled Anna with excitement. Hardly aware that she was doing it, she cupped one of Hera's breasts through the blouse she wore and toyed with the urgent nub of her erect nipple.

Guy's attention was rapt. He kept his gaze fixed on the pair of women and his expression was a combination of concentration and fervent delight.

Hera giggled softly and pushed her foot in front of him. 'Kiss it,' she said crisply.

Guy glanced from the shoe to Hera's sullen expression. A flicker of defiance flitted briefly across his face but the expression vanished swiftly. It seemed obvious to Anna that he already knew enough about Hera not to try and push her further than was necessary. Glaring angrily at her, still rolling his hand up and down his huge, meaty length, Guy lowered his lips to the tips of Hera's shoes.

'What a good little wanker you are,' Hera said cheerfully. She continued to play absently with Anna's pussy lips, her fingers teasing through the blonde curls and brushing against the tingling folds of flesh. She glanced at Guy's backside and made a soft, almost sad sound. 'What a shame I didn't bring my strap-on,' she murmured. 'I could have fucked his arse and quite enjoyed that,' she decided.

Anna shivered. She was already enjoying herself a lot more than the situation merited and the idea of Hera in a strap-on dildo was more than she wanted to contemplate at the moment. Her fingers found their way beneath Hera's blouse and she felt the delicious warmth of the leader's bare breast in her hand. An electric shock seemed to spark against her fingers and in the same instant, she and Hera sighed.

She saw Guy move his mouth from one of Hera's feet to the other. His cock was hidden from her view but she could tell, by the hectic pace of his bicep, that he was pumping it furiously. He dared to look up and his expression of concentration vanished as his gaze fixed on the activities of Hera's fingers.

Aware that he was watching, Hera smiled grimly down at him. She pushed a finger inside Anna's tight, wet hole and rubbed softly at the inner muscles. Anna groaned.

Guy released a soft, breathless sound of delight and sharply pulled his cock twice, harder than he had been doing, then stopped abruptly.

As the two women watched, a spray of white seed shot from the tip of his organ. His features tightened into a rictus of elation and he stroked the last few dollops of cream from his length. When he dared to look into Hera's face, he grinned bashfully.

In response, Hera's expression was a mask of diabolical anger. 'You've spunked on my shoes,' she observed stiffly.

He glanced nervously down and saw that a spattering of his semen had actually fallen on the toe of Hera's shoe. His expression was so nervous it was almost comical.

'Lick it off,' Hera barked sharply.

Anna drew a sharp intake of breath. She felt sure Guy would refuse, or even turn angry and violent now. Hera's last request was sure to be too much for him.

To her surprise, the gym instructor lowered his head. His mouth moved quickly over the leader's shoe and although Anna could not see a thing, she felt certain he was obeying Hera's instruction. Her thoughts were confirmed a moment later when he moved his head up. The tip of Hera's shoes glistened wetly, but there was no trace of Guy's seed remaining. Instead, dribbling from his lower lip, Anna saw a thick string of his come. Her excitement suddenly intensified.

Hera pulled her finger from the warm haven of Anna's pussy and reached forward for Guy. She brushed the fingertip against the string of spunk and pushed it to Guy's lips. Greedily, he licked at the combined juices.

Hera glared dully at him, her anger suddenly returning. 'Get out of here, Guy,' she whispered quietly. 'I've lost my interest and my patience now. Go away before I become malicious and start to mistreat you.'

Anna glanced uncertainly at her friend, surprised by the sudden change in her mood. She waited until Guy had fled the changing room, a puzzled frown etching her features. The door closed behind him with a hollow thud.

'You're getting quite strung out by this situation, aren't you?' Anna remarked, when the two of them were finally alone.

Hera sat down heavily on one of the changing-room's benches. 'That's an understatement if ever I heard one,' she agreed, running her fingers through her hair. 'I just want to get this bitch before I leave the school.'

Anna sat next to Hera and placed a comforting hand on her knee. 'We'll get her,' she said confidently. 'We have to now. You've already organised the punishment for this evening.'

Hera laughed softly. 'That was a little premature of me, wasn't it? Do you think I should cancel?'

Anna was about to make a reply but a sound at the door stopped her. She glanced up and saw the Black Garter's newest recruit standing there, a hesitant smile breaking her lips.

'I didn't know there was a meeting,' Debbie explained meekly. 'No one bothered to tell me. I just saw all the rest of the girls go filing out of here and I wondered if there was anything you wanted me to do?'

Anna grinned at her and offered her a space on the bench. 'Sit a while and talk, Debbie,' she said kindly. 'Perhaps a fresh mind can throw some new ideas up for us.'

Eagerly, Debbie took the seat that had been offered. She grinned at Anna and tried to smile into the glowering depths of Hera's solemn expression. 'Great fun,' she enthused cheerfully. 'But you don't need to call me Debbie. My family and my closest friends all call me Bunny.'

In the silence, Anna could hear her own heartbeat pulsing strongly. She glanced at Hera and saw the leader was smiling broadly.

'Bunny,' Hera repeated quietly. Her grin was so wide it looked maniacal. She draped her arm over Bunny's shoulder with heavy intimacy. 'May we call you Bunny?' she asked coolly.

'If you like,' Debbie said, still grinning cheerfully.

Hera laughed darkly. 'I'd like that a lot,' she chuckled gleefully. 'Nothing would give me greater pleasure.'

Twelve

Without looking, Jo flicked the double-headed sovereign high in the air. A frown of consternation creased her brow as she stared at the packed suitcases piled on her bed. Not for the first time in her life, she wondered if she was doing the right thing. She caught the coin absently, then flicked it again.

'A shitty end to a shitty case,' she told the empty room. She glanced at the date on her watch and did a quick mental calculation. A thoughtful smile twisted her lips as she realised she had decided to abandon the assignment before Mr Smith's cheque had been able to clear in the bank. She glanced at her mobile phone, on top of the pile of cases, wondering if she should call him. Listening to the mercenary voice at the back of her mind, she discounted the idea. It would be better to give him an update on the case once the money was safely in her account.

After all, she thought glumly, it only seemed right that she should get something for the past couple of days. Something other than heartache. She had even called the *Clarion*'s reporter, hoping she could enjoy a repeat performance of his expert cock. After all the help he had inadvertently given her, she thought she could at least give him the small pleasure of sharing her body for one last time.

He had refused her invitation, telling her he had

more important plans for the night. The rebuke had been unexpected and deeply cutting. She had even considered telling him that she was the one who had stolen his roll of film but that hadn't gone any further than a simple thought.

'Jo!' The door of her dorm burst open and Samantha stormed into the room, shouting her name.

Jo continued flicking her coin, studying the redhead calmly.

'We need to talk,' Samantha said quickly. Her eyes were red and watery, her cheeks flushed and tear-stained.

Jo felt a wave of concern and she quelled it instantly. She had already decided exactly what needed to be done this evening. There was no way Jo was going to foil her own plans by letting emotion and sentiment get in the way. 'Why do we need to talk?' Jo asked calmly. 'I thought you'd done enough talking already.'

Sam ignored the jibe. 'They know who Bunny is,' she explained urgently. She walked over to Jo's chair and knelt down in front of her. 'It's a girl called Debbie Chalmers. Hera's luring her down to the gym as we speak. You need to stop her because I don't know what the bitch intends to do.'

Jo shook her head. 'You're wrong,' she said quietly. 'Very wrong.'

Sam graced her with a puzzled frown.

'You know exactly what Hera intends to do,' Jo elaborated. 'And you're wrong if you think I'm going to intervene. My interest in this case began to wane when you started playing kiss and tell with Hera. Right now, I couldn't care less about you, Hera, Bunny or the entire fucking Kilgrimol school.'

'But I didn't . . .' Sam began.

Jo ignored her. 'Hera can cut Bunny's head off and

mount it on the school gates for all I care,' she went on. 'I'm leaving.'

Sam stared at her miserably. For the first time she saw the pile of packed suitcases and realised Jo was wearing her trench-coat. Her expression of unhappiness turned into a look of despair. The tears that had been brimming on the lower lids of her eyes began to spill. 'But I thought that you and I –'

Jo shook her head. 'You thought wrong, Sam. I could have had you as a partner if I'd been able to trust you. But you went behind my back. You told Hera what I'd discovered, and I consider that a betrayal.' Instead of hearing anger in her voice, Jo could only recognise the heavy sound of weariness.

'I didn't betray you,' Sam shouted hotly. 'I would never have done that. Melanie was eavesdropping outside the door.' She pointed at the doorway to illustrate her point. 'She's the one who told Hera. It wasn't me. Like I said, I would never have done that.'

There was something in her voice that made Jo hesitate before dismissing Sam's protestations. Perhaps it was feasible that someone could have been listening to their conversation. Remembering the previous evening, Jo realised that an eavesdropper would have been forced to listen to a lot more than just their conversation. She and Sam had made love for hours before talking about the case but, knowing the perverse view of what was acceptable in this school, Jo did not think that would present a great dilemma for any of the Black Garter girls.

The more she considered it, the more likely it seemed that Sam was telling the truth. 'You're lying,' Jo said flatly.

Sam glared at her. Her anger was a thin mask concealing emotions of frustration, rejection and sorrow. Jo could see the emotions bubbling beneath the surface of Sam's hurt expression and she tried to ignore them. She had already decided to end her relationship with Sam before it had properly begun. Whether the redhead was telling the truth or not no longer mattered. All that mattered was that Jo escape from the Kilgrimol, without a new, junior partner.

She was about to add the final touches to the farewell: a cutting, hurtful remark sufficient to make Sam never want to speak to her again. Not bothering to think if it was what she really wanted to do, Jo opened her mouth to deliver the fatal blow. The shrill ring of her mobile phone stopped her words from escaping. Jo glared angrily at the thing and caught her coin from the air. She cursed softly, stood up and answered the telephone. 'Valentine,' she growled into the mouthpiece.

'Valentine, is that you?'

Jo frowned at the telephone. 'Mr Smith?' Her thoughts turned to the cheque resting in her account and she wondered if he was phoning up to say he had put a stop on it. 'Is everything all right?'

'Everything is fine,' he assured her. 'I just wanted to make sure you were okay with the case.'

'I'm developing an understanding of things,' Jo replied carefully.

He laughed softly. 'That's as close to a straight answer as I can expect from you, isn't it?' Not waiting for a reply, he went on briskly. 'The real reason I called you is for a personal favour. I've been trying to talk to my daughter all day but her mobile seems to be playing up. Could you get a message to her and tell her I want to speak to her?'

'I'm an investigator not a fucking telephonist,' Jo barked rudely.

'And you're working for me at the moment,' Mr Smith snapped back with equal venom. 'So, you can either do this as a favour to me, or as an instruction from your client.' There was a long, embarrassing pause on the telephone. Mr Smith broke the silence. 'Ask Bunny to call me at home.'

Jo stared at the phone as though it had suddenly grown dangerously warm in her hand. 'Bunny,' she repeated numbly. She turned her back on Sam.

'I call her Bunny,' Mr Smith went on. 'She's down in the student's register as Debbie Chalmers.'

Jo sat heavily back in her chair. 'Why isn't she called Debbie Smith?'

'She uses my wife's maiden name. The same as my wife does now,' he explained tersely. 'But that's not really your business, is it?'

Jo clutched her forehead, conscious of a growing headache building up inside. 'I'll pass the message on,' she said quietly. 'Goodnight, Mr Smith.'

He did not bother with any end-of-call courtesy. He simply severed the connection. Jo was left staring glumly at the dead telephone in her hand as she tried to work out what to do next.

'Was that bad news?' Sam asked quietly.

Jo shrugged. 'It could be bad news for my bank account,' she said carefully. She glanced sharply at Sam, aware that the girl was close to spilling tears again. 'What are the chances of you getting me down to the gym?'

Sam snorted. 'Do you trust me enough to do that for you?'

Jo sighed and climbed from her chair. She placed a hand on Sam's waist and delivered a small kiss to her cheek. 'We can argue about this later,' she said, marching towards the door. She tried to ignore the grateful smile that filled the redhead's face and the tears of happiness that swam behind the lenses of her glasses.

Speaking in brash, gruff tones, she said, 'Right now, we've got to act like heroes and save ourselves a Bunny.'

Cowering inside the vaulting horse, Steven had a perfect view of the entire gymnasium. He could see the flickering candles, the circle of cowled figures and the poor, sobbing bitch on all fours that they had surrounded. A broad smile lit his lips.

Beside him, the camcorder he had borrowed from Peter whirred softly as it captured the scene. The quiet, constant sound made him think the machine was sighing with disbelief as it struggled to accept what it was viewing. If that had been the case, he could have sympathised wholeheartedly. Even though this was what Steven had hoped and expected to see, it still seemed incredible to be watching the spectacle. The air of anticipation was so heady it was electric. Each breath he drew was tainted with the flavour of expectant passion.

He had no worries about using the camcorder in candlelight. Peter had given him great assurances about its abilities to pick up clear pictures in the dark. The machine was supposedly so good, Steven believed it could have worked with the lens cap on. Not that he would have been bold enough to test such a radical theory. This piece of film was far too important for him to dare risk it.

This was going to be the story that started his career properly, he reminded himself. This piece of video was going to be the crowning glory for the scandal of the century and he was going to earn fame and fortune as the person who exposed it.

The thought was almost as exciting as the action

being played out before him and he could not decide which of these stimuli had prompted his arousal.

He could see they had Bunny in the centre of their circle. Her struggles had been weak and ineffectual against so many and now that she had been stripped naked, the ample swell of her massive breasts was displayed for all to see. The gorgeous mounds of her nicely rounded arse were thrust high into the air and he knew that if he could have moved a little closer, he would have seen the tight, forbidden cleft of her virgin hole.

The idea made his cock twitch eagerly. He felt a momentary pang of guilt as he realised she was having to suffer to help him get his story but he did not brood for too long. In the pursuit of the truth, some people had to make sacrifices, he realised. Bunny was simply doing her part for the good of his career. As he watched, he made a mental note to thank her once he had his work in print. That would be the least he could do. The idea of giving her a signed copy of his book occurred to him and he considered his own generosity carefully.

The cowled figures began to walk around Bunny, raining blows against her backside with the table-tennis paddles they carried. Her moans of protestation echoed throughout the gymnasium.

'You poor bitch,' Steven whispered softly to himself. As he briefly sympathised with her, his hand rubbed at the bulge that had grown inside his trousers. The raging eagerness of his hard-on was too great for him to ignore and the idea to wank off was sudden and unplanned but, once it was fixed in his mind, he could not get rid of the thought. He was far enough away from the cowled girls to know they would not hear him and he trusted the camcorder to catch any detail he might miss.

Determined to relieve himself, Steven unfastened his trousers and began to stroke the solid length of his erection. As his hand moved up and down his shaft, he stared at Bunny's reddening arse.

Debbie quickly lost count of the number of blows she had received. The cheeks of her arse were aflame with the dull glow of burning flesh. She could not remember how many of the paddles had actually caught the sensitive flesh of her exposed pussy lips. She was simply aware of a heat that excited her tremendously in spite of her nervousness.

Perhaps the punishment wouldn't be that bad, she thought hopefully. Debbie knew that Hera had a merciful side as well as a cruel nature and she supposed that the woman's appetite for chastisement could have been satiated.

It was a slim hope. She remembered how much Hera had enjoyed her initiation into the Black Garter, but Debbie held on to the idea with blind faith. She took a small measure of solace from the fact that Hera had not tried to penetrate her with anything. The leader of the Black Garter was one of the few women in the school who knew how importantly Debbie prized her virginity. Considering Hera's merciless nature and her justifiable anger, Debbie had been expecting the woman to exact some sort of perverse revenge that involved her defloration. She knew there was still plenty of time for that to happen but the fact that it had not occurred yet gave her more cause for hope.

Her entire body quivered with each blow of a paddle. Members of the Black Garter were circling her so quickly she was beginning to feel dizzy and the candlelight created a latticework of shadows that dizzied and disoriented her. Even when they stopped moving, Debbie could still see them circling in her mind's eye. She shook her head to clear her thoughts and stared at the motionless feet directly in front of her.

Even without hearing the woman speak, she would have known it was Hera. She had such a commanding presence, Debbie felt sure she would have recognised her under any circumstances.

'Disrobe, ladies,' Hera said crisply.

Debbie held her breath. She heard a rustle of clothing in the dark shadows behind her and realised the women were dropping their cloaks to the floor. The idea that they might be naked beneath them was darkly exciting. When she dared to risk a glance at one of them, she saw that her fears were firmly based. Each of the girls was naked, save for a black garter at the top of the right leg.

The only member of the group who had not bothered to disrobe was Hera. She stood in front of Debbie, still draped in her cowl, wearing a solemn, judicial expression on her face. A dark twinkle glinted in the corner of her eye but Debbie dared not look at this for too long. There was something too sinister and menacing about Hera's enjoyment for her to tolerate looking at it. The leader's enjoyment invariably meant suffering and discomfort for someone and Debbie knew she was the prime candidate for such activities.

Hera stepped to one side, allowing Anna to take her place.

'Kiss my feet,' Anna commanded sternly. She pushed one bare foot forward, so that the toe was just below Debbie's nose.

Debbie lowered her head and placed her lips against the woman's flesh. She could not help but feel a wave of self-revulsion as she performed the act.

Kissing Anna's feet was a humiliating gesture of her own servility and the feeling rankled deeply. Nevertheless, she delivered a small, gentle kiss to each toe before daring to strain her neck and look up. She fervently hoped that she had met with the woman's approval.

'Kiss the other foot,' Anna whispered sharply.

Debbie swallowed and, moving forward on her hands and knees, she placed her mouth over Anna's other foot and begin to kiss each of the woman's toes. She was aware of her closeness to Anna's naked body and found the nearness both exciting and unsettling. She didn't doubt that Anna's nudity had something to do with what they had in store for her, but she did not dare contemplate what it might be.

'Kiss higher,' Anna instructed firmly.

Debbie drew a short, expectant breath. She moved her lips slowly up the blonde girl's leg and kissed her shins, and calves, then her knees. Ever so slowly, hoping Anna would say, 'enough', or 'stop', she inched her lips up the soft skin of the woman's thigh.

Anna sighed softly. 'That's good,' she whispered. 'Kiss higher.'

Debbie could feel her stomach tightening with anxiety. She knew what was expected of her now. As she moved her mouth slightly higher, she wondered how long it would be possible to prolong the moment before she had to submit and kiss Anna's sex.

It wasn't that she didn't want to kiss Anna. The idea was already making her breasts throb with dull excitement. The heated skin at the lips of her sex was still tingling from the punishing paddling it had received earlier. Now, as she came ever so much closer to brushing her lips against Anna's labia, they tingled for a different reason. This, she realised, was the heady sparkle of sexual anticipation.

Unwilling to commit herself to the act, she pressed her mouth just below Anna's sex and placed one last kiss. In an act of defiance, she began to move her head away. Anna's fingers caught her hair and held her head steady.

'Kiss my cunny,' Anna said shortly. 'Kiss my cunny and do it well, or by God, you'll regret it.'

The malice in her words was enough to make Debbie realise the threat was genuine. She moved her mouth to the lips of Anna's pussy and touched her tongue against the musky folds. Anna released a pent-up sigh of delight.

Debbie tried not to think of her own excitement as she ran her tongue against the folds of flesh, tasting and moistening the subtly scented lips.

Anna drew a deep breath of satisfaction and then reluctantly stepped away. She took a step in the direction Hera had gone and another naked young woman took her place.

Debbie gazed at the triangle of pubic curls that appeared in front of her. Without waiting to be told, she nuzzled the soft, downy hairs and probed her tongue against the unknown woman's sex. The fact that she was performing such an intimacy with a stranger only added fuel to the fire of her arousal. She could feel the heat of her sex twitching with delight. The threat of orgasm was so near it was chilling and she braced herself for the climactic thrill of pleasure. The idea that she could glean so much enjoyment from simply licking another woman's pussy lips was a radical new concept for Debbie. She had almost forgotten that this was supposed to be a punishment she was enduring. When the first wave of delight rushed through her body, she pushed her tongue hard against the woman before her.

A squeal of joy escaped the woman, drowning out Debbie's own cry of excitement and in that moment the pain and humiliation of her earlier experiences were forgotten. The intensity of her sexual awakening was so strong and exciting all she could focus on was the pleasure she was receiving and administering. The circle moved around another step, and Debbie felt her enjoyment soar once again as she was allowed to tongue another stranger and taste the woman's musky perfume. The dark intimacy of her mouth on the woman's sex contrasted harshly with her ignorance of who she was licking.

That thought continued to increase Debbie's excitement as she pressed her mouth into each woman's bush and licked and nibbled at the sweet, sopping flesh. When the woman eventually stepped away, Debbie found her face being pressed against yet another woman's sex. She tongued it hungrily.

The process was repeated again and again until she lost count of how many women she had pleasured. The thought that this was supposed to be a punishment was almost forgotten. The dull burning on the cheeks of her arse had subsided to an ache that seemed to echo the throb of her eager arousal. It was only when Hera stepped before her, still draped in the cowl, that Debbie remembered that this was a punishment. The idea that her chastisement had not started properly was only just beginning to occur to her.

'Are you ready to be punished?' Hera asked softly.

Debbie swallowed and stared meekly at up at her.

Hera smiled down, her predatory grin glinting menacingly in the candlelight. Without waiting for Debbie's response, she shrugged the cloak from her shoulders. She revealed herself in all her naked glory, brandishing the thick, plastic strap-on that was fixed around her hips. Holding the length with one hand, she grinned wickedly down at Debbie. Nervously, Debbie lowered her head. All her earlier fears of penetration and the loss of her virginity returned to her. Her heart beat faster.

'Jo! Sam! Wait up!'

They both turned in the direction of the woman who was hailing them. Jo recognised Grace from the previous evening in her bedroom and she held Sam's arm to stop her. Grace hurried down the corridor to meet them and stopped. She was panting slightly after the exertion.

'Not at the meeting?' Sam asked coldly.

Grace missed the ice in her voice. 'I've been busy in the dark room,' she explained.

Jo grinned. 'That's one of my favourite pastimes.'

Grace smiled perfunctorily and shoved a handful of papers towards Jo. 'Here,' she said quickly, take a look at these.'

'We don't have time to ...' Sam began but Jo waved her into silence.

'What am I looking at, Grace?' she asked curiously, leafing through the photographs.

Grace laughed softly. 'At the risk of sounding like a prude, I'd say you're looking at hard-core pornography.'

Sam glanced over Jo's shoulder and studied the photographs.

'Those are the pictures that were on that roll of film you gave Hera last night,' Grace explained. 'Whoever took them has no morals and a very good eye for camera angles.'

'Who's that?' Jo asked, pointing to a particularly clear shot of a blonde, enjoying the penetration of a handsome young man.

Grace glanced at the picture. 'That's Anna,' she said. 'She's the most noticeable in these photos. Cassandra is barely recognisable; her face is usually hidden or out of focus.'

Jo raised her eyebrows. 'You sound like you've been studying them quite hard,' she remarked cryptically.

Grace shrugged and looked away coyly. 'I've never developed anything like these before,' she said quietly. 'I was curious, you know.'

Jo nodded absently, still studying the photographs. 'I know.'

'Could Jo borrow your cloak, Grace?' Sam asked suddenly.

Grace tightened her hand around the garment she was wearing, a frown of annoyance furling her brow. 'What the hell for?'

'It's important that Jo gets into the punishment meeting tonight,' Sam explained. 'Please,' she added. 'For old-times' sake.'

Grace looked hesitant about the idea but eventually consented. 'I can always tell Hera that I got waylaid in the dark room,' she agreed eventually, slipping the cloak from her shoulders. She still wore her gym uniform beneath the cloak and she frowned at the attire. 'I haven't even had a chance to change for the meeting,' she added.

Sam laughed. 'I have,' she said, opening her cowl and treating Grace to a glimpse of her bare body.

'Can I borrow this one?' Jo asked, holding up the photograph of Anna and the young man.

Grace shrugged. 'Will you give it back when you're done with it?'

'Probably not,' Jo said honestly. 'And I'd appreciate it if you could destroy the negatives the next time you're in the dark room.'

'That might be difficult,' Grace said. 'I could

develop a taste for working with that sort of picture.'

Jo nodded sympathetically and shrugged herself into the cloak Grace had removed. 'It might be better for the sake of the young lady in this picture,' she said encouragingly. 'Anna's in line for the leadership of the Black Garter, isn't she?'

Grace nodded.

'Then I'm sure she'll help you find other, more willing models,' Jo assured her. 'That's the way you work things in this Black Garter of yours, isn't it?'

When Grace eventually nodded her agreement, Jo knew that the woman was going to destroy the negatives as she had asked. At least that was one less worry on her mind.

'Come on,' Jo said, tugging on Sam's sleeve. 'We still have a lot of work to do.'

Sam glanced at Grace. 'Tell Jo where Melanie was last night.'

Grace glared at her and then looked away. 'How the hell would I know?' she demanded.

'We don't have time for this now,' Jo broke in.

Sam wasn't listening. 'Tell her, Grace. Tell her where Melanie had been before she went back to your dorm.'

Grace turned on her, a furious expression blazing in her eyes. 'Hera could have me punished for the help I've given you two already.'

'Then a little more won't hurt, will it?' Sam pressed.

'Really, Sam,' Jo said wishing she could go to the gym on her own. Sam had a knowledge of the Black Garter and their passwords and Jo doubted she would be able to get close to the gym without the redhead's help. 'We have to go,' she insisted.

Sam stood resolute, glaring defiantly at Grace.

'OK,' Grace said eventually. 'Melanie was eavesdropping on you two lovebirds until the small hours.' She glared angrily at Sam, resentment apparent in her eyes. She turned to Jo. 'Melanie heard you say who you were looking for,' she explained and with a dark smile she said quietly, 'Sam sat on your secret, just like she sat on your face.'

Jo studied the woman thoughtfully. 'Do they teach you nice phrases like that here at the Kilgrimol?'

'Satisfied?' Sam asked Jo.

Jo shook her head. 'This isn't satisfaction. This is a distraction. Say thank you and goodnight to Grace. We have work to do.' She turned to Grace and passed her a quick thank-you before the pair of them fled down the corridor and out into the night.

Ahead, on the horizon, the huge panelled windows of the gym flickered with the dull glow of candlelight.

'We're too late,' Jo breathed, her words tainted with soft self-disgust. 'We're far too late. They've already started.'

Sam shivered, not daring to think what might have happened. 'Let's hurry, before they let Hera loose on the poor bitch,' she said. Picking up her pace she grabbed Jo's arm and together they hurried towards the gym.

Steven could see two of the women holding Bunny and struggling to keep her still. He was deliberately prolonging the moment of orgasm, determined to witness as much of the carnal punishment as he could, before finally giving himself over to the joy of release.

Hera was bearing down on Bunny with the huge strap-on jutting menacingly from her narrow hips. The two naked girls held Bunny by the arms but she struggled feverishly away from the leader and her frightening weapon.

Steven tugged at his length lovingly, extracting as much pleasure as he could. The sight of Bunny eating pussy and licking cunt juice had been debilitating and now, watching her struggle to resist the advances of this overbearing vixen, he had to watch the pace of his hand in case he accidentally climaxed.

Not only was this evening going to win him fame and fortune, it was also proving to be the most erotic time he had spent in his entire life. The sight of so much naked young flesh, illuminated by the dull flicker of candles, was truly inspiring. He rolled the palm of his hand over the swollen tip of his cock, enjoying the deep throb of stimulation.

The women were talking now in voices so animated he could sense the mood was about to become more violent. This did nothing to hamper his arousal. Instead, he could feel his erection raging even harder than it had been before and the threat of impending orgasm was so close he could almost smell the scent of his own seed.

Hera turned around and glanced at each and every corner of the gymnasium. Her gaze paused when she looked in Steven's direction and he felt a momentary disquiet. For an instant, he thought that she was staring directly at him and as he pulled his cock in one hand, he felt sure she could see him as though he were outside the vaulting horse, slowly wanking himself off.

Hera barked an instruction and two naked girls rushed across the polished floor of the gym to where Steven hid.

He swallowed nervously inside the horse, not knowing what to expect. He could not believe she had actually seen him but it seemed like the only explanation for this unexpected turn of events. He wondered if he should jump from the horse and run but he knew that by the time he had the lid off he would have been caught. His trousers were still around his ankles and his hard cock was still in his hand.

The two women ran beyond the vaulting horse and he managed to restrain a huge sigh of relief. The danger of discovery had felt so close he wondered how he had managed to contain his fear. He had barely allowed himself a moment's reprieve to consider these thoughts when he felt the horse begin to move.

'This is fucking heavy,' one girl whispered to the other.

'Do you want to tell Hera?' the other asked.

'Shut up and keep pushing,' the first one replied.

Steven held his breath, suddenly aware of what was happening. He and the vaulting horse he was hiding in were being pushed into the centre of the Black Garter's punishment circle.

He could not recall ever having felt such terror in his life. Unconsciously, he rolled his cock back and forth in one hand.

When the vaulting horse was brought into the centre of the circle, Bunny struggled to resist the inevitable. She already felt tired. Her arms and legs ached with an interminable weariness but she still fought against the two women who pushed her against the horse. Two more joined the fight and within a moment she felt her bare body being pressed against the cool wood. Two hands held each wrist, pulling her almost over the top of the horse. Two more held each ankle, stopping her from kicking and squirming away.

She wondered if she had banged her head against the horse during the struggle. For some reason she could hear a soft whirring sound ringing in her ears.

There was little time to contemplate the thought before she felt Hera's hands fall on her shoulders and the tip of the strap-on prod rudely at the rim of her anus.

A cold dread filled her, almost vanquishing the feeling of arousal that had built up inside her. The stirring of delight returned unbidden when she felt the woman's breasts brush against the bare flesh of her back.

'Are you ready for this, Bunny?' Hera asked in a leering voice.

Bunny could not find words to respond. She simply trembled against the vaulting horse, wishing she could leave the gym and go away for ever. She could hear the excited mumbling and giggling of the girls who held her and she felt ashamed and embarrassed. She tried desperately not to think how helpless and invidious her situation was.

The dildo prodded hard against her anus. The tip was cool and wet, as though Hera had lubricated it in preparation for this moment. Debbie trembled at the woman's calculating mind and wondered if there was anything Hera had not thought of.

The strap-on pressed firmly against the puckered ring of her backside and, as Hera pushed forward, Debbie felt herself being filled. She released a soft groan as the implement plundered her brusquely. The sensation of having the makeshift cock slide into her was unwelcome and frightening but also undeniably exciting.

Hera pushed forward until the cock was filling her victim. Her hands were still on Debbie's shoulders but now her face was close enough to whisper into the woman's ear. 'Do you like it up your arse, Bunny?'

Debbie bit back a sigh of delight, not wanting Hera to have the satisfaction of knowing how much pleasure she was giving. The feel of the woman's warm breath, tickling her neck, added to the mounting excitement and she tried not to succumb to the sensations of pleasure and delight. It was a futile struggle.

For all her faults, Hera knew how to make love. She was as adept in the art of pleasuring as she was in cruelty. Beneath her hands, Debbie became a piece of clay, capable of being moulded into whatever form Hera desired.

As the cock began to slide in and out with a gradually quickening tempo, Debbie realised she would just have to endure whatever Hera had planned for her. It was an easy thought to live with as the waves of pleasure began to ripple through her body.

The strap-on was only a piece of hard, unyielding plastic but Hera used it with perfect skill. Her soft hands touched and caressed Debbie's naked back, occasionally moving to her sides. The electric touch of her fingers was a thrilling stimulus that continually sparked new and exciting sensations from the tingling depths of her erogenous zones. As the strap-on pumped into her, its broad girth stretching every tight muscle of her anus, Debbie could feel the monumental swell of a tremendous climax beginning to rise. The hands at her wrists and feet were almost forgotten as the delight welled within her. The discomfort of her position was of negligible importance. All that mattered was that Hera continued to ride her as she was doing.

A sigh of elation broke from her lips as the orgasm struck her. Each tendon in her body seemed to stretch. She pulled against the unrelenting hands that held her, enduring the delight of wave after wave of ecstasy washing over her. Her inner muscles clenched tightly against the phallus, intensifying the joy.

Hera's hands pressed tightly into Debbie's sides as the orgasm erupted and the talon-like ends of her fingernails dug deep into the flesh. Debbie was only distantly aware of the pain. Her body was glowing with the warm thrill of satisfaction and such a distraction was only peripheral.

Hera pressed her lips close to Debbie's neck, and asked maliciously. 'Enjoy having your arse fucked, Bunny?'

Debbie's shivering response was barely audible in the silence of the gloomy gym but it was enough for Hera to know it had been a yes.

'I thought as much,' Hera said, sliding the length from the quivering confines of Debbie's anus. 'That wasn't the cruellest punishment I've ever delivered, was it?'

Debbie shook her head, enjoying the slow egress of the phallus. 'I suppose not,' she breathed softly.

Hera chuckled. 'Don't worry, it's not over yet.'

Before Debbie could say a word in protest, she felt the rounded tip of the strap-on pressing firmly against the lips of her labia. The head seemed to be in the ideal position to ease into her and she struggled to move away.

The hands at her wrists and ankles held tightly and no matter how hard she pulled and twisted she knew she was not going to escape. For the first time since Hera had begun fucking her, Debbie felt her panic rising.

'You'll learn this lesson well, Bunny,' Hera hissed, her voice rich with malevolence. 'You fucked with the Black Garter, so now I'm going to fuck with you.'

'No!' Debbie whispered, shocked and frightened. 'I . . .' Her voice trailed off as she realised just how futile her words of protest would be. With a heavy air of inevitability, she braced herself for Hera's entry.

* * *

'Wait a second, Jo,' Sam said, placing her arm on the detective's. 'Before we go in there, we need to sort something out.'

Jo glanced at the gym door, then at Sam's pretty, bespectacled face. 'We're in a bit of a rush, Sam,' she reminded her. 'Like you said, we have no idea what they've done to her yet.'

Sam shook her head and moved closer to Jo. She placed her lips over the older woman's and delivered a soft kiss on her mouth. The action was sudden and unexpected, filling Jo with a chilling passion. Their tongues entwined and the thrill of excitement rose inside Jo's chest.

'This isn't the time or the place,' Jo said when their mouths broke. 'We have a case to solve.'

Sam studied her carefully in the darkness. 'Does that mean I'm a detective or a helpful schoolgirl.'

Jo rolled her eyes and looked away. 'Not now, Sam.'

'It has to be now,' Sam insisted. 'When we go in there I need to know who I am. Hera could let me back in the Black Garter if she thinks I'm on her side.'

'Is that what you want?' Jo asked quietly.

Sam stared at her levelly. 'You know damned well what I want.'

Jo could see the firm resolution in the redhead's sparkling eyes. She could still taste the kiss on her lips and with a sudden sigh, she nodded quiet agreement. 'I was wrong to blame you before,' she agreed. 'And if you still want to come and work for me, I'll take you on as a trainee.'

Sam frowned. 'Partner,' she said quietly.

Jo sighed. 'We'll iron out the details after this is over,' she said firmly. 'If we don't get in there and save Bunny, her father might not leave me with any business for you to be a partner in.'

Sam grinned and kissed Jo again. It was only a brief exchange, filled with more gratitude than passion. 'Thanks,' she said quietly.

Bunny thanked God for the moment's reprieve.

Hera had pulled the strap-on away from the lips of her pussy and instructed one of the girls to lick Debbie wet. The four women holding her had manoeuvred themselves in a quick change and pulled Debbie so that her back was now pressed against the horse. They still held her wrists and ankles.

'When my cock slides inside you,' Hera whispered into Debbie's ear, 'I want you to enjoy every inch of it.'

The words had chilled and excited her simultaneously. Now, as Cassandra's tongue worked its way up and down the heated lips of her sex, she realised her excitement was greater than she would have believed. In a bizarre way, she realised she wanted to feel the swift penetration of Hera's shaft. There was a dull longing between her legs that demanded satisfaction and even though she knew it was wrong, Debbie was prepared to accept it.

The loss of her virginity would be a violation of her father's wishes and she knew it would inevitably lead to a life of desolation and penury but at that moment, Debbie was prepared to accept all of that. She was willing to do anything to get her punishment over and done with. With that out of the way, she could get back to her dorm and start to get on with the rest of her life.

Cassandra's tongue moved roughly over the lips of her pussy, stimulating her. The tip of her tongue flicked at the pulsing nub of Debbie's clitoris, sparking a fire of desire that left her short of breath.

Debbie glanced at Hera, watching the scene with a tight smile on her lips. She was stroking her hand lovingly along the length of the strap-on she wore. The other hand toyed idly with one of her nipples, tweaking it and teasing it to a state of fierce erection. Her gaze seemed fixed on the union between Cassandra's mouth and Debbie's pussy.

'Enough!' Hera snapped sharply.

Debbie felt her stomach churn as she realised the implication of the words. She felt Cassandra move away, and watched as Hera moved towards her. It could only have been a trick of the candlelight, her rational mind knew that, but she felt certain she could see the strap-on twitching eagerly as it moved closer to her.

Closing her eyes, Debbie tried to hide herself in the safety of her own darkness. It was no protection, she realised, when she felt the tip of the dildo nuzzle against the wetness of her sex.

Hera placed a soft kiss on her forehead. 'I won't be gentle with you,' she said quietly, 'but you weren't expecting that, were you?'

Debbie dared not reply. Every muscle in her body was held tight with nervous anticipation and, as she felt Hera's hands stroke the treacherous swell of her eager nipples, she tried not to sigh with delight as the pleasure ignited inside.

'Say goodbye to your virginity,' Hera whispered.

Debbie could feel the strap-on pushing forward.

'Hold it right there!' Jo's voice carried effortlessly through the gymnasium.

The members of the Black Garter turned to face her, expressions of panic and defiance registered on their face in different degrees.

Hera glanced up from Debbie's body. 'Fuck off,

Valentine,' she called softly. 'This doesn't concern you.'

Jo walked briskly towards the woman, Sam following close behind. She glanced at Hera's strap-on and smiled quietly to herself. 'Put your dick away, Hera,' she said calmly, 'your party is over now.'

Anna rushed over to intervene. 'This is none of your concern,' she said, shrugging herself into her cloak as she spoke. 'Walk away and leave it.' She glanced at Sam. 'I thought you would have known better than to interfere with Black Garter business.'

Jo did not allow Sam to reply. She pushed a photograph into Anna's chest. 'Look at this,' she snapped, dismissing her with the gesture.

Anna glanced at it. Her eyes opened wide with horror as she realised what the picture portayed. 'Where the hell did this come from?'

Jo glanced at the women holding Debbie's arms and legs. 'Let go of her now, or I'll lose my temper.'

They stared at her uncertainly.

'Do it,' Hera instructed absently. She fixed Jo with a look of darkest fury. 'You're not making many friends here,' she growled softly.

Jo shrugged. 'Good,' she said quietly. She glanced at Debbie who was rubbing her wrists and ankles. 'Get dressed and go call your father,' she said softly.

'How did you get this picture?' Anna repeated.

Jo turned to face her. 'I stole it from a reporter,' she explained. 'A reporter who turned down the chance of a date with me this evening. There had to be a reason why and it's only just occurred to me what it is.' She glanced at Debbie. 'Where is he hiding?'

Debbie shrugged. 'He knew there was a punishment tonight but I don't know if he's come or not.'

Jo grinned slyly. 'He'll be here somewhere,' she said thoughtfully. She took a moment to cast her gaze around the candlelit gymnasium. A soft glint of light caught her eye and she smiled tightly.

Behind her, Sam was grinning broadly as she stared at the vaulting horse.

'Are you telling us that this bitch has sold us out to the papers again?' Hera demanded, pointing a furious finger at Debbie.

Jo shook her head and sighed wearily. 'I doubt she did this last one through choice,' she said quietly. 'I can imagine that her reporter friend coerced her into helping.' Glancing at Hera, she added, 'Steven isn't above a little blackmail.'

Hera's dark frown looked thunderous. 'The bitch will have to be punished for this,' she declared hotly.

'No,' Jo said firmly. 'She'll be reinstated into the Black Garter and she'll be given half a chance to do well.'

Hera snorted derisively.

'What makes you think we'd do that?' Anna asked.

Jo smiled at her. 'You'll do it, because I believe you're to be the new leader. With that photograph in your possession, you realise that you owe me a big one. A very big one.'

Anna nodded. 'You're asking a lot,' she said carefully.

'I've just given you a lot,' Jo pointed out. She glanced at Debbie. 'Go and call your father,' she repeated. 'He's expecting to hear from you.'

With a grateful smile, Debbie rushed from the gymnasium.

'Are you adjourning my meeting?' Hera asked sharply.

'Give me a hand with this,' Sam said suddenly. She had moved to the side of the vaulting horse and was trying to lift the lid on her own. Its weight was so great she could barely lift the lid from its lip. Jo grabbed the other side and helped raise the top from the horse. Steven glared angrily up at the women who stared down on him.

'There's your reporter,' Jo told Hera. She snatched the camcorder from his hand before he could see she what she intended to do. With a lithe movement, she threw it to Sam who removed the cassette and dropped it to the floor, stamping on it as hard as she could.

Fastening his trousers, Steven glared defiantly at Jo. 'It doesn't matter about the cassette,' he said angrily. 'I've got enough material for my story without that.' He glared at each of the women, his look of fury hot enough to sear flesh. 'I'm going to have you bitches as headline news tomorrow.'

Jo laughed softly. 'I don't think that's likely, Steven,' she began. 'I've read some of your notes and it seems like you're trying to expose the scandalous school lives of some of the country's leading business women. Would you say that's a fair assessment?'

'What's your point?' Steven asked defiantly.

Jo grinned. 'How many editors do you think will dare risk the libel suits that your story could provoke?'

He looked deflated as a frown creased his forehead. 'It's not libellous, it's the truth.'

'And we both know that the truth isn't likely to appear in a newspaper, don't we?' Jo responded smartly.

'Are you the *Clarion* reporter?' Hera asked suddenly.

He fixed her with an angry glare. 'What's it to you?'

Hera smiled warmly at him. 'I'd wondered when I was going to meet you,' she said cheerfully. Extending a hand, she said, 'My name is Hera Collins. As of Monday morning, I'm going to be your new editor.'

Steven studied her uncertainly.

'My parents own the *Clarion*,' Hera explained, 'along with a few other papers and magazines.' She grinned lasciviously at him and said, 'Do you know, I'm looking forward to having someone like you under me.'

Jo tapped Sam on the shoulder and tilted her head towards the door. 'It's time for us to leave,' she said quietly.

Anna turned to Sam. 'If you want to be reinstated, I can organise it.'

Sam glanced from Jo to Anna, then back to Jo. 'Thanks. But no thanks,' she said eventually. 'Jo's made me an offer I can't refuse,' she explained. 'I'm going to go with her and become a partner in her agency.'

'Trainee,' Jo corrected.

'I thought you said that was to be discussed,' Sam reminded her. Realising Jo was making no attempt to reply she said, 'You promised we'd discuss this. You promised.'

'I wish you both well,' Anna said, kissing Sam on the cheek. 'Take care and stay in touch.'

Jo nodded curtly at Anna and fixed her attention on Sam. 'As I understand it, a partner is usually someone who buys their way into a business.'

Sam shrugged. 'So I'll buy my way in. My parents are wealthy. I'm sure they'll give me the money.'

Jo paused, a smile lighting on her lips. 'How wealthy?'

Sam shrugged. 'Fairly wealthy,' she said. 'I don't know how to measure it really. They have a couple of yachts and a couple of villas. Does that explain how wealthy they are?'

Jo's grin broadened. She slipped her arm around Sam's waist and kissed her on the cheek. 'You know, Sam, I think this is going to be the start of a beautiful friendship.'